The Mystery of Swordfish Reef

ARTHUR UPFIELD

The Mystery of Swordfish Reef

HEINEMANN : LONDON

William Heinemann Ltd
15 Queen Street, Mayfair, London W1X 8BE

LONDON MELBOURNE TORONTO
JOHANNESBURG AUCKLAND

First published in Great Britain 1960
This edition 1971

434 81167 x

Printed Offset Litho and bound in Great Britain
by Cox & Wyman Ltd,
London, Fakenham and Reading

Contents

CHAPTER 1

A Calm Day

A depression which had been hesitant to move on from the south-eastern coast of Australia, and thereby had for a period of days sent mountainous seas crashing against the rock-armoured headland protecting the township of Bermagui, finally passed away over the southern Tasman Sea. Its influence rapidly waning, the wind shifted to the north, the spring sunshine became warm, the grassy slopes back from the river gleamed like velvet, and Jack Wilton and his partner, Joe Peace, continued their work on the hull of the *Marlin*.

At high tide a week earlier the sleek ocean launch had been hauled to the foot of a narrow beach well inside the river's mouth. Like many rivers along this coast the Bermaguee has teeth in its mouth in the shape of a bar, a bar perfectly safe to navigate in all weather save when the easterly gales roar across the great bay into which flows the river. The bar is something of a dividing line: outside it is the ocean, a despot of capricious moods; inside it the river provides shelter for many fishing launches, their slender jetty, a huge fish-trap, and migrating birds.

Although the tuna season was in full swing, Wilton had taken the opportunity provided by a week's gap in his engagements with anglers to clean and treat the hull of his twenty-eight-foot-long marine engine-driven launch. After the tuna season would follow the more important swordfishing season, lasting from December to April. There would be little chance for a clean-up then; besides, at the end of long days at sea the anglers liked to be speedily taken back to port.

Work on the *Marlin* was completed this calm day the third of October; at midnight when the tide was high the craft would be refloated and taken to her berth at the jetty. Of the dozen launches that lay o'nights against this splinter of iron-bolted baulks of timber, eight had been there all this day. The other four had taken anglers to sea after the vast shoals of tuna and kingfish, anglers who came from Melbourne and Sydney, and as far afield as New Zealand, England and America.

The two men at work on the *Marlin* were unable to see the river's mouth and the bar hidden from them by the low promontory protecting river and estuary. They could see a stretch of the straggling settlement of Bermagui. The main part of the township nestled in the lee of a greater headland that, like the smaller one guarding the river, pointed northward along the coast. They were able to observe the truck being driven along the road to Cobargo, see it stop at the shore end of the jetty, observe two men step from it. Even at this distance they could recognise the owner of the garage, Mr. Parkins, who was the assistant weight recorder to the honorary secretary of the Bermagui Big Game Anglers' Club, Mr. Edward Blade, who now accompanied him.

"First of the launches must be coming in," remarked Jack Wilton, owner of the *Marlin*.

Joe, his mate, stared from beneath bushy grey eyebrows at the two weight recorders now walking along the jetty to its seaward extremity where was erected the beam to take the scales and fish. Two women stood talking to a launch-man on his craft, and several day visitors followed the weight recorders.

"Likely enough to have been a good day out there," Joe

said, his voice deep and penetrating even in the open. "I think this job will do for another nine months."

He was a ponderous man, this Joseph Peace. His movements were sluggish and deliberate—until agility was demanded of him when the *Marlin* was bucking like a cork on a mill-race. The curious could not have discovered anyone in Bermagui who had ever seen Joe wearing either a hat or boots. Memory would have had to be placed on the rack to recall having seen Joe freshly shaven. The half-inch stubble of greyish beard seemed permanently halted in growth, but to balance this oddity his complexion defied the tanning effects of sun and wind; which was more than could be said of his dungaree trousers and the woollen pullover that betrayed many harsh washings. His small grey eyes were at the moment calm from mental contentment, and the strong and stubby fingers went downward to draw from the leather belt about his vast waist one of the two wooden pipes invariably carried there. Slowly, he said:

"The *Do-me* might go on the market if Mr. Ericson buys land here, and builds himself a house and buys himself a launch for Bill Spinks to run for him year in and year out."

Brown eyes surveyed Joe quizzingly, brown eyes set in an alert brown face. Jack Wilton was young and strong and lithe, of average height, and as clean as the sea which was as much part of his existence as the air. Joe became a little truculent.

"Well, if it turns out as you say Marion Spinks says so, Bill Spinks won't have no more use for the *Do-me*."

"Perhaps not, Joe. Supposing Marion's right? Supposing Ericson does buy that land and builds a home on it, supposing he does buy himself a good launch and hires Bill permanently to run it for him: supposing Ma Spinks and Marion moves out of their house and goes to live with Ericson, Ma to cook and Marion to housemaid; and supposing that Bill does think he won't have use for the *Do-me* and decides to sell her, what makes you think you'll do better as her owner than you're doing as my mate?"

The clear brown eyes had become stern and the old grey eyes shifted their gaze back again to the jetty.

"Might," Joe answered.

"You wouldn't," Wilton assured him earnestly. "Running a fishing launch is the same as running a farm or a business. You've got to put back into her a lot of what you take out of her. You're too easy-going, Joe. You'd take all out of the *Do-me* and put nothing into her as repairs and overhaul. You wouldn't escape worrying, Joe. As my mate you don't have to do any worrying at all, and you don't have to put back into the *Marlin* anything of the quarter-share you take out of her. Besides, Joe, we've been mates for a long time."

Grey eyes determinedly gazed at the jetty. A grunt was born deep in the massive chest beneath the blue pullover. Quite abruptly the grey eyes moved their gaze to cross swords with the brown eyes, blinked, and then as abruptly shifted back again to the jetty.

"Ha—well! Reckon you're right—about us being mates for a long time, an' about me being too easy to make money like an owner," Joe agreed, still truculent. "Any'ow, where'd you be if I did have a launch of me own? Lost, that's what you'd be. All you know about this coast, and the fish swimming off it, is what I've taught you, you young, jumped-up, jackanapes."

"Agreed, Mr Know-all."

"What's that?"

Wilton laughed, white teeth flashing in the amber of his face, and Joe snorted and mumbled something like:

"Know-all! Me? Too right I know all there's to know about this coast and the ruddy sea." Then more distinctly,

4

he added: "Well, do we stay here till the tide's high, or do we go 'ome for some tucker?"

"Home and tucker it is, mate-o'-mine."

"Mate-o'-mine!" Joe echoed, witheringly. "You're going to the pitchers too much, that's what you're doing. There's the *Gladious* first home."

Into their view slid a roomy launch, its white hull and brown-painted shelter-structure protecting the wheel and the cabin entrance. The owner was steering, and in the cockpit two anglers were dismantling their gear.

Joe and Wilton stepped into their dinghy and Joe rowed round the stern of the *Gladious*, as she drew alongside the head of the jetty to permit her catch to be weighed, and pulled in alongside an ancient tub which provided a step upward to the jetty. They were watching the heavy tuna being weighed, their interest in fish eternal, when a smart craft hove into sight beyond the bar. The *Edith* was gently lifted higher than the river, appeared to be powered by a force much stronger than her engine which rushed her forward over the bar and then deserted her. Like a gull she came swimming towards the jetty. Behind her, still to cross the bar, was a heavier craft named the *Snowy*.

One after the other the launches delivered up to the club secretary their biggest fish to be weighed—twenty, thirty, forty-pounders, and one after the other were moved to their usual berths alongside the jetty. The anglers hurried away to their cars parked ashore and drove round to the Bermagui Hotel. The day visitors sauntered to their cars, to gather wife and children preparatory to the home journey. Joe rolled homeward, leaving only Remmings of the *Gladious* and Burns of the *Edith* to tidy their craft before dinner. Wilton called down to the two women who were sitting on the hatch combing of the *Lily G. Excel.*

"Bill's a bit late getting in, Mrs. Spinks," he said to the

elder of the women. "Mr. Ericson may have decided to fight a shark on the way home. What d'you think of the *Marlin*? We finished up on her to-day, and we're refloating her to-night."

"She looks very nice in her new dress of paint, doesn't she, mother?" replied the younger woman, stepping lightly from launch to jetty to stand beside Wilton. He flushed faintly, and his eyes became veiled when he glanced at Marion Spinks. Gallantly he assisted the mother to the jetty, and she said, brightly:

"Yes, she certainly does. The clean-up will add a knot to the speed, Jack. Hasn't it been a wonderful day? It must have been as flat as my irons outside. There's hardly any surf at all."

Both these women were dressed with that severity and neatness which is the hall-mark of home dressmaking. Both were a fraction above average height, but further than a resemblance in mouth there were no traces of kinship. The elder woman was blonde, and hard work and the years had made her body angular. Marion was a brunette and strongly built. Her shapely figure had gladdened more than one artist, and Wilton thought her the most beautiful thing in his world of ever-changing beauty.

"Well, I must be getting along for dinner," he said, a hint of reluctance in his voice. "Do we travel part of the way together?"

"Not now, Jack," replied Mrs. Spinks. "We're to give Mr. Ericson an answer to his proposal."

"About working for him when his house is built?"

"Yes. He wants to know this evening so that he can forward his business. If Bill decides to go with him, we'll be doing the same. We all think a lot of Mr. Ericson, and I'm sure we'd be very happy."

"He's a very decent man," agreed Wilton, regarding Mrs.

Spinks and Marion alternately. "I think you'll be wise to accept his offer. Bill will have a regular screw all the year round, while you two will have an easier time. Well, I must go alone if you intend to wait for the *Do-me*. What about the pictures to-night, Marion? Coming?"

"If you'd like to take me," she replied, looking directly at him.

Wilton was optimistic as he walked the road to the township and his home. There were moments when he was exceedingly pessimistic, for Marion Spinks was not able to make up her mind sufficiently to surrender to the idea of marrying him.

He was dressed in his good blue suit when he heard his mother talking with someone in their kitchen-living-room. It was half-past seven and the evening was advanced. Through the open window of his bedroom came a cool draught of air, soft and fragrant with flowers growing in the tidy garden. Beyond the window the evening was quiet, unusually quiet. It was strangely empty of sound—the omnipresent sound of surf.

With his mother was Marion Spinks.

"Hullo! What's up, Marion?"

"The *Do-me* isn't home yet," she replied, her eyes troubled.

"Not home! Well, there's plenty of time for her to get home without you worrying."

"That's what I tell mother. But you know what she is, Jack. And—and . . ."

Her voice died away as rainwater vanishes in droughty earth. Her face was tautened by unease of mind. Mrs. Wilton echoed her son's remark about there being plenty of time still for the *Do-me* to reach port before the need for worry. Wilton crossed the room and stood close to the girl.

"Well?" he asked softly.

7

Into the wide blue eyes entered an expression of entreaty. Her right hand grasped his left arm.

"I haven't felt too good all afternoon, Jack. Now I feel that there's something wrong with Bill and young Garroway and Mr. Ericson. You know how it is with me and Bill."

"But what could be wrong?" argued Wilton. "The sea all day has been as calm as a park lake. It's not yet fully dark, and even if it was as black as the ace of spades Bill could navigate the *Do-me* across the bar and up to the jetty."

"Still . . ."

The blue eyes now were compelling. The small nostrils were slightly distended, and the hand which grasped his arm was now clasped by her other hand.

"I feel—I know—I feel that something's happened to the *Do-me*," she said, slowly and softly. A strange power seemed to emanate from her which he felt. "There hasn't been a breath of wind all day, and Alf Remmings said it's been hazy, too. There's no wind now. I've just been up to the headland. The sea looks like new-cut lead. Supposing the *Do-me*'s engine has broken down—the sail would be useless. She might be current-driven to the coast rocks."

Wilton said, gazing into the fearful eyes regarding him pleadingly:

"There may be something in what you say. I don't think it's likely, though. Bill knows his engine, from sump to tank. Tell you what! If the *Do-me* isn't home when we come out of the pictures I'll get Burns and Remmings to go out and patrol. The *Marlin* not being ready for sea, I could go with one or other. But—still—by that time the *Do-me* will be home. Hang it! Bill's one of the best launchmen here."

The girl bit her lower lip.

"I wouldn't enjoy the pictures, Jack, thinking, thinking——"

8

"All right! If that's how you feel I'll change back into my sea clothes and go after Burns and Remmings now. You slip back home and stop your mother worrying."

"Yes, dear, that's best," Mrs. Wilton said in support. "You can leave the rest to Jack."

An hour later the three launches, *Edith*, *Gladious* and *Ivy*, crossed the bar and slid like shadows over the bay swell towards the tip of the headland and the ocean. Marion and her mother waited at home until their anxiety would permit them to wait there no longer. It was close to midnight when they walked along the road to the jetty.

There they found the *Snowy*, with other launches moored against the jetty, and they went aboard her and took possession of the two uncushioned anglers' chairs. They could see nothing, but it was comforting to sit there.

The familiar sounds of the river were infinitely more soothing than the empty silence of their home—the cry of a gull, the honking of swans far up the river, now and then the plop of a small fish followed by the surface movement of heavier fish chasing it. All about them life was unseen but prolific, familiar. Outside, the ocean was as quiet as if it had been withdrawn to the very stars that gleamed in the velvety sky. From it came no sound save the faint music of surf on sand. It was not the voice of the sea they knew so well—the heavy pounding and thudding of league-long rollers.

At 2 a.m. the *Edith* came in with Eddy Burns and Joe Peace on board. They reported that they had patrolled up and down Swordfish Reef without sighting the *Do-me*. At daybreak the two women were still on the jetty when the *Edith* went out again, after which they hurried home for a meal and then walked to the front of the great headland protecting the township. At noon all the searching launches returned to port. The *Do-me* had not been sighted, nor could her wreckage be observed on the coast. Silently, Marion and her mother were eating lunch when Wilton entered their kitchen-living-room.

"It's no use worrying," he told them. "A wire may come through from somewhere."

Marion crossed to him, for the first time to hold out her hands for him to take.

"Tell us, Jack, what you and the others thinks," she pleaded.

"We think that the *Do-me*'s engine broke down when they were trolling along Swordfish Reef," he answered frankly. "As the current's been setting to the south'ard for more than twenty-four hours, the *Do-me* would have been taken south. We think she might have been taken past that trawler that's been working off Bunga Head since yesterday morning, and by now she ought to be somewhere off Eden."

"Oh! Then what had we better do?" urged Mrs. Spinks, whose face was white and drawn and in whose eyes was a strange light.

"I was thinking of getting Constable Telfer to telephone the police at Eden to ask one of the launchmen there to make a special trip to sea to look for the *Do-me*. Remmings spoke the trawler early this morning, but they haven't seen the *Do-me*. Still, she must be down south somewhere, and Joe says that as there's been no wind the currents wouldn't have taken her ashore.

"Anyhow, it's no use you two worrying. I'm taking the *Marlin* to sea directly we can get her loaded with oil. We mightn't be back to-night, because Joe is going to follow the currents down from Swordfish Reef till we *do* find the *Do-me*. Excepting for a broken engine the *Do-me* must be all right. The sea's like a pond. Haven't seen it so calm for years. Some ship or other is bound to sight Bill and give him a tow to port, or at least wireless his position."

"It's good of you—and the others, Jack," Marion said.

"It is that," added Mrs. Spinks. "We'll never be able to repay you all, I'm sure."

"Yes, you can," Wilton told her, and then stared at Marion. "You can repay us by not worrying. And, remember, Bill would be the first to go out after any of us. Well, so long! And no worrying, understand."

He stood for a moment regarding the girl's haunted face with lifted eyebrows and a smile that was forced. Impulsively she squeezed his hands, and he felt himself rewarded for a night's vigil. He wanted badly to draw her to him and kiss her, to wipe away from her blue eyes the expression of dread. He said to her:

"How do you feel now about Bill?"

"He's in great danger, Jack. I know he's in great danger."

Wilton nodded. He said nothing more. He knew that Marion and Bill Spinks were twins.

CHAPTER 2

No News is Bad News

Having been honorary secretary of the Bermagui Big Game
Anglers' Club from its inception, Mr. Edward Blade had at
his finger-tips a wide knowledge of game fishing in the waters
off the south coast of New South Wales, and of men, launches
and tackle. It is doubtful if anyone better could have been
found for this position, for Blade was that rarity among men,
a born club secretary combining a business education with
charming social qualities. His life at Bermagui was of even
tenor, due more to his personality and temperament than
to outside influences such as the non-arrival of important
gear or the difficulty in fitting an angler's application for a
launch into an extended busy period. This, of course, was
prior to the disappearance of the *Do-me*.

It was first realised by Mr. Blade that something most
serious had happened to the *Do-me* when Constable Telfer
entered his office at four o'clock in the afternoon following
that night of vigil conducted by the two Spinks women.
Constable Telfer, big and tough and red of face, accepted
the chair offered by the club secretary who was shorter in
stature, pink-complexioned and quick in movement.

"I don't like this *Do-me* business," was Telfer's announcement.

"It will probably be cleared up about sundown when the
Do-me comes home with the other launches," Blade said.
"Spinks is a good boatman, a good seaman, and a good fisher-
man. He wouldn't take risks with an angler aboard the

12

Do-me. Likely enough, he'll report that owing to trouble of some kind the *Do-me* had to spend the night in some cove or other."

"Why?" bluntly asked Telfer.

"Engine trouble. Or exhausted petrol supply."

The policeman removed his cap and set it down beside the typewriter on the paper-littered table. While his heavy fingers pressed tobacco into the bowl of an ancient pipe his prominent dark eyes noted the details of the room as though it were the first time he had been in it. He was acquainted with every picture on the wall—pictures of swordfish leaping high above water, of sharks being weighed at the head of the jetty, of world-famous anglers who had sat in the chair he now occupied. He knew the contents of heavy leather cases —huge ball-bearing, geared, steel reels capable of taking nine hundred yards of number 36-cord, and that inside the long cylinders resting on wall hooks were heavy rods which even he found difficulty in bending against a knee. He had never once been out after the giants of the sea, being too fearful of sickness, but he was a fishing enthusiast on the river.

"Alf Remmings, of the *Gladious*, tells me that Spinks yesterday morning took on board enough fuel to keep the *Do-me*'s engine running for thirty hours," he said deliberately. "The *Do-me* left port yesterday morning at eight o'clock, and her petrol supply would have run out at two o'clock this afternoon. Spinks would know his petrol supply in hours, and he would have been back some time this morning, making sure to give himself a good margin—if he had agreed with his angler to stay out fishing all night."

"Have you been in touch with the other stations up and down the coast?" asked Blade.

"Yes. I've been in communication with all police stations within a hundred miles north and south of Bermagui. Not one can report anything concerning the *Do-me*."

"I suppose you know that the *Gladious* and the *Ivy* were out at sea all last night, and the *Edith* part of the night, searching for the *Do-me?*"

"Of course," replied Telfer.

"And you know that Wilton, on his *Marlin*, went out this morning to follow Swordfish Reef to the southward because yesterday's current set to the south, and it is known that Spinks suggested to his angler trying for sharks over the reef?"

"Of course, I know it. Ain't I a policeman? The *Ivy* has gone south to-day, hugging the coast, and the *Dorothea* has made out towards Montague Island. I've just come down from the headland. The wind is freshening from the east'ard. I saw the *Gladious* and the *Edith* both well out, heading for home. There's no sail in sight to indicate the *Do-me* making to port with the wind."

Constable Telfer produced his notebook.

"Mrs. Spinks and the girl state that William Spinks took no extra clothes and no food other than what Mrs. Spinks put into his lunch-basket," he read in a monotone. "At seven-thirty yesterday morning the garage truck delivered six six-gallon drums of petrol to the *Do-me*, and the driver states that Spinks said he would then have a full load of fuel and wouldn't require none for to-day's fishing. At the hotel they state that Mr. Ericson took only tucker and his thermos-flask for his lunch; and, further, that he left instructions that if Martin, the Cobargo solicitor, arrived at Bermagui before he got back he was to be entertained at his, Ericson's, expense. It's evident that Mr. Ericson and his launchmen did not think they would not get back to port last evening. And they're still not back, being twenty-two hours overdue."

Blade offered a remark.

"That's certainly not normal in the calm weather we've had."

14

"No, it isn't. If it had been blowing a nor'-easter we could say that the *Do-me* was sheltering at Montague Island, with which there is only semaphore communication, and that possible only in clear weather. But, Blade, the sea has been calm, extra special calm."

The club secretary found a packet of cigarettes in the table drawer and lit one. Then he rose to his feet and crossed to the barometer, which he gently tapped with a finger-nail. The pointer moved steadily to halt at the figures 29.95.

"Hum! Barometer beginning to fall. You say that the wind is from the east. The *Do-me* might well show up before night."

"Hope your guess is correct," Telfer said dryly.

"And," went on Blade, "if she doesn't, then one or more of the Eden launches may have word of her when they get in this evening. I'm not worrying a great deal as yet, because of my confidence in Bill Spinks. He knows as much about this coast, and the currents off it, as any man bar old Joe Peace."

"I still don't like this *Do-me* business," persisted Constable Telfer. "Listen to me. Yesterday there were three launches out at sea with the *Do-me*. As you know, they were the *Gladious*, the *Snowy* and the *Edith*. The last of those three to sight the *Do-me* was the *Gladious* just after eleven o'clock. The *Do-me* was then still trolling to the east, towards Swordfish Reef."

Blade regarded the policeman steadily.

"You have been busy to-day," he said. "Go on."

"An hour after he last saw the *Do-me*, Remmings on the *Gladious* was five miles farther south. There was a haze on the sea, reducing visibility to a few miles, and the current at the south end of Swordfish Reef was setting south. If the *Do-me*'s engine had broken down after Remmings lost sight of her, she'd drift southward fairly fast because there wasn't no wind to fill her sail. In which case a trawler, working six or seven miles south of the *Gladious,* and as far off the land, might easily have seen the *Do-me.* Unlike the launches, that trawler would work all night in that same area. And last night, or rather early this morning, Remmings ran alongside the trawler and spoke with the captain. No one on the trawler had sighted the *Do-me.*

"This morning the trawler was working a little north of Eden and about eight miles off shore. The Eden police got a launchman there to go out and speak her. He spoke her at a little after twelve o'clock, and she hadn't sighted the *Do-me* up till then. The Eden launch then patrolled for an hour or two without result. She has just returned to port, and I have just had her report through the Eden station."

After this long and detailed statement Constable Telfer stared at Blade with a positive satisfaction in his prominent eyes. Blade looked away and gazed thoughtfully at his typewriter. A period of seconds passed, when he said:

"That doesn't sound so good."

Telfer snorted and continued.

"Before I came here I walked down to the jetty and had a talk with Harry Low. The *Lily G. Excel* didn't go out to-day. Low reckons it don't sound any too good, either, because this morning the sea was flat and the visibility was extra good. The men on the bridge of the trawler would have been looking for the *Do-me,* and they could have seen her mast at eight miles, if not a mile or two more."

The two men fell silent, Telfer vigorously drawing at his old pipe, Blade drumming the fingers of one hand on a paper lying on the table. In his mind the affair of the *Do-me* was now growing big with portent. After a while, Telfer asked:

"What could happen to a launch out on the ocean, alone, cut off from human sight and contact by a haze?"

"Happen! Oh! . . . She could catch fire. But if the *Do-me*

had caught fire yesterday, the smoke would have been observed by Remmings, and perhaps, by the trawler. And then the *Do-me* carried a small boat, and those on her could very easily have rowed ashore."

"Low says——" Telfer began. "Low one time was whaling down at Eden, and he says that a whale could come up to blow under a launch and capsize her without giving any warning to those on board."

"I suppose that could be possible," conceded Blade. "But it would be by no means probable. I have never heard of such a happening. It would be as unlikely as a launch being attacked by a sea-serpent or a gang of mermen."

"Could the *Do-me* have capsized through any other cause, do you think?"

"Not through any cause due to the launch herself," replied Blade. "It was a very calm day, remember. The *Do-me* is as seaworthy a craft as any at Bermagui."

The policeman's chair scraped noisily on the floor and he rose to his feet. With slow deliberation, he slid the note-book into a breast pocket whilst he looked down at the club secretary.

"We'll know what happened to the *Do-me* some day—perhaps," he said. "It's rough on the Spinks women, this not knowing what has happened. They're up on the head-land now. They've been there since breakfast this morning, and they were up there before daybreak. See you later."

After Telfer had gone Edward Blade thought to note the time. It was four minutes to five. The sunlight was slanting into his office through window and open door. He began to type a letter to a sports firm, gave it up and walked to the doorway, where he paused and searched the sky. It was streaked with faint gossamer ribbons. Re-entering the office he again tapped the barometer. The pointer indicated a drop to 29.5. Standing in the doorway once again he looked to the north past the township, over the inner bay and across the great bay to Dromedary Mountain, backing it. Thin clouds crowned its summit. Opposite the office, across the road and the un-built-on land, the river's estuary came from the low promontory protecting its mouth to curve eastward past the launch jetty. The stretch of sheltered water was covered with dark cat's-paws.

"Going to be a dirty night," he murmured, summing up all these weather signs. "Ah!"

Coming towards him, to pass his office on her way home, was Marion Spinks. The wind on the headland had blown her hair into disorder. Even here in the street it teased the hem of her skirt.

"Any sight of the *Do-me*, Miss Spinks?" he asked her.

She shook her head.

"I'm going home to make tea and take it to mother," she said. "She won't leave the headland. She won't come home and wait." Her control gave way at last under the long strain, and in her voice was a sob. "Oh, Mr. Blade! I'm afraid . . . I'm afraid."

"But, Miss Spinks, this wind will bring the *Do-me* to port somewhere."

"Yes, I am hoping that about the *Do-me*. I am afraid now for mother. She's taking on so. I can't do anything with her, and she won't come home. She says she must stop on the headland looking for the *Do-me*."

"Have you both been up there all day?"

Marion nodded her head, dumbly miserable, even desperate. Blade was quick to make a suggestion.

"Well, then, while you are home getting the tea, I'll slip off home and ask the wife to go with you and persuade your mother to come home. Mrs. Blade once was a trained nurse, you know, and she would know how to manage your mother."

"Oh, if Mrs. Blade would!"

18

"She will, I'm sure. I'll have her here when you pass with the tea."

Blade smiled encouragement at the girl, and she went on her way. Looking after her, memory of her eyes big with dread stayed with him, but he could not help noticing her poise and dignity.

His wife was with him in the office when Marion returned carrying a basket and a billy of tea. He stood in his doorway watching them pass along the street, pass the hotel, gain the end of the road and take the path to the summit of the headland.

The first of the launches in this evening was a smart craft named *Vida*; its owner reported that the sea was rising before the wind and predicted a stormy night. He had no news of the missing launch and, as the other launches were all hurrying in, he thought no news of the *Do-me* had been gained.

The last launch in was the *Myoni*. Williams, her owner, told Blade that he had taken his angler as far south as Bunga Head, and that he had not sighted the *Marlin* since nine o'clock that morning. This was shortly after six when the roar of the surf was louder than the whine of the wind about the mast stays of craft moored to the sheltered jetty. The river's mouth was foaming, and now and then the sea on the bar and beyond it lifted high above the water in the channel.

"Another easterly making," complained Alf Remmings, his moustache salted by sea spray, his darkly tanned face brightened by the spray's stinging lash. "Why can't it blow from any other quarter but the east? Looks like we're going to be kept in for days. If Jack Wilton and Joe don't soon turn up in the *Marlin* they won't risk the bar and they'll have to punch away out to Montague and shelter there."

"Trust them two to look after themselves," said Burns, as he was about to pass on his way to his home. "They went down south and they'll likely enough run in to Eden for the night. And that's where the *Do-me* is going to turn up, too, under her sail. This wind'll bring her in even if she drifted fifty miles out."

A little after seven o'clock the anxious Mrs. Wilton was relieved of growing anxiety by a telephoned message stating that the *Marlin* had reached Eden and would stay there the night.

Her son and Joe had seen nothing of the *Do-me*.

At seven-thirty Edward Blade locked his office and went home to find his wife absent and no dinner prepared. He changed into warmer clothes and walked to the headland. The sea was a restless pattern of black and white. The sky was ribbed with black cloud streamers, pointing to where the highlands made a bold silhouette against the sunset glow. The endless procession of rollers, surmounted by a film of spray, swept past the headland into the great bay, their left flanks wheeling into the inner bay to smash with ghastly whiteness against the promontory protecting the river, their centres rushing onward to hurl themselves far up the sand slopes beyond.

Blade's wife was with Mrs. Spinks and Marion. Mrs. Blade was almost beside herself, the girl tearfully beseeching her mother to abandon the vigil.

Mrs. Spinks was screaming:

"Leave me alone! I'm staying here to see the *Do-me* come home. I won't go. I tell you I won't go down. My Bill's out there, and I won't go home."

The woman's appearance shocked Blade. His wife and Marion could do nothing to pacify her, and his own efforts were of no avail. He hurried back for Constable Telfer. They were obliged to use force. All the way down the path to the road Mrs. Spinks continued to scream. She screamed until the doctor came to her house and administered morphia.

CHAPTER 3

Flotsam

The predictions of the local weather experts were wrong. On the following morning the sun rose in a clear sky and a light southerly already was having effect on the ugly white-capped rollers. Day was breaking when Joe called his partner to the breakfast he had prepared on a primus stove.

"Weather's cleared, Jack, me lad," he announced. "We can get away any time."

An hour later the *Marlin* was running up and over the water mountains, both men standing in the shelter of the glass-fronted structure protecting the wheel and steersman, the cockpit and cabin entrance. The wind was cold. The sea had the appearance of having been washed, for the valleys were dark blue, the mountain crests light blue, and the breakers brilliantly white. Astern, beetling cliffs bore the everlasting attacks of the foaming breakers. Above the cliffs were green caps of grass. Beyond rose dense timber, and farther back the distant blue-black highlands.

Wilton had interviewed the police at Eden—some forty miles south of Bermagui—for possible news of the *Do-me*. There was no news from ship or shore station, no discovery of any wreckage. In his heart this morning hope was almost dead: in Joe's heart hope was a corpse.

"She's foundered, Jack, that's what she's done," he growled, hands lightly resting on the wheel-spokes, teeth biting upon the lacerated stem of one of his two pipes. "All yesterday we looked for the *Do-me*. To-day I reckon we'd better look for oil and flotsam."

Wilton nodded, saying nothing, his eyes stern, his face seemingly fixed into a mask. Presently he passed into the cabin. A glance at his barometer told him that the pressure was steadily rising. He adjusted the engine running to maintain a steady seven knots, greased the bearings of the propeller shaft. On rejoining Joe, he said:

"We'll look for oil and flotsam. You're boss to-day. The general current is setting to the nor'ard. When d'you reckon it changed?"

"Not till some time after midnight. I was up then and the wind was still easterly."

"Well, I'll leave the course to you. You're better able to nut out the currents working south from Swordfish Reef from the time the *Do-me* was last sighted by the *Gladious*. It would give me a headache, and then I'd be wrong."

"All right," assented Joe.

Wilton rolled a cigarette, lit it, inhaled deeply. Then he clambered for'ard past the protruding shelter structure, and stood against the mast, his feet planted far apart. This day he would be the mate and would have to maintain a constant look out, not for a fin but for relics of a tragedy which had surely engulfed his lifelong friend and might engulf his own hopes of happiness centred upon that friend's sister. He left in charge at the wheel a man whose knowledge of the sea off this coast, its feminine whims and its masculine habits, was almost uncanny. They had looked for the *Do-me* with more guesswork behind the search than would be employed this day in the hunt for a patch of oil and possible flotsam.

The trawler had vanished, having left for Sydney to unload her catch. The coastal steamer, *Cobargo*, was coming south to call at Eden, whilst far at sea a trader was making for Melbourne, smoke from her solitary tall stack lying low upon the water astern of her.

Noonday found the *Marlin* fifteen miles north of Eden and some ten miles off land. The trader had been captured by distance and the *Cobargo* had gone in to Eden to unload and pick up cargo. The sea was empty. Even when the *Marlin* was atop a water mountain Wilton could see nothing afloat. The rollers were becoming mere swells, shrinking fast under the energetic influence of the low chop set up by the southerly wind.

He went aft to bring back his lunch and tea thermos. He ate whilst sitting on the forward hatch, his gaze never on his food, always on the sea. Once he saw the fin of a mako shark, and now and then a shoal of small fish whip-lashing the surface in frantic effort to escape bigger fish. A school of porpoises came to gambol about the bow, grey-green symbols of streamlined speed.

Having disposed of his lunch, he repacked the basket and took it down below. Only a minute did he give to tending the engine, and then gained Joe's side to take a trick at the wheel.

"Keep her there for a bit," Joe said. "I'll go for'ard with me grub and keep a look-out. Might alter course from time to time so's to come in to the tail of Swordfish Reef from the east. Keep an eye on me."

Wilton heard him moving heavily beside the shelter structure, saw him waddling forward to sit on the hatch-covering he had just vacated. Joe's thin grey hair was whipped by the breeze, but his body seemed as immovable as a rock. He was a man of whom a first impression was always bad and always in error.

In his turn he was repacking his tucker basket when he paused to stare landward, and then to thump the decking with one calloused hand. Through the glass Wilton saw him pointing to the west. He heard him shouting but could not distinguish the words, and he left the wheel to raise his head above the shelter structure by standing on the gunwale.

"Aireyplane," shouted Joe, again pointing.

Wilton saw the machine. It was flying low above the sea, and its course quickly informed him that it was on no normal flight. It was searching for the *Do-me*, or it's wreckage.

So the fact of the *Do-me*'s disappearance had been broadcast, for the plane must have come down from Sydney. Although it was a twin-engined machine, the pilot was taking a chance by flying so far from land. It was coming towards them now on a straight course; Wilton was able to watch it and steer the launch with his left foot on the wheel-spokes.

Joe stood up to wave, and when the machine had passed over and began to circle there could be seen two men, one of whom waved back whilst he examined the *Marlin* through binoculars. After that, like an albatross, it 'drifted' northward.

Joe came aft with his lunch basket.

"Sooner be here than up in that thing," he said, with the conservatism of the sailor. "Shift her four points to starboard, and we'll follow up a current running between two reefs."

"Telfer must have got to work reporting the absence of the *Do-me*," surmised Wilton, again standing before the wheel and obeying his partner's order. "That plane's from Sydney all right. She's an Air Force machine."

"Hell-'v-a-'ope of sightin' the *Do-me* now," grumbled Joe. "And not much chance their sighting oil after last night's weather. Any'ow if they seen a patch of oil they couldn't tell if it came from the *Do-me* or a steamer."

"How do you think to tell it if we come across any?"

"If we come across oil, Jack, the chances are that it came from the *Do-me*. 'Cos why? Cos we're follering tight the sea-

drift from where the *Do-me* must have gone down. Oil anywhere away from the drift would be steamer's oil, likely
enough. Any'ow, after last night's weather it won't be easy
to look at from aboard here, let alone a plane, low as that
one was working. Better let me take the wheel. I'll have to
do a bit of dodging about. If there's anything to be found it
will be within a mile or two of this position."

Wilton was standing beside the mast when, some forty
minutes later, he abruptly turned aft and raised both his
arms. Instantly Joe pushed the engine clutch into neutral,
and raised himself to look over the shelter structure. Wilton
was pointing to the sea about the launch.

"What d'you make of it, Joe? Is it oil?"

Joe's eyes widened. Then he sprang down into the cockpit, bent low to bring his eyes on a level with the gunwale to
squint across the low chop-waves on the slopes of the greater
swells. Perhaps for half a minute he remained thus before
clambering for'ard to join his partner in staring downward
at the surface of the water. Then:

"Yes, that's oil, Jack. Film's thinner than ordinary due to
last night's rough weather. It's oil, all right, and it's in the
drift coming from Swordfish Reef. Now lemme think."

His face became a study of mental concentration, the
expression not unlike that of a schoolboy trying to remember
a lesson. In fact his brain was working on a problem that
would have defied a professor of mathematics, for he sought
the answer to the question: How far from an oil patch which
offers exceedingly slight resistance to wind might be found
flotsam from the same craft from which came the oil, when
the velocity of the wind was such and such for so many hours,
when it blew from such a quarter before changing to such a
quarter, when this current would flow at so many knots to
the hour, and that at so many knots, to join another current
moving at such a speed?

"We'll move on a bit," he said sharply. "You stay here and keep a look-out. Don't pass by as much as a splinter of wood."

The aeroplane was still out over the sea, out from Bunga Head, ten miles south of Bermagui. The *Marlin* was six miles south of the great headland and seven miles off the small settlement called Tathra. They could this clear day see the hotel at Tathra.

Joe brought out from the cabin a petrol drum, and standing on this he could see on all sides above the shelter roof whilst he steered with his naked feet. He sent the *Marlin* forward at a mere two knots to the hour, scanning the coast about Tathra and taking constant bearings from Bunga Head. The upper part of his body rested on the roof of the shelter and his hands protected his eyes from the near light. Apparently undirected, the *Marlin* began a series of zig-zags, curves and giant circles.

Steadying himself by holding to the mast and the port mast stay, Jack Wilton ceaselessly scanned the sea with greater mental concentration than ever he had watched for a fin. His craft's extraordinary antics perturbed him not at all, for his confidence in his partner was supreme when it was a question of the currents controlled by the wind and the reefs far below the surface. He did not permit himself to gaze landward, or to watch the plane, giving every second of time to the surface of the glittering sea.

The wind was dying. The chop from the south was falling fast, and the now unopposed swells were flat topped and smooth sloped. Minutes mounted to an hour, the hour grew to two hours, and still Joe stood on his drum and steered with his naked feet. He watched not the sea but the land and Bunga Head, for that Head and points of the land gave him his constantly changing positions.

The plane had at last gone from the sea. There was a

launch far away to the nor'-east, its hull below the horizon, its mast standing stiffly on the horizon like a hair on the head of a bald man.

Both Wilton and Joe were confident that if the *Do-me* had gone down there must be flotsam and oil to betray its fate. The oil they had passed over was more likely than not to have come from the *Do-me*, for Joe was following an invisible road to Swordfish Reef above which the missing launch was assumed to have sunk. On this same invisible road would be objects which would float away from the *Do-me* if and when she sank; objects such as the angler's chair-cushion, the wooden bait-fish box, hats, lunch basket and wooden tucker box, thermos flasks and milk bottles. If the door giving entry to the engine-room cabin was open at the time of the catastrophe, a good deal of gear would wash out and float to the surface. Somewhere along Joe's narrow and invisible road would be floating flotsam from the missing launch—if she had sunk—and Joe's ability to keep to this track zig-zagging across the trackless sea was something extraordinary.

Ah! There was Jack still standing against the mast, but now loudly stamping on the deck to attract his partner's attention. He did not look back, but continued to stare away over the starboard bow, as though he knew that once he shifted the direction of his gaze the object would be lost to him. Joe altered course in accordance with the orders given by Wilton's outstretched arm, his feet taking the place of his hands on the wheel-spokes.

Presently he came to see ahead a line of suds, thin and broken. As he well knew, it was the division line between a current setting landward and one making seaward, a dividing line forming a no-man's-land on which floated the chalky backs of cuttlefish, the bodies of dead crabs, and other offal of the sea.

Then Joe saw that which was exciting his partner. It was

reflecting the sunlight, winking as the water moved its angle with the sun. Joe pushed the clutch into neutral, and the *Marlin* lost speed and glided towards the sun-reflector. Wilton shouted:

"It's a thermos-flask!"

He raced aft to leap down into the cockpit, where he crouched over the gunwale whilst Joe expertly 'edged' the craft alongside the flask. With his booted feet hooked about the side rail of the starboard angler's chair, Wilton leaned far out and down to snatch from the sea this piece of flotsam. Joe helped him inboard, and together they regarded the flask.

The cap cup was screwed on tightly and yet was not rusted on. There was no rust on the screw of the flask, which was new and obviously had not long been in the water. The cork was firmly pushed into the glass receptacle, and on being pulled free permitted Wilton to pour a little of the contents out on to a hand palm. It was tea, and when he tasted it, he said, looking at Joe:

"Might have been brewed this morning. Hullo, what's this?"

On the bottom of the flask had been scratched two letters. The scratching was still bright. Only recently had it been done.

"Who-in-'ell's B.H.?" demanded Joe. "Them's someone's initials."

"Yes. B.H. Can't be Hooper of the *Lily*. His are M.H."

"No. And B.H. don't stand for Ericson, or for Spinks, or for Garroway, Spinks's mate. She couldn't have come from the *Do-me*."

There was vast disappointment in Joe's voice. He turned back to the wheel, put in the gear, climbed to his petrol drum and resumed his crouching attitude above the shelter roof. It was as though he blamed Wilton.

Wilton placed the 'find' in his lunch basket in the cabin, and resumed his place at the mast. Slowly the *Marlin* was sent on her way parallel with the winding line of suds. When at the end of the suds line, the craft continued her apparently aimless wandering about the sea. During the next hour Wilton retrieved a caseboard, which, however, had small shell fish adhering to it, proving that it had been in the water for some considerable time, and a butter-box with similar evidence.

Nothing was seen or retrieved of vital importance to the fate of the *Do-me*; and the flask was not likely to have any bearing on it, either.

Time passed quite unnoticed by the searchers until the sun, having travelled down the sky's flawless bowl, rested for a moment on the horizon and then was swallowed by the sea. Still the *Marlin* crawled along the invisible road, and still the two men maintained their stations and their attitudes. Only when increasing dusk decreased visibility to a few yards did Jack Wilton come aft, to say:

"We'll go home and come out again to-morrow."

"All right! We can start from Swordfish Reef to-morrow," Joe agreed. "If we don't find anything to-morrow, then the *Do-me*'s still afloat somewhere."

It was close to midnight when the *Marlin* approached the now invisible bar, kicked herself over the tumbling water into the channel, and crept along the river to the jetty.

Three men stood on the jetty, evidently waiting for them.

"Any luck, Jack?" inquired Mr. Blade.

"No. Don't think so, anyway."

"Don't think so!" echoed a man whose dark shape against the starry sky informed the seaman that he was a stranger.

"What 'ave you got to do with it, any'ow?" demanded Joe, climbing to the jetty with a mooring-rope.

"This is Detective-Sergeant Allen," said Constable Telfer.

"Coo!" snorted Joe, as though Detective-Sergeant Allen had no moral or legal right to breathe.

Wilton gained the jetty, to say to the waiting three:

"We've seen nothing of the *Do-me*—only that aeroplane. We've been looking for wreckage, flotsam, where Joe reckons flotsam from off the *Do-me* ought to be if she had sunk. We found nothing belonging to her. All we found was a new thermos-flask. Here it is. On the bottom is scratched the initials B.H."

"Ah!" murmured Allen with immense satisfaction. "B.H. stands for Bermagui Hotel. The morning that the *Do-me* last went to sea, one of the maids at the pub dropped Mr. Ericson's flask and broke it. She filled and gave him one of three flasks bought a couple of days before by the hotel. The barman scratched the initials on all three of 'em."

CHAPTER 4

A Clue Among Fish

Before the construction of the Prince's Highway, Bermagui was an isolated hamlet aroused only at Christmas and at Easter by the small influx of visitors from inland farms and the market town of Cobargo. Even after the opening of the Highway it suffered to some extent through the disadvantage of being seven miles from it at Tilba Tilba. It was His Majesty the Swordfish that 'made' Bermagui.

The discovery of swordfish in the waters off the southern coast of New South Wales was due to chance, for their swift-moving dorsal fins when seen by the fishermen were thought to be a species of shark. A fisherman when out for salmon, using a hand line with a feathered hook attached, one afternoon was bringing to his boat a fine fighting salmon which was followed by a huge fish. The big fish came to the surface close to the boat—to reveal not only its dorsal fin but its 'sword'.

For some time this was thought to be only a fisherman's yarn, until Mr. Roy Smith determined to test the story, and on 2nd February, 1933, proved its authenticity by capturing with rod and reel a black marlin weighing 262 pounds. Still, doubt remained general that swordfish regularly visited the coast of southern New South Wales, although the fishermen declared that the swift-moving fins had been seen every summer. When Mr. Roy Machaelis and Mr. W. G. Wallis between them captured nine swordfish in the one day, deep sea anglers the world over began to take notice. The subsequent visit of Mr. Zane Grey resulted in Bermagui becoming famous as a centre of big game angling.

When Angler Ericson and his launchmen on the *Do-me* vanished, Bermagui suffered a slight setback, for it naturally followed that when an unexplained catastrophe overwhelmed a small launch the other launches were considered to be too frail for the open sea, or too likely to be the victims of whales or mermen, or too liable to strike an uncharted reef. Proof of this came quickly in the form of cancelled bookings of the launches and hotel accommodation.

The search for the *Do-me* achieved nothing but the reclamation of one thermos-flask from the sea.

Detective-Sergeant Allen's reputation was high, but he was unfortunately a poor sailor. Jack Wilton and Joe took him out to show him the position of the *Gladious* when Remmings last sighted the *Do-me*, and the position of the *Do-me* when she was last sighted, but poor Allen became frightfully seasick and unable to maintain any interest. Thereafter he confined his investigating to the land.

One man in Bermagui came to wonder just who and what Mr. Ericson had been—and was, if still alive. The secretary of the club followed the intensive and extensive search with both hope for its success and gratification that officialdom was trying so hard, incidentally, to remove the stigma the mystery put upon Bermagui.

A second plane was sent down from Sydney to assist the first in its thorough examination of the sea and the coast. Allen recommended the employment of the *Marlin*, and her crew, to continue making a search for flotsam, and for a little more than a fortnight Wilton and his mate enjoyed government pay. On shore, Sergeant Allen organised two searchparties to explore the base of cliffs and those parts of the coast barred to launches, these men primarily concentrating on the discovery of small items of wreckage not likely to be observed by the air pilots. At the end of three weeks the only clue to the fate of the *Do-me* was the thermos-flask retrieved from the sea by Wilton.

Even the flask was not a clue that proved anything. That it belonged to the licensee of the Bermagui Hotel, and that it had been filled with tea and put into Ericson's lunch basket, was, of course, established; but, there was no proof how it came to be floating in the sea; whether it had been washed off the *Do-me* when she sank, or had been lost overboard. General opinion favoured the first theory; for, as Joe Peace maintained, had the angler or one of his launchmen accidentally knocked the flask overboard it would have been retrieved. It appeared unlikely that an article such as a thermos-flask would fall overboard unobserved. The angler would take it from the basket, and pour tea from it, whilst he was in his rightful place—the cockpit.

Joe's claim to the wide knowledge of the local sea currents, and his ability to follow them, even to 'back-track' them, was given little credence by Sergeant Allen, or by Detective-Sergeant Light, who came down to assist him. The small army of reporters were even greater doubters. For a while Bermagui accommodation was taxed to its utmost, and the official search was maintained for three weeks.

No wonder that Mr. Blade began to think that the missing angler was a world figure incognito. After Light went back to Sydney in one of the planes, and the search parties were disbanded, Wilton and Joe continued to search for evidence of the fate of the *Do-me*, and Constable Telfer confided in Blade when telling him that Sergeant Allen had received instructions to remain on the 'job' until recalled.

October passed out in calm and warm weather. But November quickly produced a nor'-easterly which raged for days and kept the launches idle and the few anglers in the hotel bar.

After that one terrible night and day of vigil Mrs. Spinks became almost normal. Almost but not quite, for her mind appeared to have become permanently deranged on one matter. She refused to believe that the *Do-me* was lost and that her son was dead. She took advantage of every opportunity to escape from the watchful care of her daughter and would hurry to the headland to search the ocean for sight of her son's launch coming home. Often she called in on Mr. Blade to request him to send to a passing ship a wireless message asking the captain to tell her son to return at once as his underclothes were due to be changed.

The neighbours and others felt pity and little wonder because in her belief that the *Do-me* had not gone down Mrs. Spinks was firmly supported by Marion, whose mind had not been affected by the tragedy. The only change to be observed in Marion was the absence of her flashing laughter. She would shake her head when people proffered sympathy and say:

"Bill's not dead. I'd know it if he was dead."

The sixth day of November was indelibly printed on Blade's mind by visits he received in the afternoon from Jack Wilton and, later, a visiting angler, a Mr. George Emery. Wilton did not expend time in preliminaries.

"I've come to see you about Marion and Mrs. Spinks," he said, his brown eyes a little troubled but his mouth determined. "They're in a bad way—about money. As you know, old man Spinks was a boozer and left the family well in debt when he died. It was only then that Bill got a square deal from life and began to pull things together. The building of the *Do-me* put him in debt again, but he had cleared this off just before the *Do-me* vanished.

"Other times Marion would have got a job somewhere, but now she has to look after her mother more than ever she did after the old man pegged out. I'm in love with Marion.

Been that way since we were kids at school. And I wanted her to marry me—want her to marry me now—but she couldn't make up her mind about it. And now she's not trying. I want you to do me a favour. Will you?"

"Of course, Jack."

"Well, I've been thinking of getting up a subscription to help them two, but it wouldn't do for me to run it, Marion being a bit proud and independent. I've got here a hundred quid. Just took it out of the bank. You could say you had received it from a rich sympathiser in Sydney or somewhere."

Placing the money in a compact bundle on the table, he put down beside it a smaller sheaf of notes, saying:

"This is from my partner, Joe Peace. There's twenty-seven quid in it. That makes a hundred and twenty-seven. If you could raise another twenty-three to make the total a hundred and fifty, it could be suggested to Marion that she take over Nott's shop. Mrs. Nott wants to go to Melbourne to live, and she's willing to sell for a hundred and fifty and the balance at interest."

Blade's gaze moved from the eager face to his typewriter. He did not look up when he asked:

"Would Miss Spinks go into that business, do you think?"

"I think so—so long as I had nothing to do with it. We were talking about it last night. She says she thinks her mother wouldn't be so restless if she had to prepare the teas and suppers and make the meat-pies."

"Very well, Jack. I'll raise the balance."

"Thanks, Mr. Blade. I thought you'd help. You'll keep me and Joe out of it?"

"Yes, as you wish it."

Blade saw that his visitor waited, but hesitated, to suggest something further.

"You can depend on me to do everything I can to help Miss Spinks and her mother," he said encouragingly.

"Good! And—and would you keep an eye on the books and things? You see, Marion and me aren't good at that part of it."

"I shall be glad to, Jack."

Wilton rose to his feet, his face swept clean of trouble.

"Things is going to be droughty with us this summer," he said, thoughtfully. "Not with the ordinary people, but with us launchmen. Two of my bookings for the swordies have been cancelled and the others have had bookings cancelled too. Me and Joe will have to take to the beach-netting for salmon for the factory. It's a blasted shame we can't sell tunny. There's millions of 'em about now. All from six- to fifteen-pounders."

Blade smiled.

"I don't think we need worry much, Jack. This *Do-me* affair will blow over by Christmas now that the newspapers have shut down on it."

Wilton had not been gone ten minutes when Mr. Emery entered. He was portly, important, and now burned scarlet by the wind and sun and sea-spray. He advanced with hand outstretched.

"I'm leaving for Sydney, Blade. Business calls and all that. Blast business! Should have gone yesterday, you know, but this fishing gets into a man's very bones."

"Well, I hope you will come again soon."

Mr. Emery beamed, but was explosive.

"Come again! Hang it, Blade! I couldn't keep away if every launch in Bermagui disappeared. I'm coming down for the swordies early in January. It's a bit rough on those women, anyway. Saw them last evening on the headland when we were coming in. The daughter was trying to persuade the mother to go home with her, or it looked like it."

It was then that Blade had inspiration. He first bound Mr. Emery to confidence and then related what had transpired between Wilton and himself. Mr. Emery said, less explosively:

"Give me a pen."

He wrote his cheque hurriedly, and rose to his feet, saying:

"Give them two fellers back their savings. If I can't still make three hundred pounds before breakfast I'm losing my punch. So long, and if you can spare a minute any time drop me a letter saying how the fish are going. I'm only living for the swordies in January."

He shook hands, beamed and departed, leaving Blade a little breathless and staring down at the cheque he had drawn in Marion's favour for three hundred pounds. The figures were written with extreme care, but the signature was familiar to the secretary, although he was unable to read it. Blade was astonished but not amazed, for swordfishing is a rich man's sport, and rich men sometimes are philanthropic.

Marion Spinks and her mother were in possession of the refreshment shop and small store by the middle of November. The girl's hopes were justified; so long as Mrs. Spinks could be kept busy she appeared not to worry about her son's clean underclothes. There were occasions, however, especially towards evening, when Mrs. Spinks would slip away to the headland, and then Marion had to run to Mrs. Wilton and ask her to 'mind' the shop whilst she went after her mother.

Shortly before four o'clock on the afternoon of the 20th, there appeared rounding the headland to reach the steamer wharf a rusty and disreputable ship of some two thousand tons. The only respectable portion of her was her bridge, white-painted and almost entirely glassed in. On either side of her blunt bow was the cipher *A.S.3*.

It so happened that, when the *A.S.3* hove into sight of those about the only street of Bermagui, Edward Blade was talking with Detective-Sergeant Allen and Mr. Parkins, the garage proprietor, outside the club secretary's office.

"Hullo! What does she want in here?" demanded Mr. Parkins, a keen-eyed man of fifty. "I haven't seen one of those trawlers here for a long time."

"So that's a trawler, is it?" mildly inquired Sergeant Allen, the very sight of this ship arousing memory of his excessive sea-sickness.

"Yes," Blade answered him. "It might be that one of her crew has met with an accident. There must be something serious, for her captain to call here. Let's go along and find out."

The three men walked along the street, past the hotel, deserted at this time of day and of the week, and so reached the edge of the wharf as two men in a small boat were returning from having taken a rope hawser to the mooring buoy. The captain was giving megaphoned orders to his crew.

The ship was being gently 'edged' to the wharf front with the aid of propeller and winch. The actions of the men hinted that the ship's stay at Bermagui was not to be overlong. Immediately aft of the bridge was the wireless cabin, and in the doorway of this was standing the operator, a young man who appeared either delicate in health or still suffering from sea-sickness. The captain having done with his megaphone, Blade shouted:

"Anything wrong, Captain?"

"Nothing much," came the shouted answer. "I'm wanting the constable. Suppose he's about?"

"Well, no, he's out of town this afternoon. Had a mutiny?"

The crew were passing a gangway from ship to wharf. The captain left his bridge, gained the deck, and passed along the gangway to Blade and his companions.

"When will the constable be back?" demanded the trawler captain. "Can't stay here in port all day."

"Not until this evening, Captain. But if you have trouble

of any kind, here is Detective-Sergeant Allen, who will take charge of it."

"Oh, good day, Sergeant. Please follow me."

The captain recrossed the gangway, followed by Allen with Blade and Parkins. The small procession made its way across the littered deck to the bridge entrance where it was calmly surveyed by the first mate. Blade had noticed whilst they were on the main deck how the crew stared at them, and as he mounted to the bridge he noticed the fixed expression on the face of the wireless operator and received a shock from the look of stark horror in the young man's eyes. The captain halted beside the ship's wheel at the foot of which a piece of old tarpaulin lay heaped as though it covered a small object. Grimly the captain said:

"At two-thirty this afternoon, I gave the order for the trawl to be brought inboard. The trawl had been down on the sea bottom for one hour thirty minutes, when the course of the ship had been roughly parallel with Swordfish Reef and half a mile inshore of it. Among the fish and other stuff in the trawl was this——"

He bent down swiftly and snatched up the piece of tarpaulin.

Mr. Parkins cried loudly:

"Good lord!"

Blade whistled, and Sergeant Allen hissed between his teeth.

Grinning up at them from the bridge flooring was a human head.

Its aspect was much more horrific than those polished relics to be found in museums. Although the flesh had been removed by the crayfish and the crabs and small fish the scalp still covered the cranium, and to the scalp was still attached dark-grey hair.

Blade knew that he felt much like the wireless operator

was still feeling. He regarded Allen as a strong man when the detective bent down the closer to examine the fearful object. Mr. Parkins did not move. The captain's voice appeared to reach him from great distance.

"This head has been in the water less than months and longer than days," the captain was remarking. "It might belong to one of those poor fellows on the launch *Do-me*."

"There was only the head—no body?" asked Allen.

"No, Sergeant, there was no body . . . only that. I haven't yet figured it out how it came to get into the trawl, the lower edge of the trawl being slightly above the sea bottom, if you know what I mean. By rights the trawl ought to have passed over it. Just a fluke, I suppose. Funny how murder will out, isn't it?"

"Funny!" gasped Mr. Parkins, and the captain glared at him.

"Murder!" Allen said softly.

The captain again stooped, and this time when he straightened he held the relic between his hands. He held it high; held it level with the eyes of the three men. Just behind the right temple they saw a neat round hole. The captain reversed the head, and then they saw much farther back from the left temple another hole, larger and less neat.

"Bullet-holes," said Sergeant Allen.

"Bullet-holes," echoed Blade.

"That's what I think," agreed the captain. "The poor feller who once had this head on his walking body wasn't drowned. He was shot, murdered."

"And he was on board the *Do-me*," Mr. Parkins added. "Look at the hair! It must be Mr. Ericson's head."

CHAPTER 5

Inspector Bonaparte Arrives

Detective-Sergeant Allen would have made a secret of the recovery of the human head had not so many persons known of it. Besides, the officers and men of the trawler, the captain had wirelessed his owners the fact and his decision to take the relic to the police at Bermagui. Allen, however, kept the *A.S.3* in port for longer than two hours whilst he took statements from the captain and first officer, the wireless operator and four of the men. When the *A.S.3* was rounding the headland on her way back to her lawful business, Allen was starting in a hired car for Sydney with the head boxed and set at his feet.

The first thing done by Blade after he left the ship was to call on Marion Spinks so that she would hear first from him of the finding of the head, and to be assured that it had not been torn from her brother's body. The girl, neatly dressed in a blue print overall, stood quite placidly behind her counter whilst he related the bare facts, her big dark eyes concentrated on his. Still feeling shock, he was able to wonder at her calmness.

"I don't believe Bill is dead," she said. "I feel that he's in great trouble but not dead. He's calling to me for assistance, and it makes me so that I can't sleep at night. You see, Mr. Blade, Bill and me were always kind of close to each other. When he was happy so was I, and when anything upset me he was upset, too. No, Bill's not dead."

"But, Miss Spinks——"

41

Blade stopped, for how could he press the assertion that the *Do-me* had gone down and all with her in face of that sublime belief that Spinks still lived? The import of her belief when allied with the bullet-holes in that head burst in his mind like a star. Who could have killed Ericson save Bill Spinks or young Bob Garroway? One or other must have shot the angler, and then if he had not shot his mate, too, taken the *Do-me* out to sea away from all craft for the remainder of the day; returning after dark to hide her somewhere from the searchers.

Sergeant Allen did not return from Sydney; but a detective-inspector named Handy came down, to go out with Wilton and Joe Peace for three days. He spent two days inquiring into the past life of William Spinks, during which he often interviewed Marion, and tried to interview the mother, but was prevented by that woman's quick and probably unreasoning hostility. After being satisfied about the origin of the money which had set Marion up in business, he returned to Sydney to the relief of many people in general and Constable Telfer in particular.

As far as concerned the people of Bermagui, it seemed that the police investigation into the disappearance of the *Do-me*, and those with her, had been a failure, and was recognised as such. Much to Blade's relief opinion remained strongly in favour of the missing launchmen. In such a small community everyone was familiar with everyone else's affairs, and everyone at Bermagui knew that neither Bill Spinks nor his mate owned a pistol, only a rifle which discharged a .32 bullet, and was used for dispatching sharks brought to the gaff by anglers. No motive for killing Mr. Ericson could even be imagined; for everyone knew what he was planning to do and how the Spinks family were to benefit by those plans.

The first swordfish of the new season was brought in for

weighing by a Mr. Rockaway, who had settled at Wapengo Inlet, ten miles south of Bermagui, where he had built himself a fine house and a jetty to take his fifty-foot launch. Thereafter Bermagui tried hard to get into its busy stride for the very important big game fishing season. Christmas passed. Then on New Year's Day six anglers between them brought to Mr. Blade's scales six swordfish and two mako sharks. It certainly appeared that Mr. Blade's hope that the shadow on Bermagui would quickly pass was to be realised.

A little after three o'clock on 10th January, a man of average height and weight, dressed in a smart double-breasted suit of light grey tweed, entered the club secretary's office. The visitor's eyes were blue, his hair black and inclined to waviness, and his skin dark. A good-looking man, yet he was not a white man.

"Mr. Blade—Mr. Edward Blade?"

"Yes. Will you sit down?"

"Thank you. May I smoke?"

A cigarette was rolled more swiftly than Blade had ever seen done. He was entranced. Then he was again hearing the pleasantly modulated, clearly accented voice.

"Detective-Sergeant Allen has spoken to me most highly of you, Mr. Blade. He tells me that you are a man to be confidently trusted, and one eager to be of assistance to all and sundry. Also that you are conversant with everyone here, the history of the place, its geography, and that you will gladly advise me on how to become the compleat angler."

"Sergeant Allen is generous. I shall be delighted to assist you in any and every way."

Blade was experiencing slight awe of this visitor to Bermagui, who was so immaculate, so easy in manner, and still so unusual. He looked not unlike an Indian prince. He spoke, as they do in Dublin, the purest English. Even more

43

remarkable than his appearance and speech was his obvious self-confidence.

"I do not think you have ever heard of me. My name is Napoleon Bonaparte."

Blade bowed from his chair behind the table. The famous name claimed his interest, but did not enlighten him. Had his visitor said he was Marco Polo or Nero he would have wondered no more than he did at any man having such a name in this year of grace when it could be so easily changed for another by deed poll.

"May I be encouraged to rely on your discretion?" inquired Mr. Napoleon Bonaparte.

"Certainly."

"And to hope that you will regard what I want to say with the strictest confidence?"

Blade nodded his agreement, and Mr. Napoleon Bonaparte's blue eyes beamed upon him. Despite his 'backing and filling', the visitor was a likeable chap.

"It is not my intention to announce my profession, Mr. Blade, and therefore I have taken care to inform those at the hotel that I am a cattleman down from the Northern Territory on a prolonged holiday. Fame is so apt to become a devouring fire that I keep mine under a quart-pot. I see that you do not associate me with the police, although I have told you my name. I am a detective-inspector from the Queensland Criminal Investigation Branch; now attached, by arrangement with my Chief Commissioner, to the New South Wales C.I.B."

"Indeed!" murmured Blade.

"My visit to Bermagui is a dual-purpose one. Having been asked to investigate the affair of the missing *Do-me*, I see my way quite clear to the indulgence of what I am told is the finest sport in the world, swordfishing, at someone else's expense."

The features of Inspector Bonaparte's face were immobile, but in his eyes gleamed humour which made Blade suspect impish cynicism. It occurred to him suddenly that this Bonaparte man was really quite charming.

"So the police have not yet given up the mystery," he said.

"By no means. In fact, they are only beginning on it by asking me to take over the investigation. Poor Sergeant Allen admitted defeat, complaining of the paucity of clues and leads, and cursing the sea and a particular launch named *Marlin* which he did not seem to favour. Then Inspector Handy agreed with him in all but the sea and the launch. And so, having read all their reports and having gone through their collection of statements, I decided that this was a meaty bone for me on which to try the teeth of my brain.

"It is certainly an out-of-the-way case. I have to admit that I shy clear of crimes of violence where there are finger-prints and revolvers, bodies and missing valuables, and a nark or two in a thieves' kitchen waiting to inform for the price of beer. I like my cases minus bodies and minus clues, if possible. Which is why this *Do-me* case so attracts me. Three men go to sea in a fishing launch, and neither launch nor men are ever seen again. Then the head of one of them is brought up in a ship's trawl, and it is seen that its owner was murdered with a pistol bullet. There is no motive to account for the killing, and everything points away from either the launchman or his mate having done the killing."

"I am glad to hear you say that, Inspector," interrupted the club secretary. "I have known the Spinks family for several years, and young Spinks was a hard-working, dependable man, frank and straightforward. As for his mate, Bob Garroway, a lad of only nineteen, he has been hereabouts for five or six years and was well liked."

"Well, it will be all cleared up one day, Mr. Blade. I have

never failed to finalise a case, and it would be unthinkable for me to have any doubt regarding this one. I suppose you don't know who Ericson was?"

"No."

"I will tell you, Mr. Blade; because I shall want your collaboration, as this case will take me far from my usual background. I am not familiar with the sea. Now, Ericson retired three years ago from New Scotland Yard, London, where he was a superintendent, in fact, was one of the famous Big Five. Years before retiring, he had met the present New South Wales Chief Commissioner of Police, and these two men became warm friends.

"When he retired Ericson was a wealthy man, having inherited money, and he built himself a house at a place called Warsash, bordering Southampton Water, where he owned his own yacht and spent much of his time fishing. It was after reading an article on swordfishing here at Bermagui that he wrote his friend out here asking for further details of life in Australia, and the result of that was his acceptance of an invitation to come out here, make the Chief Commissioner's home his headquarters, and from there test this sport of swordfishing.

"He arrived on September the third, and four days later visited the Commissioner's dentist to have work done on his teeth. Thus it was that his head was identified. Here he paid all debts with cheques. He paid the hotel weekly with a cheque and he paid Spinks weekly with a cheque. His cheque-book and pocket wallet containing only a few pound notes were found among his effects in his room at the hotel. Robbery as a motive for the crime appears to be quite ruled out. The idea Ericson was putting into shape of settling here and buying a launch for Spinks to run for him, as well as to employ Spinks's mother and sister, smashes any theory connecting Spinks with the disappearance of the *Do-me*. Ericson was robbed of nothing but his life. There is nothing in his character that would lead one to assume that he could or did double-cross Spinks for any reason, whilst his death would be the cause of certain loss to Spinks.

"There is a man here, a Joseph Peace, who is going to be of great assistance to me. Officially he is regarded as being a crank because of his claim that he can define the direction of a succession of sea currents. Possibly I have been termed a crank for the reason that I can follow tracks not to be seen by ordinary men. Peace, I understand, is mate to a Jack Wilton, who owns a launch named *Marlin*. I would like to engage those men and that launch."

"Wilton will be glad of the engagement," Blade hastened to say. "The *Do-me* affair has cast a shadow over Bermagui and the place is not popular just now. If you can remove the shadow, everyone here will be grateful to you. How long will you be requiring the launch, do you think?"

"During the whole of my stay here, which may be for several months. As I told you, my expenses are to be paid from Ericson's estate."

"What about tackle? I assume you will require that."

"Sergeant Allen told me I could hire the tackle from you. I must rely on you for what I want, for I know nothing about swordfishing."

"Well, then I can let you have a complete set of tackle for five pounds a week: rod and reel, line and trace and hooks, body harness and teasers. I will get you to sign for the items, and then Wilton can take charge of them and have everything ready. Will you be going out to-morrow?"

Bonaparte's face was alight with anticipation.

"Assuredly," he replied, to add with a smile: "A detective's first duty is to examine the scene of the alleged crime, and so I must visit Swordfish Reef, and . . . perhaps . . . catch a swordfish. Meanwhile I am a cattleman from the Northern

Territory. I will study Wilton and his mate before taking them into my confidence. They tell me, Mr. Blade, that catching a swordfish gives a greater thrill than buffalo hunting, even tiger shooting."

Blade sighed, and Bonaparte saw ecstatic memory leap to his eyes.

"Life doesn't hold a bigger thrill than the 'feel' of a two to three hundred pound swordfish at the end of five hundred yards of line," he said slowly. "The rougher the sea the more intense the thrill. Are you a good sailor?"

"I have authority for thinking so. Nothing will——"

The sound of flying feet on the sidewalk outside the office put a period on what Bonaparte was saying, and in through the open doorway dashed a small boy.

"Mr. Blade! Mr. Blade!" he cried pipingly. "The *Gladious* is coming in with a swordie."

"Oh! Is she flying the blue flag?"

"Yes, Mr. Blade. Can I go with you on the truck down to the jetty?"

"Certainly. You run in and tell Mr. Parkins. Are you coming along to the jetty, Mr. Bonaparte? I have to go to weigh the capture."

Bony was on his feet.

"I could not possibly do anything else, Mr. Blade," he replied.

CHAPTER 6

"Fish-oh!"

Bony breakfasted at seven o'clock the following morning in company with that Mr. Emery who had set up Marion Spinks in business and whose capture of the last evening was now suspended on the triangle at the entrance to the town. The small grey eyes regarded Bonaparte for a fraction of time.

"Morning! You going out fishing to-day?"

"Yes. This is to be my first sally after the swordfish. What are the prospects, do you think?"

Again that stabbing glance was directed at the half-caste, but the heavy, reddened face successfully masked the thought relative to Bonaparte's birth. An educated man is stamped by his voice and accent, and both were weighed and judged by a mind used to lightning decisions. Although Emery was ageing and probably knew better, he bolted his food and spoke with his mouth full.

"You never know how the day will turn out," he said, in a manner reminding his table companion of a marionette show. "This is my third swordfishing season at Bermagui. It's the uncertainty of the fishing which makes it so great a sport. If a feller could catch 'em all day long and every day he'd want to be as strong as one of those wrestlers—as you will, I hope, find out. A feller's lucky to get three swordies a week, and sometimes, when the shoal fish are away, you can go a full week and never see a fin. You using your car?"

"No. I came down by plane."

49

"Well, then, hurry up and I'll take you along to the jetty in my 'tub'. Ordered your lunch basket?"

"Yes."

"You get sick?"

"Never."

"You're lucky. Me, I'm terribly sick the first day or two." The food was shovelled into the wide mouth. Then: "Being sick don't stop me fishing. First day this time I was as sick as a dog and not keeping proper watch on my bait-fish, when a hammerhead took the bait. Great brainless pig of a fish is that kind of shark. Won't fight, you know. Anyway, time I'd bullocked with him, and he wanted to go down deep and drown himself, I forgot all about being sick." Another silence followed these somewhat inapt remarks. Presently: "If I ate like this at home I'd have indigestion for a month and a doctor's bill to pay. Go on, man, hurry up. The days are short enough without wasting time on breakfast."

They ate rapidly, Bonaparte feeling the thrill of a race.

"Fighting a swordfish must give a terrific thrill," he said, anxious to know all that was to be known about swordfishing in the shortest possible time.

"Swordfishing gets you like whisky," Emery stuttered. "One time I used to down two bottles a day, so I know what I'm talking about. Once you bring a swordfish to the gaff you become a slave to a drug worse'n whisky. I've landed ten fish so far. Years ago I used to day-dream of fighting blackguards to rescue a girl; now I day-dream of fighting a swordie in a half-gale, one that'll weigh a thousand pounds. Australian record was one going at six-seven-two pounds, a black marlin captured by a Mr. J. Porter, of Melbourne. There must be a thousand-pounder somewhere to be caught."

"We will hope that one of us will capture him."

"We'll hope like mad."

"A great place this Bermagui," Bony remarked a moment

later. "Fish everywhere, they tell me, and no mosquitoes."

"Bermagui becomes a man's Sharg Grelah, or whatever was the name of that place in *Lost Horizon*. A feller's never happy away from it. You finished? Good! Come on!"

They rose to dash across to the sideboard for their prepared lunches and thermos-flasks, Emery the more disreputably dressed of the two. Outside the hotel, where it had been carelessly parked all night, stood the tub, a three-thousand-pound affair in charge of a uniformed driver. From the hotel to the jetty was less than half a mile, and the walk after breakfast would have done Emery good, but time was precious, or so he said.

"What launch have you booked?" he asked when they had taken their seats. "Drive slowly past the fish, Fred. I want to look at it."

"The *Marlin*."

"Oh! Good craft, that, and they tell me that young Wilton's a good man. Want a tip?"

"All you can give me."

"In a minute, then. What d'you think of my fish? Took me fifty-three minutes to bring him to the gaff. Nice striped marlin, isn't he?"

"Yes, a beautiful fish, Mr. Emery," Bony agreed, sighing.

"You can say you've got a good fish if you land a striped marlin weighing two-eight-three pounds," Emery said. "They're better fighters than the black marlin, I think, but there's some who will argue about it. Look at that head, and the sword that's like a needle! All right, Fred, get along. . . . About that tip, now."

"Yes," urged Bony.

"Well, here's a good one. Give your launchman to understand that he's to go where he likes, that he's the captain who knows more about the fishing along this coast than you do.

He'll be glad to do as you ask, because he's out to land the greatest number for the season. Want another tip?"

"You are being kind. Certainly."

"Then tell your launchman that as you know nothing about the game you will be glad of his advice. Lots of fellers come here who've caught a tiddler or two and think they know all about angling for swordies. They don't want advice from any low-browed launchman, you understand, and so the launchman is mortified to see 'em get excited and break their rods or lines and lose the fish he's been counting on to bring his tally ahead of the others. Then we hear 'em talking loudly in the pub how they missed the fish. The odds are always in favour of the swordie, remember. Here we are. Come on!"

The crews of half the launches moored to the slender jetty were busy preparing for their anglers: winding on to the heavy steel reels from the drying frames the lines used the previous day; watching every foot of the nine hundred yards for a possible flaw that would lose a fish; stowing away drums of petrol and oil; affixing the heavy rods to the seat-edge of the anglers' swivel chairs; and generally making all ship-shape.

"Well, so long and good luck," Emery cried, stopping above the *Gladious* on which Remmings's mate took down the lunch baskets and thermos Emery was not too proud to carry from the car.

"Good luck to you, and many thanks," Bony said, before moving on to meet Jack Wilton, who was waiting above his *Marlin*.

The light wind failed wholly to cover the river's water. Beyond the bar the ocean appeared lazy this morning. The air was softly warm and crystal clear, bringing Dromedary Mountain to within rifle range. Launch engines were thudding sluggishly. Gulls sometimes cried their harsh notes. A small boy lying on the jetty floor, perilously balanced, was fishing with a hand line and small hook, and every time he dropped the baited hook into the crystal-clear water, tiny black fish swarmed about the bait until they became a compact mass the size of a football. The small fisherman never caught a fish. The tiny fish sucked off his bait before it could sink to the bottom where swam the larger perch.

"Morning, Mr. Bonaparte!" Wilton said, coming to stand beside the detective who was watching the efforts of the boy to get his bait past the attacking fish.

"Good day, Jack," replied Bony, handing over his lunch and thermos to his launchman who insisted on taking it from him. "Is everything ready?"

"Yes. My partner, Joe Peace, wet your line and wound it on the reel. It's faultless, and the reel runs smooth as oil. Going to be a good day, I think. The glass is steady."

"I am glad to hear that," Bony said, smilingly. "Before we go on board I am going to ask you to grant me three favours. One: that you will understand that I am a new-chum angler, who will gladly accept any advice. Two: that I don't really mind where we go to fish. Three: that when we are away from this jetty you will kindly drop the 'mister' and call me Bony."

"None of 'em will be hard to grant—Bony. You want swordies: I want to see you bring 'em to the gaff. The angler's art isn't difficult to learn, but some will lose their blocks, get excited, and then something has to go west. The best anglers never become excited. The fish are out there in the sea, all right. And here's my mate, Joe Peace. He's likely to call a fish a cow, with trimmings, but he knows more about the coast and the swordies than I do. Meet Mr. Bonaparte, Joe, and remember when we're at sea that Mr. Bonaparte wants to be called just Bony."

Bony was delighted with this barrel of a man who was

glaring at him with his light grey eyes, his right hand resting on the two bowls of the pipes thrust through his belt.

"Day!" he rumbled.

"Right-oh, Joe. Cast off!" Wilton ordered. Then Bony followed him down into the cockpit of the *Marlin*.

For a moment or two Joe still held the attention of the detective. Bony was interested in Joe's enormous calloused feet and his agility which seemed, when needed, to uncoil like the quickening of a sleepy snake. Then other things claimed Bonaparte. The engine of the craft on which he stood roared with power and the jetty slid away. The scene turned half circle, and they were moving down-river towards the narrows. Joe came aft as lightly as a cat, to unwind a light line and to toss its feathered hook overside.

"Get a holt, mister," he rumbled, proffering the line to his angler. "Want bait-fish."

A second line he let go astern, and to Bony it seemed that the rock-footed promontory on the one side and the steep-sided sand-bar on the other were closing in to pinch the *Marlin*. The water under them began to boil. Little wavelets darted over the cauldron as though animated by hidden springs. The stern of the *Marlin* sank downward and then the bow thudded and spray hissed outward. They were on the bar and the entire craft lifted above the river water they had left. Now they were over the bar and in the bay, and the action of the *Marlin* was regular—rising and falling.

The promontory protecting the river's mouth fell astern, and Bony saw the white sweep of the little inner bay extending round in a white-edged crescent to skirt the township and to end at the base of the great protective headland jutting northward. Eastward beyond that tongue of rock-armoured land lay the Tasman Sea. Northward he gazed across the great bay to Cape Dromedary, blue in the distance and guarded by the tall mountain of the same name.

The long ground swells were advancing majestically shore-ward, smooth-sloped and dull green in colour. Up and over them moved the *Marlin*, two craft ahead of her, another coming out round the promontory.

"Fish-oh!" shouted Joe, and in that instant of time Bony's line was tugged so heavily as to be almost taken through his clenched hand. The launch engine at once accelerated when the propeller shaft was put out of gear by Wilton. Bony found himself frantically hauling in his tautened line, was conscious that Joe was acting similarly. Now both lines were cutting the water as the hooked fish swam powerfully to the right and left. With a heave Joe jerked his catch into the cockpit, but Bony permitted his to jump the side of the launch and so lost it.

"Lift 'em clear, or you'll lose 'em every time," Joe urged.

"I'll try to remember to," assented the smiling Bony, and it was then that Joe summed up this new angler. Here was no haughty know-all.

Out went the bait lines and onward went the *Marlin*. In the bait-box the two-pound salmon snapped like a machine-gun.

"You see, as the boat's going when we hook 'em don't begin to haul 'em in until the speed of the boat slackens," advised Joe. "Now look out! We're coming to another shoal."

This time Bony joined Joe in the shout of "fish-oh", and waited until the launch lost speed before beginning to haul in. He lifted into the cockpit a blue-green bonito, a species of tuna, weighing about a pound and a half, and he was astonished to see Joe taking from his hook a similar fish of the same weight.

"That's the sort," chortled Joe. "Just the right size for the swordies, and their favourite. Going to try 'em again, Jack. There they are!"

Wilton swung the *Marlin* round again to cross over the shoal, and two more bonito were added to the bait-box.

"That'll be enough," called Wilton. "We're lucky this morning to get bait-fish so quick. Come and take the wheel, Joe. We'll go straight out as the wind might move to the east'ard during the day."

Beyond the tip of the headland, the chop from the south caused the *Marlin* to roll as she climbed up and over and down the endless swells. Other launches were still engaged getting bait-fish, trolling close to the ugly rocks, obedient to the master at the wheel. Out here the surge was attacking the *Marlin*, taking her high and dropping her low, her white wake lying astern like the track of a scenic railway. Bony stood leaning back against the stern rail, watching the other launches, the receding coast, and Wilton, who was pushing outward to either side from amidship a long pole from the point of which fell a light rope line. To these lines were attached brightly painted cylinders of wood which, when tossed overboard and dragged by the lines, darted beneath and skimmed over the surface like torpedoes gone mad. Teasers, Wilton explained to Bony, and then came aft to join him.

To the end of the cord line on the drum of the huge reel fixed to the butt of the rod, which in turn was swivelled to the edge of one of the two anglers' chairs, Wilton fastened one end of a twenty-foot long wire trace. At the other end was the hook, almost the size of a man's hand. On the hook he placed one of the recently caught bonito, further securing it with a section of cord. Finally he slipped the bait-fish over the stern and it dropped back some thirty odd feet and skimmed the surface like a small motor-boat, escorted either side by a darting teaser.

"D'you see, Bony, the bait-fish and the two teasers look to a shark or swordie just like a small shoal of fish following the launch for protection," Wilton explained. "Now you sit here with a leg either side the rod. That's right. You leave the rod resting on the stern rail. This spoked wheel at the side of the reel is the brake, and you must remember that you can easily put on brakage enough either to break the line or the rod. Just you work it for a bit, and try it for yourself. Have on only sufficient brakage to resist the water on the bait-fish."

"Oh! Ah, yes! I see! I've mastered it. What else?"

"It's the angler's job to watch his bait-fish and the sea on the stern quarters. It's our job to keep watch on the sea for'ard and on both beams for a fin, or for shoal fish where its likely a swordie will be.

"All you'll see of a swordie will be his fin sticking above water and cutting it like a knife. When you see one you yell out 'fish-oh', but for crikey's sake don't lift the rod or do anything with the line or reel. Let him come after the bait-fish. Let him take it, and the moment he does you whip off the brake and prevent the line over-running by pressing on the revolving drum with your left hand. Have a glove on, of course. Anyway, before then I'll be with you, and if you do just what I tell you, and don't get excited, we'll get him."

"A fish may come after the bait-fish any second?" pressed the thrilling Bony.

"Any second. And you may have to wait only a minute or as long as a week."

"All right."

"Now just you have a practice with that brake, and when done troll the bait-fish at that distance astern. I'll go for'ard and see what I can see."

When Bony was satisfied that he understood the action of the brake on the reel, he gazed out over the sea—to landward to observe the headland shrinking downward and becoming submerged in the general green of the coast; to the north where on a 'pimple' he could see the white stick of Montague lighthouse; to the east as far as the faint line of the horizon; to the south beyond the battlemented Bunga Head.

The wind was freshly cool. The sea was a bluish-green. The white caps surmounting the southerly chop were quite gentle in action, and appeared to be impishly daring the mighty swells coming from the east and ignoring them.

Bony filled his lungs with the clean salt air—and thought of his eternal cigarettes. He thought, too, of poor Sergeant Allen, who could not appreciate this riding over the sea on a horse of wood encased with copper. For the first time in his career the thrill of hunting a man was subordinated to the thrill of hunting a giant fish, and he blessed his lucky star for directing his footsteps to Sydney at the moment when the Chief Commissioner was despairing that his friend's murder would remain for ever a mystery unsolved.

This new assignment had certainly resulted from fortuitous circumstances. In Sydney on research work connected with the agitation of sand-grains by wind, he had been asked to call on the Chief Commissioner who had admitted the defeat of his best men to solve this mystery of the sea. Then it had been suggested to the Queenslander that he take over the investigation.

Bony asked for the history of the case and all the statements obtained, and for a day to study this collection of matter. It became obvious that the *Do-me* and those on board her had not been destroyed by natural causes. The recovery of the angler's head from the sea bottom did more than suggest a murder: it raised the probability that one or both of the launchmen were still alive and that the launch itself was hidden somewhere along the coast. The lack of flotsam supported this idea, but the known history and character of the launchmen, as well as Ericson's plans for settling at

Bermagui, raised another probability that they as well as the angler had been murdered.

A survey of the investigation conducted by Allen and Light, then by Handy and his assistant, produced the belief in Bony's mind that the attack on the mystery had failed because one sector was weak. Assuming that the crime had been committed at sea, then the scene of the crime had not been thoroughly examined when it ought to have received the closest attention. The fate of the launch and the three men in her had been attacked from the wrong angle.

Although Bonaparte was the vainest of men, and one of the proudest, he never failed to understand his own limits, and when he decided to accept the assignment he clearly saw that the sea was not his element as was the Inland of Australia. The sea might easily defeat him when the bush had never done so; and, in undertaking this case of the missing launch, he would be accepting a grave risk of defeat. This in itself would be a small thing in his amazingly successful career but one of vast importance in its psychological effect upon his future.

Detective-Inspector Napoleon Bonaparte, the son of an aboriginal woman and a white man, was what he was this day, here on the sea angling for swordfish off Bermagui, because of the pride based on continued success in his chosen career. It was this pride of accomplishment which sustained him and prevented the bush from claiming him body and soul as it claims all whose heredity is rooted in it. It was as though pride was a plank floating on the Ocean of Life, and he a castaway clinging to the plank. Should the plank become water-logged he would sink into the depths there to perish as Detective-Inspector Bonaparte and to exist as Bony, a half-caste nomad.

Sitting there in the angler's chair and waiting for a fin to appear and come racing after his bait-fish, he realised the risk of failure, and its inevitable result, which he had entailed when accepting the assignment. Nevertheless, he felt pride in his pride, was thankful that he had taken the course he had taken, and knew that had he declined the assignment through fear of failure fear for ever would be a positive menace.

Oh no, this was not his natural background, this heaving water which retained nothing on its surface for long. This was 11th January, and the genesis of the case, dated 3rd October, was out here far from land. Life and the elements leave their records on the bush for years; but here on sea life and the elements left no record for even such as he to read.

In all his bush cases he had had many allies: the birds and the insects; the ground which was like the pages of a huge book wherein were printed the acts of all living things; the actions of rain and sunlight and wind. And greater than all these added together was his ally Time. And now of all his former allies only Time was with him.

He had recognised this, too, when accepting the assignment, for there was no hint of compulsion about its acceptance. Here was a case which would truly try his mettle by reason of the fact that he would be removed from his background to one quite unfamiliar, and this was recognised by the New South Wales Police Commissioner as clearly as by Bony himself. When he decided to accept it, Colonel Spendor, his chief, was asked for the loan of his services, and this time had not put a period to Bony's absence from his own State.

There had been raised the subject of abnormal expenses; for Bony saw that to reach the point of being able to reconstruct the affair of the *Do-me,* even in theory, would mean the engagement of a launch and fishing for swordfish, the imbibing of sea lore from men familiar with it from childhood, and the making of this sea background almost if not quite as familiar as his own background. To achieve this his expenses would be high: three pounds a day for the launch, a fiver a week for the tackle, four guineas a week for hotel accommodation, items rarely found in a detective officer's expense-book.

"Among Ericson's effects was his will," began Mr. Mac-Coll. "He had neither wife nor kin to whom to leave his money, and he left it to me. I shall not object, Bonaparte, if all that money is spent on finding the man who killed my friend. Do not think of the expense: give all your thoughts to finding Ericson's murderer."

So Time, limitless Time, was his, even if Time demanded much money. He could ignore Time and Time would be his ally. He could impinge himself upon this unfamiliar background, and make this changing and yet changeless sea give up its hidden clues.

The soft and pleasant hours passed, during which one part of his brain considered the problem of the *Do-me* and the other part remained alert for the coming of a giant fish. But no fin appeared to come knifing after the skimming bait-fish seemingly so detached from the launch and always so frantically swimming after it as though fearful of being left behind to the mercy of hidden monsters. Joe was relieved at the wheel and he went for'ard to stand with one hand gripping the mast to assist balance whilst scanning the sea. When he came aft again to take over the wheel, Wilton brought Bony's and his own lunch and sat in the vacant angler's chair.

The conversation during the half-hour he was there was—swordfishing.

When Joe took his place to eat his lunch, his conversation was—swordfishing.

Bony learned a great deal and hoped he would remember at least a little of what he had learned if a swordfish ran away with the bait-fish. He was impressed by the quiet enthusiasm in the voices of these two men who might well have been expected to be bored with this incessant chase after fish to be caught by other men. He was struck by the extraordinary similarity of these seamen with bushmen who are such keen observers of their background, men who think and reason and wonder, and he became glad that he had undertaken this investigation and had laid down the conditions of himself becoming an angler.

By lunch-time the morning chop had abated and the wind had become a cooling zephyr. When one of the escorting teasers dived deep the clarity of the water amazed him. The coast was a mere dark line above and beyond which rose the inland hills, the whole dominated by Dromedary Mountain. They were seven miles out and not far from Swordfish Reef, although Bony did not know it.

He was standing over his rod when he fancied he saw a surface shadow beside one of the teasers. This shadow fell back a little and drifted across the stern to the port teaser. But there were no clouds to-day, and the birds were absent. And then just behind the port teaser rose a streamlined triangular fin.

"Fish-oh!" he shouted.

Upward along his back flashed an exquisite sensation. The blood rushed to his head and drummed in his ears. His feet and finger-tips tingled, and a coldness took charge of his brain. The fin was apparently attempting to nuzzle the teaser, and it created a little wave as though it were the sharp bow of a fast ship. He heard Joe shout. He heard Wilton's rubber-shod feet thud into the cockpit. He wanted to turn and draw their attention to the fin, and found himself unable.

"Pull in that starboard teaser, Joe. Quick! Sit down Bony! Pull on your gloves. Watch him. Off with the brake if he takes the bait-fish. Remember what I told you."

Inboard came the coloured cylinders of wood, leaving the

bait-fish alone to fall victim. The fin sank, vanished. Joe
stood with one hand on the wheel and the other on the engine
clutch. Wilton stood now behind his angler, slipping about
Bony's body the leather harness which he clipped to the rod
reel.

"That's right! Stay quiet. Don't raise the rod. Whip off
the brake when I say so, and press on the cord on the drum
when it runs out so that it won't over-run when the fish
stops."

The division of Bony's brain now gave attention to the sea
about the bait-fish and the quiet voice behind him. He was
fastened to the rod and reel, but the butt of the rod was
swivelled to the chair and there was no possibility of his
being dragged overboard.

"Ah—there he is!" Wilton cried. "A nice fish, too! Here
he comes. Don't move the rod. Let him take the bait and
run, and be ready to off with the brake. Remember what I
said. He'll go like hell with the bait-fish in his gummy
mouth, then he'll stop to chew it a bit and swallow it head
first. Then, when he feels the hook or the trace, up he'll come,
and that will be the moment to strike. He's got to come up
to get rid of the hook, or try to, 'cos he can't swim backward,
and you mustn't let him swim forward."

A shark's fin has a zigzagging action, ungainly and brutish.
This fin maintained a comparative straight course. It had
again appeared a hundred yards astern the launch, and now
it came on with astonishing speed after the bait-fish. Bony
imagined the bait-fish imbued with life; imagined its tortured
instinct to escape; realised the hopelessness of out-distancing
that pursuing fin. The fin came on to keep pace for a fraction
just behind the bait-fish. It appeared to hover there for
many minutes which actually were split seconds. Then it
vanished.

"The ruddy cow!" roared Joe.

"Never mind," Wilton urged quietly. "He'll come again. He's a bit suspicious; that's all."

When Joe again spoke his disgust had become fury.

"He won't come no more," he shouted. "It was them teasers what done it. Just our luck he'd want to take a look-see at one of them and not the bait-fish. Pity we never seen him. Didn't you see him before he came under them teasers, Bony?"

"No. And I only saw him under the water, not his fin. He looked like a dark shadow.

"Take a circle, Joe. We might pick him up again," Wilton ordered.

The launch circled for ten minutes, but the fin did not again appear, and the *Marlin* continued her trolling.

"Bit of bad luck, what," Wilton cheerfully informed his angler. "Never mind. There's plenty more between here and New Zealand."

Bony mastered a bitter disappointment but suffered from reaction. It had been an experience he would never forget. Up from the seemingly empty and sunlit sea that fish had materialised to be a part of the upper world for a few moments, to evince curiosity and suspicion, to vanish again into its element, to be somewhere under that cloth of gold all studded with diamonds.

Hour after hour chugged the *Marlin,* mile after mile. The sunlight on the ocean tended to dull the thought of things that lived deep under the passing craft, things that darted and streaked and looked upward at the passing launch and the imitation shoal of small fish frantically following it for protection.

The sun was low to the sea, again disturbed by an evening breeze, when they passed the tip of the headland. The two women standing on its green head were clearly visible. Wilton waved to them, but he did not smile. They waved

back, and the elder woman cried something the wind prevented them from hearing. The younger had her arm
through her mother's: she was urging her away, but she
would not leave.

CHAPTER 7

Swordfish Reef

Late in the evening of Bony's first day at sea in a small fishing launch, he introduced himself to Constable Telfer at that officer's house. Bony's first impression of Telfer was good and was to last. He discovered a man who was ambitious, and one who on being assured that merit would have its reward was anxious to collaborate. Unlike many of his fellow members of the C.I.B., Bonaparte did not adopt an attitude of lofty superiority towards uniformed men. Consequently he never failed to get their generous support and co-operation.

The results of this conference with Telfer were many and varied. He learned much of the private lives of the launch-men and their families, and so was able to add considerably to the general reports made by his predecessors. He found they were without exception steady in their habits, and reliable, decent citizens. They deplored the disappearance of the *Do-me*, and the queer twist to that disappearance given by the recovery of the human head from the floor of the sea, mainly on account of two of their number, but also for the adverse effect it had on big game angling at Bermagui. It was almost as bad as the river bar being made dangerous through a whim of the sea.

Recognising the forces arrayed against him, Bony understood that working incognito on this case would be a decided disadvantage, and he temporised with himself by deciding to admit several of the launchmen to his confidence and so seek their aid. It was arranged that those launchmen who were at sea when the *Do-me* vanished should meet at Telfer's house late the following evening. Bony decided to take Wilton and Joe along, also.

At seven o'clock next morning he sat down to breakfast with Mr. Emery, who was in great cheer because the barometer he had brought from his own house indicated rising pressure and fair weather. Previous to this meeting at the table both men had stood in their dressing-gowns on the hotel balcony from which they could observe the lazy water of the great bay which appeared as flat as the proverbial mill-pond. Later, they parted on the jetty to go to their respective launches after wishing each other the best of good fortune.

"Well, Jack, what is it going to be to-day?" Bony asked when he stepped down into the *Marlin*'s cockpit where Wilton was securing the butt end of the heavy rod to the seat of the angler's chair.

"The day's going to be good. Glass is as steady as a rock at 30.1. The wind's coming from the south-east—what there is of it. Here, Joe, stow Mr. Bonaparte's lunch and thermos. We'll get away and show 'em how to catch swordies."

"Right-oh, Jack! And you keep your eyes on them blinded teasers, Mr. Bonaparte. If you see shadders or anything, you bawl and scream and we'll have them teasers inboard in two ups."

The breakers on the bar this morning would not have upset a row-boat, and having thrust past them the *Marlin* crossed the low ground swells of the bay as a car might the land waves of a road. Even beyond the headland the swells were bare of the suds of the lesser waves riding them.

In company with four other launches, those on the *Marlin* trolled off the headland for bait-fish, securing half a dozen two-pounders in ten mintues. Joe grumbled because they were too big: he liked them one and half pounds in weight, and he liked bonito in preference to salmon.

"Not much shoal fish about this morning," he observed as though he had been insulted. "The place is going to the devil. Looks like the shoal fish have cleared out again."

"If they have they'll be back to-morrow, Joe."

"To-morrer's not to-day, is it? Any'ow, we've got enough salmon for now, and there's yesterday's bonito in the box."

Bony, who was standing with his back resting against the stern rail, overheard this conversation and wondered what the small fishing hereabout would be like when the fish were plentiful, as in ten minutes he and Joe had caught ten pounds' weight of fish for bait. The early wind had died and the short chop waves above the ground swells seemed painted with a green shellac.

"*Edith* and *Vida* going to try up around Montague," observed Wilton, thoughtfully. "*Gladious* doesn't seem to know what to do. Alf Remmings is artful. He's got some place in his mind to go to, but wants us to clear out first so's we shan't follow him. What about trying down at Bunga Head?"

Joe regarded the sea with a scowling face, and the sky with squinting eyes.

"It'll be quiet out along Swordfish Reef," he said slowly. "Likely day to pick up a striped marlin out of there. Seems to me the shoal fish have all gone to sea. . . . Yes, out to sea. Might run acrost 'em on Swordfish Reef, or a bit farther out."

"Right-oh! Take her out sou'-east and then when we hit the reef we can follow it up to Montague. Wind might get up a bit and blow from the nor'ard or nor'-east'ard."

The engine revolutions increased and the speed of the launch was raised to five knots. To Bony, Wilton remarked, softly:

"When Joe makes up his mind there's no fish inshore then, according to him, there is none. We're just as likely to pick up a swordie here as anywhere. I'll knock her back when we've got everything set."

Proceeding to trail the two teasers and prepare the angler's bait-fish, he went on:

"Me, I like a rough sea for fishing. When the spindrift is being whipped off the white horses, the swordies seem to be more active. But you never know. They're a blinking gamble. We might raise the record swordie any minute, no matter where the place and the weather. I wouldn't mind seeing you land a hefty mako shark to-day. They give a feller plenty of sport."

"Hope we catch something big, anyway," Bony said, smilingly. "I'm just itching to feel a big fish. I suppose they are, though, generally where the shoal fish are?"

"Yes, when the shoal fish are about the big 'uns are about, too. You haven't seen a shoal yet. Wait till you do. The shoal fish lives mostly on a very small crab-like fish no bigger than a flea, and no one seems to know what controls these small fish. They come along in countless billions, spreading over miles and miles of water. Then in a night they will all disappear; where to, not even Joe can tell us. We get days sometimes when we won't see a fin, or a shoal fish, or a single one of those tiny chaps. Then one morning, or one afternoon, the mutton birds are flying thick, the sea's alive with the small fellers and being lashed to foam by the shoal fish that's after them. Often, you can see a swordie at work among the shoal fish, leaping after them above the surface and smashing down at them with his sword. Now everything's right, I'll go for'ard and keep a look-out. Shout 'fish-oh' if you see a fin or a shadow."

He left Bony to stop for a second beside Joe, and the speed of the launch was reduced to three knots. A little sternly Bony looked away over the glittering sea, for a sentence from the Book of Sea had been translated for him and he was conscious of his inability to read a writing foreign to him.

They were heading for Swordfish Reef, and now and then Bony gazed eagerly ahead expecting to see water suds surging over semi-submerged rocks. There was nothing between him and the sharply defined line of the horizon. He could just make out the 'pimple' of land and the white pencil of the lighthouse on Montague Island. A light haze already masked the receding shore, but above this haze stood clearly the summits of the distant hills and the upper slopes of Dromedary Mountain dominating the great bay. The *Vida* and *Edith* were low upon the water, while the *Gladious*, making to the south, was barely discernible. Beyond her, Bunga Head stood out, stained by the haze, and beyond Bunga Head would be other headlands between it and Twofold Bay of historic interest.

Standing beside the mast, Wilton stamped a foot on the decking and pointed away to the port bow. The watchful Joe immediately altered course in obedience to the order, and Bony heard Wilton shout:

"A fin! Can't make it out yet. Might be shark."

Two minutes passed before Bony saw the fin, and at that instant Wilton cried:

"Sun-fish! Go 'way out, Joe!"

The fin slowly wagged. It was triangular and would mean shark to anyone unable to read the Book of the Sea. A huge skate-like fish of enormous weight and no pugnaciousness; fishermen and angler ignore them.

Thirty minutes later Wilton again stamped a foot on the deck, and the drowsing angler sprang to his feet to look forward, glad of the distraction to banish the almost mastering desire to sleep. The relaxing sea air was like a narcotic.

He saw the object towards which the launch was now being steered, a blackish thing that raised what appeared to be long and hairy arms. It was not a fish, and it was not a castaway clinging to a piece of flotsam. Steadily the launch neared it, and then quite abruptly the grotesque object resolved into a thing of slim-curved beauty and disappeared. Four seconds later it reappeared to lift itself half-way out of the water like a man 'treading water', to gaze at the oncoming craft with curious placidity. Almost contemptuously the seal dived again, and when next it came to the surface it was well astern of the *Marlin*.

"He was enjoying a bit of sun-bask," Joe announced to the angler, pride of showmanship in his voice.

An albatross arrived from nowhere to maintain its splendid poise above Bony at less than fifty feet. Never did it flap its great wings: it moved their angles to the air currents: and for an instant or two it inquiringly examined the launch and its occupants before 'floating' away without effort, supremely master of its element.

"We want to see mutton birds, not 'im," called Joe. "Ain't seen a mutton bird all morning. They keeps with the shoal fish."

Another hour passed during which Bony often was compelled to close his eyes against the sea-glare for a moment's relief. He was pressing his hands against his eyes when Wilton came aft and entered the cabin.

"Try these dark glasses," he said, on joining Bony. "The light is extra bad to-day, and they will save your eyes. You'll feel like sleeping for a month after the first few days' fishing. Like to come for'ard to see Swordfish Reef?"

So Bony clambered forward to stand with Wilton against the mast.

"Where is it?" he asked.

"There, beyond that white line drawn on the water."

A thin white line of suds, or what appeared to be foam but which may have been composed of the dead bodies of minute creatures, extended as far as could be seen to the north and to the south. The launch was passing over tiny choppy wavelets most certainly not created by the wind, steadily advanced to the white line which itself appeared immovable. Beyond the line was a water lane where the sea gently boiled in expanding discs, and beyond the lane, some hundred yards wide, the same choppy wavelets were barred back as though by a cement and stone breakwater.

Over the white line the *Marlin* passed and quarter-circled to the north until it was treading along the pavement of the sea. It was almost as steady as though it were moored to the jetty seven miles distant. The low swells seemed not to touch this lane, and Bony imagined that royalty, driving along a road made empty by authority crowding the people to the sidewalks, would be used to such an experience as now was his. The progress of the launch was deliberate and steady: the sun-kissed wavelets on either side of the 'road' could have been the hands and handkerchiefs of a cheering populace.

"It's not often we see the reef like this," Wilton was saying, in his voice the evidence of a man entranced by his own environment. "She's pretty rough here even in moderate weather, for the surface of the reef is only a few dozen fathoms down under. It's like a lake, isn't it? And the reef lies for several miles to the south and all the way up to Montague Island."

Swordfish Reef! Seven full miles from land, away out in the Tasman Sea, and the launch he was on as steady as though it were moored to the jetty. Bony had not the need to hold to anything for support. The sound of the engine was low and indistinct. He gazed around in a circle. He saw not one launch or ship: only the plume of oily smoke rising from the southern horizon betraying a steamer's position. A sensation of vast loneliness possessed him, and this was replaced by a twinge of fear. If anything happened to the

Marlin! What chance was there of survival? No more than if on a twenty-thousand tonner.

"Didn't the *Do-me* vanish somewhere out here?" he asked Wilton.

"So we reckon," came the reply. "She was last seen heading this way. A bit farther north and west is where the trawler brought up the head. Funny about that. Sharks must have fought over the body, and during the scrimmage the head must have been torn off and then sunk unnoticed by the brutes. Inside the reef that was. Two miles farther out, shallow water ends at the Continental Shelf. Beyond that the bottom is miles down."

"The weather was calm, too, that day the *Do-me* disappeared?"

"It was as calm as this, in fact calmer. I wasn't out that day. We were working on the *Marlin* that we'd hauled up the beach, but the other fellers said it was the flattest sea they ever saw."

"Would the *Do-me* have had a compass on board?"

"Oh, yes. All the launches have compasses and barometers. But the *Do-me* wouldn't want her compass that day, although it was a bit hazy. At only four miles out the haze hid the coast, but sticking up above the haze was the summit of Dromedary Mountain which is our best landmark. We can see her when thirty miles at sea."

"Why do you go out that far?"

"After swordies, striped marlin chiefly. I don't believe in going out there, you know, but some anglers like to."

"And observing the sea over Swordfish Reef like it is to-day is a rare phenomenon?"

"Eh?"

"Sight."

"Yes. Too right it is. When she blows an easterly this place isn't worth a visit, I can assure you. Just take a squint at the water. You don't see water so blue as that, and so clear, every month of the year. You don't——— Cripes! There's a fin. A swordie! He's coming to meet us. Jump for your rod, quick!"

There was no mistaking the fish whose fin cut the water so cleanly and swiftly. It was following the sea-lane southward and so would meet the *Marlin,* the tip of its fin a bare nine inches above the pale-blue pavement.

Rushing aft, Wilton and Bony swung themselves down by the cabin roof into the cockpit. Wilton's voice became brittle.

"Swordie, Joe! Coming south. Keep her dead ahead and be ready to inboard the port teaser."

Now Bony was in his seat, slipping the canvas gloves on to his hands. Wilton snatched up the leather harness and assisted his angler to strap it about his body and fasten the clips to the rod reel.

"He went below," Wilton said, the excitement under which he had spoken to Joe now replaced by cool deliberation. "He saw the launch and dived. He's watching us now, the teasers and the bait-fish. Look out for him."

Now perforce crouched over his rod which he did not raise from the stern rail, Bony's left hand caressed the wide band of cord on the reel drum, whilst the fingers of the right hand maintained light contact with the spokes of the brake wheel, ready instantly to relieve the slight strain keeping the bait-fish from being taken away by the water. His pulses were throbbing, but his brain felt cold and his eyes were like points of blue ice.

"There he is to starboard!" Wilton cried. "He's coming round to follow us."

Again Bony saw the triangular fin, now cutting the surface in a wide arc to come in behind the launch a hundred odd yards away. The sun glinted on the stiffly-erect, greyish-green triangle now keeping even pace with the launch, watched by three men to whom the world and all it contained for them was nothing. Thirty seconds passed before the distance between fin and launch was decreased. The fish came on the better to examine this shoal of wounded 'fish', following a moving rock for protection. Power was epitomised by that fin: now it epitomised velocity as though it was passing through a vacuum, not water.

"He's coming! Ah—a nice fish, too. Might go three hundred pounds," whispered Wilton, and Bony sub-consciously wondered how the devil he knew how much the fish might weigh on observing only the fin. Velocity became mere speed when the fin gained position a few yards behind the bait-fish, a position it maintained.

"He's taking a bird's-eye view of the bait-fish," Joe said. "What about them teasers, Jack?"

"Right! Bring 'em in, Joe. This feller isn't extra hungry, and we don't want him to play the fool with 'em."

The brightly-coloured cylinders of wood jerked forward and disappeared from Bony's range of view. He saw them go, dragged forward by Joe, although the focal point of his gaze had become a fixture to the fin. Then with terrific acceleration the fin came on after the bait-fish.

For a split second Bony experienced pity for the fish which had been dead for hours and now was impaled on a hook. There was no swerving of the giant fin now, no hesitation. It came to within a yard of the bait-fish over which rose a grey-brown 'sword'. Bony saw an elephantine mouth take the bait-fish. There was a gentle swirl of water, but no sight of body or tail. The bait-fish vanished, and the rod reel began to scream its high-pitched note.

The launch had been proceeding on a northerly course, but immediately the swordfish took the bait Joe swung the *Marlin* hard to port and slipped out the engine clutch, bringing the stern round to the north-east. A swordfish invariably runs with its capture to the north-east, and Joe's manœuvre brought the angler to face that direction.

Bony had swiftly removed brakage on the line which now was being torn away from the reel at yards per second. He became aware that the launch was stopping, that the engine-beat was different, that Wilton stood just behind him, and that Wilton's mouth was close to his neck. It seemed that it was only one part of his mind that registered all this: the other part was like a gun barrel through which he was looking to see the line running away and down into the sea.

The fingers of his left hand protected by the glove were pressing gently on the revolving reel drum, keeping the line just sufficiently taut to prevent the whizzing reel giving up line faster than the fish took it. His right hand caressed the spokes of the brake, ready to apply pressure immediately the fish stopped—if ever it would stop.

"Let him go," Wilton breathed on Bony's neck. "He thinks he's got a win, and he's highly delighted. He'll stop soon. He's taken three hundred yards of line. He won't want much more. There! Careful."

The music of the reel abruptly ceased. Abruptly it began again, to continue for three seconds before again ceasing its high note. The ensuing silence was remarkable. The pulsations of the running engine seemed to come from a great distance, far beyond the silence pressing hard upon Bony's ears. The line was falling slackly. There was no movement on it. It entered the sea through the suds line, on one side of which the tiny chop lapped it, and on the other side of which began the flat water pavement.

"What next?" he asked, feeling that this waiting was intolerable.

"Wind in a little of the slack," came the suggestion, and Bony put on brakage sufficient to master the freedom of the drum. "He's all right, down there. If you strike now you'll lose him, pull the bait-fish out of his mouth. He's down fathoms and rolling on his back like a playful kitten, just munching the bait-fish, turning it round so's it will go down his gullet head first. He'll go to market in a second when he feels the hook or the wire trace, and then he'll come up to throw it. Give him time. Get in that bit of slack. That's right. Keep it there. Now look at the line!"

Bony saw that the angle of the cord line was becoming less acute, that inch by swift inch more of it was appearing between rod tip and the water.

"He's coming up. Strike him!"

Trying desperately to remember all the careful tuition he had received, Bony's right hand left the brake and gripped the line above the reel, while his left hand raised the rod tip upward in a flashing arc. Then with right hand again on the winder handle of the reel he wound in the slack of the line gained when the rod tip was flashed downward. He could 'feel' the weight of the fish at every sweep of the rod tip, but the slack threatened to beat his effort on the winder handle.

"Give it to the cow!" yelled Joe. "Sock it into him!"

"That's right, Bony. Give it him quick and plenty. Careful not to put on too much brake. That's it. Ah—look at him!"

Joe uttered a yell of delighted triumph, and implored the world to: "Look at him!" But the novice was too preoccupied with the confounded reel brake and the line, and the rod and himself on the swinging chair, to accept the plea, for he was constantly raising the rod tip, and winding in slack or holding to the line above the drum. That secondary part of his brain was registering the intense enthusiasm of the launchmen and was anticipating the unbearable disappointment of losing the fish through a stupid mistake on his part.

Between three and four hundred yards away the fish was dancing on its tail, dancing on a circular 'spot-light' of foam.

It was dancing with its sword thrusting towards the cobalt sky, and its form enshrouded by a rainbow coloured mist. It appeared to dance like that for a full minute when in fact it was a fraction of a second. Then in a great sheet of spray it fell forward on to the 'pavement' and was engulfed in a bath of white foam.

"I can't hold him," Bony gasped, and Wilton, who could do nothing else but watch the fish, again forced his mind to his angler.

"Don't try. Let him go. He'll come up again. Just keep the line taut. There! He's coming up."

Again the fish appeared, but not this time to dance. It shot out from and above the water pavement, and fell with barely a splash.

"Now he'll fight you," Wilton hissed. "Brake a bit, but not too much or the line will part."

Along the line came a succession of heavy tugs, each tug tearing line off the reel against brakage. Abruptly the line went slack and frantically Bony wound line on to the drum which began to cascade water. Then again came the weight on the line and another series of tugs when all the wet line he had gained was lost to him.

"He's gonna breach again," Joe shouted.

"Too right, he is," Wilton said in agreement. "He can't get rid of the hook down under by belching like a dog 'cos he can't swim backwards and must always go for'ards. Only in the air can he get rid of it, and that's when an angler's likely to lose him if the fish has a slack line. Get me?"

Bony nodded his head vigorously. Perspiration was running down his face, and his left forearm was beginning to be filled with lead. The fish appeared on the surface of the water, threshing it into a smother for three seconds. Then down it went and, despite brakage, it tore fifty yards of line off the reel.

Bony was gaining confidence. He recognised that patience and correct judgment with the brake were the two essentials of success. To have struck before the psychological moment would have taken the bait-fish out of the mouth of the sword-fish; to have permitted the line to slacken when the fish was out of the water would have permitted it to disgorge the hook; and to have too much brakage on the line when those terrible tugs were given would have snapped the rod or have parted the cord able to withstand a breaking strain only of eighty-eight pounds. And away down there in the depths fought a fish weighing hundreds of pounds, and a power strength much greater than its weight.

"You've got him fast, I think," Wilton said, loudly, triumphantly. "You're doing all right. He won't come up again. Just take your time. Give him line when he wants it bad. Get it back on the reel when he gives you a chance. That's the ticket. You're gaining yards and losing only feet. Bring her round to starboard a bit, Joe. Bony's gonna be a Zane Grey yet."

"Too right, he is, too ruddy right," Joe chortled, and again one part of Bony's mind registered the extraordinary enthusiasm of men who were only looking on. His left arm now ached badly, and his face and neck were dripping sweat. But his blood was on fire and his pulses beat like Thor's great hammer. Confidence was strengthening, and for half a minute he permitted himself to rest, merely 'holding' the fish. Then up again went the rod tip, to fall once more and so permit slack line to be wound in. His knees were dripping with salt water from the wet line on the reel. His mind was bathed in the water of pure ecstasy.

"He's coming to!" cried Wilton. "He's not far away now by the amount of line on your reel. Look!—There's the swivel. When you get the swivel near your rod tip, bring it 'way back for'ard to me. Starboard a bit, Joe."

"Starboard it is. How's she coming?" demanded Joe, meaning the fish.

"Coming in well. Leave the wheel, Joe, and bring the gaff and ropes."

Wilton pulled leather gloves over his amber hands, and Joe nimbly came aft with the gaff on its pole handle, and like a cat he placed gaff and ropes in readiness for use. Bony wanted to shout, but was too breathless. There to the surface of the water, only ten feet from the launch, rose the dorsal fin of his fish, and behind it the long back fins all erect like the 'prickles' along the back of some lizards. There was no fight left in the fish. It was drawn easily alongside the launch and Wilton grasped the wire trace with his gloved hands.

"Careful. Watch out! He's not ours yet and he might want to take another run," Wilton said. Joe laid the gaff under the torpedo-shaped body and hauled on pole and rope attached to the gaff. Out came the pole. Joe leaned back on the gaff rope while Wilton snatched up another and leaned overside to slip a noose about the flailing tail. When he stood up his head and shoulders cascaded sea-water. He was smiling; and Joe began a chuckle that made his whiskers expand like the quills of a porcupine.

"Take it easy, Bony," he shouted. "He's ours. Congratulations."

Both men had to shake hands with Bony, who smiled his appreciation, and was then asked to stand aside. The rod was unshipped and put away for'ard for the moment. Then followed five minutes of hauling by the launchmen to drag the fish up and across the stern of the *Marlin*, where it was securely lashed.

"Ah!" breathed Wilton, when the three stood to regard the capture. "A nice striped marlin. Two hundred and forty pounds, eh, Joe?"

Joe squinted at the fish from sword point to tail fins. He

grimaced; pursed his lips. He might have been a butcher judging the weight of a store bullock.

"Might go a bit more," he said slowly. " 'E's in good nick. 'Is tail's round as a barrel. Yes, might go two hundred and forty-eight pounds."

"Well, we'll have to get under way," Wilton ordered. "May be another swordie or two about here on the reef."

The gaff and ropes were stowed. Joe went back to the wheel and the *Marlin* continued her trolling at three knots to the hour. Bony's arms and legs ached from the exertion, but no man was ever more proud of his bride than he was of that beautiful fish, gleaming green and blue and grey. He stretched himself, yawned and rolled a cigarette whilst Wilton reset the rod, and baited the hook. Joe began to sing about a fair 'may-den' who sold her beer in gallon pots.

Overboard went the bait-fish to begin its spell of skimming the surface after the launch. Overboard went the teasers to skip and dive and dart. Wilton went for'ard to stand beside the mast, and slowly the *Marlin* sauntered along the pavement this day laid down above Swordfish Reef. In his angler's chair Bony relaxed and smoked. Constantly his gaze rested on the fish, its sword protruding over one side of the launch and its tail over the other.

"Ahoy!" shouted Wilton, pointing aloft.

And there fluttering lazily at the masthead flew the coveted flag with the small white swordfish on the blue background.

Bony stood and gravely raised his old hat to it. He had never dreamed that life had in store an experience like this.

CHAPTER 8

The Conference

It was dark when Bony entered Constable Telfer's office to see there, other than the policeman, the owners of the *Gladious*, the *Edith* and the *Snowy*, and Joe and Wilton. Setting a suit-case and a brief-case on the table, previously cleared by Telfer, Bony smiled at the seamen and asked them to draw chairs to the table and be seated. Not a man answered his smile: every one of them was wondering why he had been asked to attend and what he had to do with the reason actuating Telfer's request that they attend.

"Gentlemen," Bony began, seating himself at the head of the table. "I have an explanation to offer and then a favour to ask which I am confident you will grant. It is known that I am a cattleman from the Northern Territory here on a fishing holiday. My name, indeed, is Napoleon Bonaparte, but I am as insignificant as the great Emperor was mighty until disease, not his enemies, destroyed him. I am a detective-inspector from Queensland come here to Bermagui to solve the mystery of the *Do-me* and the fate of those who went to sea on her."

The men stared for a fraction of a second at the dark and handsome face supported by the encircling starched collar. Then they glanced at each other and at Telfer, who sat at the other end of the table. As though accustomed to addressing meetings, Bony waited until their attention was again directed to him. Then:

"All of us here have a common interest. Constable Telfer

and I hope to succeed in bringing to light the fate of the *Do-me* and those three men, not only because it is what we are being paid a salary to do, but because, as normal citizens suspecting foul play, we desire to see justice done. Your interest in the matter is also of a dual nature. You want to see justice done on behalf of Spinks and his mate, as well as on behalf of the unfortunate angler, and you want to see lifted the shadow this mystery has cast on Bermagui and big game angling here. You will, I know, be anxious to have this mystery solved, having reasonable hope that the solution will prove that it was not the sea or the normal conditions of deep-sea angling off this coast which accounted for the disappearance of the *Do-me*."

This produced confirmatory exclamations.

"I have taken the liberty of making the usual inquiries about all of you, and these inquiries produce the belief that you are one and all decent fellows who, when my request is placed before you, will gladly consent to assist me. I know that the average man and woman is suspicious of a detective, dreading to be associated with a criminal trial with all its inconveniences and worries. I am aware that there have been detectives whose ethics were not above reproach, but to-day they are exceedingly few in number. I am not going to ask you to make statements, and tell you to be careful what you say, and then cross-examine you as though I believe you to be liars.

"My Chief Commissioner often tells me that I am a cursed bad policeman but a damned good detective. As a fact, I am an investigator who once I am able to say how it was done and who did it, leaves the arrest and charge to other officers. I am interested less in the fate of a criminal than in his psychology.

"I am convinced that neither the sea nor its hazards were responsible for the disappearance of the *Do-me*. The recovery of the human head by the trawler crew indicates murder, and the wound in the head was caused by a .45 pistol bullet and not a .32 rifle bullet fired from the rifle Spinks always had with him on the *Do-me* with which to dispatch sharks. That Mr. Ericson was shot and his body thrown overboard to be partially devoured by the sharks may be taken for granted. Placing last things first, the question is: Who killed Ericson?"

In the short ensuing silence the men relaxed, but their supple bodies again tensed when he continued speaking.

"You all knew William Spinks and his mate, Robert Garroway. You will hasten to assure me that neither killed his patron. I incline to agree with you because of the absence of any motive for the crime, and because Mr. Ericson intended to settle here and benefit the entire Spinks family. It is possible that Garroway had a motive for killing Mr. Ericson, for Garroway was not included in Ericson's plans for settling here and he may have resented the prospect of unemployment. I used the word 'possible' not the word 'probable', which please note.

"And now for my request. A study of the reports compiled by the Sydney detectives indicated that they sought for wreckage and bodies along the coast and confined their investigations to the land. Aeroplanes searched the sea, we know, and Jack Wilton and Joe Peace, on the *Marlin*, hunted for flotsam: still the main investigations were confined to the land.

"It is my intention to concentrate on what happened to the *Do-me*. She put to sea that fine and calm morning, and she was seen later making towards Swordfish Reef. Because the *Do-me* was a vehicle of the sea and not of land, I find myself at a great disadvantage, not being a seaman as you are. Away beyond the railways, in my own country, I'd lose you in five minutes, but here on the sea you turn the tables on me. Now, will you join me in a free and easy discussion of

84

this mystery, like business men discussing a deal, without thought of anything said being recorded and checked and——" Bony smiled—"used in evidence against you?"

This raised a general laugh and one after another the launchmen promptly assented.

"Thank you." Bony reached forward and drew to him the suit-case: "Before we begin, gentlemen, I want you to join in drinking a toast to my first swordfish. Mr. Telfer, glasses, please."

Telfer departed for the glasses. Bony beamed on the conference, and produced bottles of beer.

"If the usual run of detectives used more tact—with beer—they'd get on better," observed Eddy Burns, owner of the *Edith*, and on whose face was the indelible stamp of Anzac. "This is going to be the first time I've drunk beer in a police station."

"I don't care where I drink," rumbled the vast Joe, to add as an afterthought: "Providin' it ain't water or tea."

A stout man, whose face was perfectly round and whose eyes were small and blue-grey, chuckled but said nothing. His facial expression was one of eternal peace with himself and the world. Owner of the *Snowy*, his name was Edward Flandin. Telfer came in with the glasses, and Bony filled them and himself handed them round to his 'collaborators'.

The toast was drunk with enthusiasm.

"May Inspector Bonaparte catch many more," said Remmings, a dark, red-faced man and owner of the *Gladious*.

"May he land the biggest yet," said Eddy Burns.

"The second biggest," interposed Flandin. "I promised the biggest to those Americans booked with me for next week."

"Thank you, gentlemen," Bony said, smilingly. "This is the first investigation I have conducted permitting me pleasure with work. Now let us begin."

From his brief-case Bony produced a wad of papers and a bundle of sharpened pencils. Then, lighting a cigarette, he exhaled smoke and looked through it at the conference.

"I am aware," he said, "that you three men who were at sea the day the *Do-me* disappeared have already been severely questioned by the detectives. You, Remmings and Burns and Flandin, state the time you left the jetty and the time you got back to it, and the time each of you last saw the *Do-me*. Although your respective statements are positive, the details are few and confined to those on which you were questioned. You can, I think, supply me with many more details of what happened that day. And your statements, when correlated, may well give me a lead. And a lead I must have.

"On one point I owe the Sydney men something: by their questioning of you they must have fixed in your minds a mental picture of everything you did that day the *Do-me* failed to reach port. You have had much time to think of that day, to discuss its generalities among yourselves.

"Now, here on these sheets of paper I have drawn a rough sketch map of the coast for twenty miles north and south of Bermagui. By the way, why is the town spelled Bermagui and the river Bermaguee?"

"The Postal Department named the town BERMAGUI," replied Remmings. "It was a long time ago. Why, no one can tell."

"And what does the word 'Bermaguee' mean? Do you know?" pressed Bony.

"Yes. It means, in abo language, a meeting-place."

"Ah! I like to know these small details. Now for my maps. I want you, Flandin and Remmings and Burns, each to take a map and a pencil, and to plot on your map, as accurately as possible, the course your launch followed throughout the whole of that vital day. Take your time. There are several bottles still to be emptied. I want you, Jack, to sketch on this map the position of Swordfish Reef, the edge of the Continental Shelf, and any other reefs of which you are familiar. And you, Joe, you are a man after my own heart, for you can track at sea as well as I can track on land. Do you think you could plot on this sketch map the drift a piece of flotsam would take assuming it came from the *Do-me* which sank above Swordfish Reef?"

Joe grinned with pleasure at the implied compliment.

"I'll give 'er a go," he said, and accepted paper and pencil, to examine the paper with his eyes screwed to pin-points whilst he sucked the point of the pencil.

"Were you able to borrow the weather records from the postmaster, Telfer?" asked Bony.

Telfer nodded, placed a wad of official forms before the detective—and then filled all glasses. The others worked industriously at their maps, and Bony fell to studying the weather records. One by one the maps were passed to him. He gave Flandin another sketch map of the coast, saying:

"I want you to plot the course of the *Do-me* till the moment you last sighted her, marking her position then, and your own position, with a cross and noting the approximate time."

Flandin having done this the same map was passed to Burns, the *Edith* having been the next launch to have lost sight of the *Do-me*, and after he had continued the *Do-me*'s course and marked his own and her position when he had last sighted her, Remmings was asked to continue the tale, as he on the *Gladious* was the last of all to see the *Do-me*."

"When I am in my native bush, gentlemen," Bony began in explanation, "everything I observe, except the clouds, is static. On the sea nothing is static. A ship does not leave tracks on the sea, but when I have transferred the courses of your launches and the ships you saw that vital day to one key plan we will see how the sea was tracked by their wakes for a few seconds.

"You have been patient with me, and I am going to present each of you with yet another blank sketch map and ask you to plot the course of any ship or other craft you saw during that day the *Do-me* disappeared."

Whilst the men were working he thoughtfully watched them, noting how each bore the same stamp of the sea upon his face and neck and hands whilst retaining marked individuality. The colour of their eyes was different, but the manner in which all eyes were employed was exactly the same. Here in the lamplight all eyes were wide open, and all were as clear as the sea which was their background. When their maps had been returned to Bony, he gave several minutes to studying them. Then:

"So the mail steamer, *Orcades*, passed northward that day. How far out from shore was she?"

"About fourteen miles," replied Burns, and Remmings agreed.

"You, Remmings, saw a trawler working south of the *Gladious*. I assume that that was the same trawler which was spoken of the following night by you?"

"That's so."

"There was only the one trawler working off the coast hereabouts that day?"

"Only that one."

"She was the *A.S.1*, not the *A.S.3*, which recovered the angler's head?"

"Yes, she was the *A.S.1*," confirmed Remmings.

Bony produced a telegram from his suit-case, and, glancing at it, said to Remmings:

"You did not that day see a launch about fifty feet in length, without a mast, and painted a silver-grey?"

"No."

"That day, Mr. Remmings, you worked southward of Bermagui, and the *Edith* and *Snowy* worked about Montague

Island which is north of Bermagui. I want you to be quite
sure that you did not see that launch painted silver-grey.
Think."

"I'm quite sure about it," Remmings said, positively. "If
I had seen her I would have remembered because she must
be the *Dolfin*, Mr. Rockaway's launch."

"Oh! I have not seen her."

"No. She hasn't been in with a fish since you've been
here."

"Where, then, is her headquarters?"

Telfer answered this question.

"Mr. Rockaway has a house near the mouth of Wapengo
Inlet, a mile or two south of Bunga Head. He's been living
there for a few years now. Built his own private jetty."

"Great angler," supplemented Burns. "Mr. Rockaway's a
member of the Bermagui Anglers' Club, and when he catches
a fish he brings it here to be weighed and recorded."

"Hum!" Again Bony studied the sketch maps last filled
with detail. "I see here that you, Burns and Flandin, have
noted the presence of several launches in the vicinity of
Montague Island, but have not named them. Where did
they come from?"

"They came from Narooma, a bit north of Montague,"
replied Flandin. "None of 'em were this side or east'ard of
the Island."

"So I see. And you, Burns, who that day was well east of
Montague Island, would have seen any Narooma launch that
was east of Montague Island, would you not?"

"Yes. I was trolling out there east of the Island most of
the day."

"Hum! Can you tell me why Spinks named his launch the
Do-me?"

The question produced smiles and chuckles, and Remmings answered the question.

"When Bill Spinks and Joe, here, were building her we'd go and have a look at their work and chiack 'em about the ideas Spinks was putting into her, and he used to say: 'Well, she'll do me, anyway.' "

"And I suggested to Bill when the naming came up that he call her the *Do-me*," added Wilton.

"Well, I am most grateful to you men for your interest and assistance," Bony said, smiling at them in turn. "We have certainly laid foundations more solid than those put down by the Sydney detectives. What I would like agreed upon is the limit of visibility that day the *Do-me* vanished. I mean the limit of visibility beyond, say, five miles off the coast."

"There was more haze that day than there was to-day," Flandin said, with slow deliberation.

"Yes, there was," confirmed Burns. Then he asked: "Visibility of what, Mr. Bonaparte? We'd see a liner farther away that day than a launch, you understand. We seen the *Orcades* quite plain at about six miles, but we'd have found it hard to see a launch at four miles."

"Quite so, Burns. I am thinking of small craft sighted from small craft."

"It wouldn't be much more'n four miles," Remmings contributed, and Flandin agreed with him.

Bony proceeded to question them about the *Do-me*. All stoutly resisted the suggestion that the *Do-me* was unseaworthy, or that her engine and petrol feed system was faulty and likely to cause fire.

"She was only three years old," Wilton said. "I helped to install her engine which was a new one, and her petrol-tank was away up in the bows. Spinks always stowed his supply of extra petrol up for'ard, because he and young Garroway were great cigarette smokers and he was naturally cautious. Anyway, if she'd caught fire someone would have seen the smoke."

"And I'd have found drift wood or something when me and Jack follered the currents to Swordfish Reef the next day," added Joe.

"Nothing happened to her like that," Burns said, with solemn conviction. "Even if that head hadn't been found I'd never believe that the *Do-me* disappeared through natural causes."

"What were the odds against the trawler bringing up the head?" asked Bony. His confreres regarded the ponderous Joe who had once served aboard a trawler.

"Smaller than you'd think," answered Joe. "The sea bottom is as plain to a trawler skipper as a paddock is to a farmer. The trawler man knows all the reefs, and all the bottoms that are clear of reefs and rocks. The only thing about that head being found in the trawl is that it was found in the trawl when the bottom bar of the net is higher than the ground on which it is dragged."

"Then, how do you acount for it?"

"Well, it's like this here. It seems to me that after Mr. Ericson was shot he was tossed overboard, or his body fell overboard after he was shot. There was a shark or two about and they fought over the body, tearing it to pieces, you understand. They missed the head what sinks while they're fighting over other bits, and the head comes to rest on thick seaweed a few feet above bottom."

"It wouldn't be feasible to send a diver down in the locality where the head was found—to search for, let us say, the *Do-me*?"

"No. Because they don't know where the head entered the trawl. They only know where the trawl was brought up. That trawl was down one hour and thirty minutes, and it had travelled over the sea bottom four or five miles along a zigzag course."

Bony rose to his feet.

"Well, gentlemen, the night is ageing and we all have to go to sea early in the morning. Permit me again to thank you, and to make a final request. That is, that you will continue to think of me as a cattleman from the Northern Territory, and not to disclose my profession. Good night!"

Left alone with Constable Telfer, Bony wrote on a sheet of blank paper. Then, regarding the constable intently, said:

"Get this message off to Headquarters first thing to-morrow. We must know if the officers of the *Orcades* saw any small craft far off land that day the liner passed up this coast. One of them may have remembered seeing such a craft. No note of it will be in the log, but yet one may remember."

"That'll be done, sir. Why did you ask about Rockaway's *Dolfin*?"

"Because the captain of the trawler *A.S.1* has reported seeing her early that morning, and I think it important to have noted, on the key plan I will be preparing, every craft at sea that day."

CHAPTER 9

The Key Plan

The following morning, instead of joining Emery at the breakfast-table at seven o'clock, Bony sent a message to Wilton saying that he would not be going out that day, and asking him to call on him at eleven.

From the hotel balcony he watched the majority of the Bermagui launches appear from beyond the promontory hiding the bar and the mouth of the river, pass across the inner bay, skirt the headland for bait-fish, and so set out to sea. He now knew them all by name, and he instantly noticed among them a strange craft. It was a sleek cruiser-type launch, some fifty feet in length and painted silver-grey.

"Do you know the name of that launch?" he called down to the yard-man who was sweeping in front of the building.

"That's the *Dolfin*," came the reply. "She belongs to Mr. Rockaway who lives down at Wapengo Inlet. She brought a swordie in this morning to be weighed."

"Indeed!"

"Yes. A black marlin. Weighed two hundred and ninety-one pounds. Miss Rockaway caught him south of Tathra."

Watching the tail end of the procession of launches, Bony felt keen-edged regret that the *Marlin* was not among them and he in its cockpit, for that drug which Emery had said was worse than alcohol was already his master.

He was in the lounge studying his sketch maps when Wilton arrived.

"They tell me that that smart launch which went out this

morning was the *Dolfin*?" he said, query in his soft voice.

"That's so, Mr. Bonaparte. Miss Rockaway landed a nice two-ninety-one-pounder. Black marlin. That's her third fish this season. She's pretty good at game fishing."

Bony led the way outside to the sidewalk where he faced his launchman, and said smilingly:

"I thought we'd give Joe a spell to-day. There are a few matters I have to attend to, and I thought you might like to assist me."

"Only too glad to."

"Well then, I would like to meet Miss Spinks to whom you could give me an introduction. While I am talking to her you could engage the mother with small talk. Confide in her my profession."

"All right."

An expression of doubt touched the keen brown eyes regarding Bony, and Bony's blue eyes became abruptly hard. Wilton recognised in them that indefinable something stamping all men who have made their mark on the world, several of whom had been 'his' anglers.

"I shall not upset Miss Spinks by severe questioning and a too vulgar probing into her family relationships," Bony said, slowly moving off along the street in the direction of Nott's Tea Rooms. "I am not going to hold out any hope that Spinks is alive, although we have no proof that he is dead. If, however, he is alive and should one day return home, Miss Spinks might consider herself in a more favourable position to accept the suggestion of marriage, don't you think?"

Glancing sideways at Wilton, Bony noted the expression of strain.

"I know, Jack, how matters are with you. In fact, I know about you more than you may think. My first impression of you is wearing very well, and had I not been born a detective-inspector I would have been a great match-maker."

Marion Spinks turned from dusting the shelves and glass containers beyond the counter to welcome her prospective customers, and instantly the susceptible detective was charmed by her freshness and gipsy beauty. There was no guile, only a pleasing frankness in her dark eyes.

During the introduction, Bony noticed the flash of hostility in those expressive eyes, replaced almost instantly by friendliness. He bowed in his own inimitable way, and said:

"I thought, perhaps, that Jack could interview your mother, and himself bring me a pot of morning tea, while you and I enjoyed a little chat. I would like to prove to you that chatting with a detective can be enjoyable." Bony spoke in his grand manner which, although probably overdone, never failed to charm. "There appear to be no customers requiring your attention just now. Shall we sit at one of these little tables?"

She nodded and, passing round the end of the counter, sat down opposite him. Wilton departed.

"I want you to understand, Miss Spinks," Bony began, "that I do not believe your brother had anything to do with the killing of unfortunate Mr. Ericson. Further, as the *Do-me* evidently was not a victim of the sea, I am inclined to the opinion that your brother was killed with Mr. Ericson."

"He's still alive, Mr. Bonaparte," she said quietly, confidently.

"Do you know that for a fact or do you just feel it is so?"

"I don't know it and I don't feel it."

"Then——"

"I would have felt it had he died," she proceeded earnestly. "Bill and I are twins. When he was caned at school I used to feel on my hand the cuts he got on his. If he got them on his right hand, then my right hand would sting and on it would appear a dull red mark. Father used to drink a lot, and one day he hit Bill with a billet of wood and knocked him unconscious. I was away picking blackberries when it happened, but I knew the instant Bill was hit. I could tell you about other things showing how close Bill and I are together. If Bill had been killed I'd have felt it. As it was, that afternoon the *Do-me* vanished I felt unsettled, and then, when mother and I were waiting at home before we went down to the jetty, I felt that Bill was wanting me badly."

"Have you felt like that since?"

"Often," she replied, nodding her black-crowned head. Then she clasped her hands tightly together on the table and she cried out as though made desperate by all the people who had refused to accept her belief. "Bill's not dead, Mr. Bonaparte. I know he's not. I'd have known it if he was. And I know he had nothing to do with the shooting of Mr. Ericson. He's too fine to do anything like that."

"And you are twins, I think you said?"

"Yes."

Bony stared at her and she wondered why.

"Tell me, Miss Spinks, did you know beforehand that your brother and Mr. Ericson intended to fish along Swordfish Reef?"

"Oh, yes. Bill told mother and me at supper the night before. It wasn't finally decided then, but when mother took Bill's and Robert Garroway's lunch down to the jetty the next morning, Bill and Mr. Ericson had decided on Swordfish Reef."

At this moment Wilton came with Bony's morning tea which the girl set out on the table. To Wilton, Bony said:

"When did you know definitely that Bill Spinks and Mr. Ericson were going out to Swordfish Reef?"

Wilton hesitated to reply.

"I don't remember," he admitted. "I'll have to think back. Ah—yes, I know. It was when Joe and me rowed to the jetty from the *Marlin* at lunch-time. We stopped for a chin-wag to Martin Hooper and Fred Penny. Fred Penny was saying that Swordfish Reef was as good as anywhere off Montague Island for sharks, the argument coming about because the *Do-me* had gone out to Swordfish Reef that day."

"Oh!" Bony sipped his tea. "It was then fairly general knowledge?"

"Yes. There was no secret about it, anyway."

"Hum! Now you go back and talk to Mrs. Spinks. Tell her that the tea is just how I like it." To Marion, Bony said after Wilton had left them: "Your brother did not have any enemies?"

"No. Everyone liked Bill."

"And you all three liked Mr. Ericson?"

"Oh yes. He was a wonderful man. Bill said he was so kind and considerate. He even let Robert Garroway have his rod for half an hour catching tunny."

"I understand that Robert Garroway boarded with you. How did you get along with him?"

"Very well. Robert was quiet and he was always polite to mother and me."

"He wasn't in love with you?"

For the first time the girl smiled. She shook her head.

"Then he was backward for his age, Miss Spinks," Bony told her, softly chuckling. "How did Robert Garroway accept the idea of your brother working Mr. Ericson's prospective launch, and you and your mother going to live in Mr. Ericson's new house? That would have meant that Garroway would have had to seek another job and another home, wouldn't it?"

"But that wouldn't have happened, Mr. Bonaparte. At least I don't think so. Bill thought a lot of Robert Garroway. He was quick to do what he was told at the wheel, and he was always polite and obliging to anglers. It wasn't settled, but

Bill was going to ask Mr. Ericson to let Robert be his mate on the new launch."

"Then you can think of no reason whatever for Robert Garroway to have shot Mr. Ericson?"

"Of course not."

Bony then conducted the conversation into generalities. He learned that the business was thriving; that Mr. Blade continued to act as a business adviser; that Mrs. Spinks suffered only two delusions, and that Marion 'rather liked' Jack Wilton.

Later that morning Bony interviewed the club secretary, and related to Blade the details of the conference at the police station the night before. He agreed to meet Bony on the *Marlin* at two o'clock that afternoon.

At one o'clock Bony received a long telegraphic message from the Chief Commissioner at Sydney.

At two o'clock he found Blade with Wilton in the cabin of the *Marlin*. He asked for a rough table to be erected. Wilton went one better by borrowing a collapsable one from the *Vida*.

"I have brought my sketch maps, Mr. Blade, and I want you to assist me in transporting all their details to one key plan showing the movement of all craft at sea the day the *Do-me* disappeared. We shall want your advice from time to time, Jack. By the way, did you have a picture taken of my swordfish hanging on the town triangle?"

"It was taken this morning," replied Blade.

"Good! I shall want it to convince my wife and children that I caught that fish. Now to work. I have divided these maps into two classes. We will each reduce a set to one map, and finally we will reduce the two resultant maps to a grand final plan. Here are blank sketch maps showing only the coast for use in plotting details from all the other maps."

For an hour they worked carefully plotting the course of

every launch out from Bermagui that fatal day. Times and positions were marked relative to each other, the *Orcades*, the trawler working south of Bunga Head, the several launches out from Narooma. From this the final map was drawn giving all details except the actual courses. In silence the three men studied the key plan.

Presently Bony murmured:

"What can we learn from this? It might contain clues I cannot see but which can clearly be seen by such a man as you, Jack. Look at it carefully. Search for any absurdity, any abnormality. But wait a moment. It will help us if we sub-divide this plan into three areas."

With a coloured pencil he drew curved lines circumscribing his three areas. The one at the top, which included waters about Montague Island, he marked 'North'. That one east of Bermagui he marked 'Central', and that one off Bunga Head south of Bermagui, and which included Wapengo Inlet, he marked 'South'. The 'South' area showed the position of the *Gladious* with that of the *Orcades* and the trawler, *A.S.1.* In the 'Central' area were marked the position of the *Gladious*, *Edith* and *Snowy* with that of the *Do-me* from the time that craft left port until last sighted by the *Gladious*. In the 'North' area the positions of *Edith* and *Snowy* with each other and the *Orcades* were given. After consideration Bony removed the launches from Narooma because, none having been off shore more than two miles, he felt sure they were unimportant.

"Well, Mr. Blade, what do you make of it?" he asked, when again they were silently studying the final drawing.

"Not much as yet. The plan is most enlightening, for we get a kind of aerial view of all craft at sea."

"That is not quite correct, for we have yet to plot in the part-course of the *Dolfin*. The trawler saw her first at seven-fifteen in the morning making south-eastward across her bow.

She lost sight of the *Dolfin*, still making to the south-east, at about eight o'clock. I will pencil in those details. You see, the *Dolfin* emerges from Wapengo Inlet and heads straight to the south-east until lost sight of by the captain of the trawler.

"We appear to possess two premises from which to build two structures of theory," he went on. "The first is that the owner of the *Do-me*, William Spinks, murdered his angler and his mate, or the mate murdered Spinks and the angler, and then steered the launch farther out to sea for the duration of that day, to return at night to the coast where he sank the *Do-me* in shallow water and reached land in the small boat. So far we need not trouble with motive, but we have to recognise the difficulty of disposing of the small boat. The second theory, which seems to contain probability, is that a craft unknown attacked those on the *Do-me*, murdered them all, and then sank the launch. Here again we are without a motive. But we will leave motives alone and concentrate on what could have happened to the *Do-me*.

"If we adopt the first theory, then Spinks or his mate when taking the *Do-me* out to sea for the remainder of the day would have had to hide from the *Orcades* for at least an hour and a half whilst that ship was passing up the coast. If we assume the second theory to be more probable, then the craft that accounted for the *Do-me* had to escape the attention of those on the *Orcades*, the *Gladious*, and the trawler; and it would presume knowledge that Spinks and Ericson had decided to fish along Swordfish Reef. Well, then, what craft on our map, without being observed by the others, was able to dodge north or south and so come in from the east to Swordfish Reef and the *Do-me*?"

After a period of further study, Wilton said:

"The *Gladious* could have done that. *Gladious* could have seen *A.S.1* in the distance; but it was hazy and being a small craft the trawler wouldn't have seen her at half the distance."

"And up here in the north area the *Edith* could have come south after the *Orcades* had passed her at twelve-forty," Blade contributed.

"I think we can absolve the *Edith*," decided Bony, "because Flandin on his *Snowy* checked the course of the *Edith*, after Burns checked his course with the *Snowy* and either one would have noted error in the other's map-plotting. Which leaves us *Gladious* and *Dolfin*."

"Yes, both could have reached the *Do-me* without being seen by those on the trawler—and, too, without being seen by anyone on the *Orcades* after twelve-thirty p.m."

"I agree with you, Jack," Blade said, reluctantly. "Phew! For Remmings on his *Gladious* to have done that would mean that he had to make confederates of his mate and his two anglers who are professional men in Melbourne. As for Rockaway on his *Dolfin*, he would have had as confederates his crew of three men and his daughter if she went to sea that day. Hang it! Rockaway has been living at Wapengo Inlet for years, seven years. He built himself a fine house. He owns several cars and the *Dolfin*. He built a comfortable jetty to take the *Dolfin*. No, no, no! It couldn't have been *Gladious* or *Dolfin*."

Once again silently they studied the plan. Now and then footsteps sounded on the decking of the jetty outside. Through the cabin entrance drifted the low murmur of human voices, the cry of sea birds, the eternal roar of surf. Then Bony said, softly, taking pleasure in throwing a bomb into the works of the plan:

"Do either of you know a launch about forty feet in length, steam driven, with a black funnel and no mast, and painted warship grey?"

Both his hearers stared at him, and then both answered in the negative. Bony smiled a little when he went on:

"I received a message to-day conveying the information that the officer of the watch on the *Orcades* when she passed up this coast, as well as the quartermaster at the wheel, remember seeing such a craft approximately due east of Bunga Head by fourteen miles. They remember seeing this craft because they passed it by only a couple of hundred yards. The two men on it waved to the passengers lining the ship's rails. The time of passing this craft was about twenty minutes after twelve o'clock, and, you will see by our map, seventy-five minutes after *Gladious* last saw the *Do-me* still making to the east in the direction of that steam launch."

Wilton whistled. Blade offered no comment.

"Never even heard of such a craft," Wilton said. "Did the *Orcades* say which way she was making when they saw her?"

"She was making to the south."

"She will have to be located," Blade said.

"The police of Australia are now searching for her," Bony stated. "I think it is too late now to discover her, because she will have been disguised. However, by no means do I think our work on this key plan wasted. The next step is to write history from the day that Ericson arrived at Bermagui to the day after the *Do-me* disappeared. I have made a copy of the weather records, and from your books, Mr. Blade, other items can likely enough be obtained to go into the making of the history."

The secretary's grey eyes were shining when he said, eagerly:

"My books would give a great deal of information, because they concern fishing and items that will recall incidents from which other items of information can be built up. We could, I think, make the history of those days fairly comprehensive."

"Good!" exclaimed the half-caste. "We'll make it a personal history, as though it were a diary kept by the unfortunate Mr. Ericson. From it might emerge a lead. I am beginning to feel that the motive behind the destruction of the *Do-me* was the killing of Ericson, and that the motive for the murder of Ericson might be discovered in those twenty-nine days."

Swiftly he gathered the plans together and placed them in the brief-case. It was five o'clock and the first of the launches was coming in over the bar.

"I want to go fishing to-morrow, Mr. Blade. Could we devote a couple of hours to the History of the Twenty-nine Days, say after nine o'clock to-night?"

"Yes. Certainly."

"You're a brick. I will be at your office at nine. Jack, to-morrow we sail for the open sea and the big fish."

Blade chuckled.

"It's a great sport, isn't it?" he said.

"Sport!" Boney echoed. "It's a grand passion!"

CHAPTER 10

Real Angling

When the procession of launches left Bermagui the following morning, the *Marlin* was a unit of it and Bony was in her cockpit.

"I 'ates these calm glassy days," Joe informed him, dropping over the stern his feathered hook which had just been removed from the mouth of a two-pound bonito. "Gimme a good rip-snorter for swordfishing: a man's got to keep his fingers out of 'is nose when a swordie takes a good holt on a bait-fish in a half gale."

They were crossing the mouth of the inner bay towards the tip of the outer headland, three launches ahead and two astern with another coming round the promontory. A heavy ground swell was running into the great bay, the low water mountains ridged by a short chop set going by the wind coming off the land. Against the green back of the protecting headland Bermagui township appeared as newly-washed clothes drying on a line.

Outside the headland the swells sent back by the rock-armoured land created a chaos of water that took the launches high and dropped them low; but once away from this disturbance they rode easier. Some went towards Montague Island, others straight out towards Swordfish Reef, but the *Marlin* trolled southward, passed the Three Brothers rocks and towards Bunga Head.

Overboard went the teasers to skip and dance on and under the surface of clear water. Overboard went the bait-fish to come skimming after the *Marlin* like a small speed-boat. Each successive roller took the craft high, permitting Bony to view the coast less than a mile away, and then dropped her low, allowing the departing roller to hide the land for a little space. The methodical labour of the engine never varied, never faltered.

"Funny kind of morning," Wilton observed as he sat on the gunwale rolling a cigarette. "Glass as steady as a rock at twenty-nine point seven inches. Been like that all night. Must have been rough weather 'way out towards New Zealand for these rollers to be coming in. Have to keep an eye on the glass. It might mean an easterly and we don't want to be too far off Bermee if she comes."

"What are the chances of getting a fish, do you think?" Bony asked.

"Not bad. There's more birds about to-day. See that gannet working inshore? The mutton birds are making south, too."

"Which means?"

"That the small fish are on the surface, and that the shoal fish are coming north. The birds are going to meet 'em. That's why Joe agreed easily to make down to Bunga. Those birds whisper yarns to him all right. Look at that gannet."

Bony saw the gannet, a large and graceful bird, circling above the sea only a hundred yards away. Then it quickly tilted forward and fell like a dart, its wings partly extended to maintain direction until the last fraction of a second before it plunged into the sea.

"You'd think it would break its neck, wouldn't you?" remarked Wilton. "I wonder at times how often they have to dive to get a meal. Not many. That fellow's got his breakfast. He wastes no time in getting it down his gullet and being a-wing again."

From the gannet Bony's interest was transferred to the

launches, all now at varying distance from the *Marlin*. He was beginning to understand the language in which the Book of the Sea is written. But sea distances still baffled him: he asked how far away was the *Dorothea*.

"About four miles," answered Wilton.

So only four miles separated. *Marlin* from *Dorothea*, and only now and then could Bony see *Dorothea*. That was when she rode the back of a roller when the *Marlin* was doing the same. Otherwise Bony could see only her bare mast. All the launches had masts and carried sails to be used in case of engine break-down; often it was the mast above the horizon which indicated the position of another launch.

"Assuming, Jack, that you wanted to keep out of sight of another launch but wished to keep in touch with her, could you do it by taking down your mast?" he asked.

"Too right! A launch with her mast down could fox another with her mast up, all day and never be sighted."

"It would be easier to do if there was a haze?"

"Of course. Neither that black launch nor the *Dolfin* would be seen, if their skippers didn't want 'em to be seen. The mystery launch had no mast standing, according to the *Orcades* and the mast on the *Dolfin* is hinged and can be hauled up or lowered to the deck in no time. In fact, Mr. Rockaway had her mast fixed like that because he reckoned a mast spoilt her lines. He wouldn't have a mast at all only he wants one to fly a capture flag as well as to hoist a sail on in case of engine trouble."

Bony pondered on this before asking:

"This Wapengo Inlet—has it a bar?"

"Yes. It's as easy to navigate, though, as the Bermaguee bar. But the same easterly gales that close the Bermaguee River also close the Wapengo Inlet. They very seldom blow this time of year, but in winter they keep going for days and there's no getting in or out."

"In those circumstances what would happen if a launch attempted crossing either bar?"

"She'd be dumped on the bottom if she wasn't rolled over. But we never take risks on that stunt. If we can't get in—and I've been caught by an easterly more than once—it means punching away up to Montague Island and taking shelter in its lee until the gale blows out. We take good care not to run the risk of that when we've an angler aboard.

"Me and Joe got caught once down off Tathra. It was our own fault in a way because we saw it coming. We just got over the bar at Wapengo Inlet in time. I was scared stiff, but Joe took her over without turning a hair. Inside, there's enough shelter for a dozen liners. It blew hard for a week, but, as there were millions of ducks about, we lived on ducks and nothing else. Afterwards I wouldn't look at poultry for a year."

"Was that before Rockaway built his house there?"

"Yes."

"Why did he elect to live there, do you know?"

"For the shooting as well as the fishing, I expect. It don't seem to be any different living there than at Bermee when a feller can afford to run cars and a truck. What's a few miles, anyway? Besides, he was able to buy up a lot of land that one day is going to be dear. Not a bad sort, Rockaway. Pretty generous. And keen in a business way. Well, I'd better go for'ard and take a look-see. Shoal fish coming up from the south all right by all these working mutton birds."

Slowly the morning passed, and they were just south of Bunga Head when Wilton came aft for the lunch baskets. Bony noticed Joe gazing earnestly to the east. He looked that way himself, but could see nothing of import or interest. Then Wilton emerged from the cabin and said to his partner:

"The guts have fallen out of the barometer. Turn her

round and make for home. The nearer port we are if heavy weather comes the better."

"I thought somethin' was happenin'," Joe rumbled, bringing the bow of the *Marlin* round to point northward. "These rollers are gettin' bigger. Still, the sky's clear enough. No sign of weather that I can see, unless, yes, there's a bit of darkness low on the horizon to east'ard."

"Probably come quick. Keep a look-out."

Wilton was seated in the starboard angler's vacant chair eating his lunch in Bony's company when Joe shouted:

"Fish-oh!"

They swung round to the quarter at which Joe was pointing, and Joe was shouting exultantly, ten times louder than he need have done.

"Look at that fin! By heck, look at it!"

The hair at the back of Bony's head felt as through it stood outward stiffly, at its roots a sensation of prickling. He saw the fin at the instant Wilton shouted. The fin was passing the launch to come in round astern of it. Already it had begun the movement. But what a fin! It was standing out of the water as high again as that of his first fish, a thick-based, symmetrically-tapered grey slab of streamlined speed. There was no mistaking it for other than what it was, the fin of a big swordfish.

Joe continued to shout, but now Bony's brain did not register the words. He did not see the enormous Joe dancing with naked feet, or Wilton standing on the gunwale and supporting himself against the side of the cabin structure. The falling barometer and the threat of bad weather were forgotten by all. The fish was curving well astern of the launch, coming in and on to follow the wake.

Wilton sprang to the back of Bony's chair and began to fasten on his angler the body harness. In this harness clipped to the rod reel, Bony was compelled to crouch over the rod, gloves now on his hands, the fingers of the right hand gently working at the brake spokes, feeling the drag of the water on the bait-fish. Wilton's voice in his ear was like the hiss of the sea.

"Six hundred pounds if an ounce, Bony. Take him easy. Oh—what a beauty! He's after the bait-fish. He's seen it. Look at him, just keeping pace with it, eyeing it, smelling it. He's a bit suspicious. We're leaving the teasers out till the last second. That's right! Be ready to take off brakage, and be careful not to let the line over-run when he's taking it away. Come on, you beauty! What's stopping you? Come and take it. It's just waiting for you. Ah! . . . Look!"

Like an arrow sped straight and sure, the fin streaked forward, came on up the slope of a water mountain, up and up after the skimming bait-fish. The *Marlin* began to drop down into the water valley, and there on the summit of the huge roller, silhouetted against the steely sky, rode the bait-fish, sending outward to port and starboard its 'bow' wave, and there immediately behind it, sticking upward like the keel of an overturned racing yacht, sped the dorsal fin of the swordfish.

Down came the bait-fish, following the *Marlin* into the valley. And now the men could look through the slope of the roller and see the black shape beneath the fin, slim and long and superb.

They were in the valley when a brown spear of bone rose out of the sea. An elephantine mouth rose up beside the bait-fish. It seemed to jerk forward like the open jaws of an eager dog, then sank with the bait-fish gripped by it. The fin disappeared. The reel began to scream.

Immediately Joe spun the wheel to bring the stern round to the north-east. The line from the rod tip ran out directly astern, watched by Bony, the angler, crouching over the screaming reel. Wilton jumped back to whisk inboard the two teasers. Then he sprang again to crouch over Bony from behind the chair.

Every second yards of line were torn off the reel. There had been nine hundred yards wound on it. Now there were only seven hundred yards. Three seconds later there were but six hundred yards. The reel was being emptied of line. There was left only half of the nine hundred yards of line when the reel abruptly ceased its screaming and the line between rod tip and water lay slack.

"Wait!" pleaded Wilton. "No brake, yet. He'll run again."

Wilton was right. Again the reel screamed and the line again ran away into the sea. Bony's gloved fingers continued to press on the revolving drum. The fingers of his right hand itched to turn the spokes of the brake wheel, to stem that terrific outgoing of precious line. Wilton's nerves were frozen solid. He watched the emptying reel first with unease and then with growing despair. Six hundred yards of line lay buried in the sea. Now six hundred and fifty yards of line had been taken overboard. Now only two hundred yards of line remained on the reel.

His angler couldn't wait longer for the fish to stop and chew the bait-fish before swallowing it, no not with only a hundred and fifty yards of line in reserve, and this reserve being eaten up at every split second. The last foot of line to leave the reel would mean breaking the rod or snapping the line, in any case losing the fish. Better to strike before the right moment and chance hooking the fish than to leave it too late and certainly lose it through the line being snapped off the drum.

"Strike him, Bony! Strike him now!" he shouted. "You'll probably lose him, but you'd lose him anyway with no line left on the reel in reserve."

Bony struck, sharply, felt the weight, was unable to hold

the line racing away under his finger-tips. He struck again, bringing the rod tip up and back over his head, braking as hard as he dared.

The scream of the reel stopped.

He wound in the slack line, felt the weight of the fish, and again struck.

"Give it to him," yelled Joe.

"Come round, Joe. Speed her up. Follow the fish. Line's short!" shouted Wilton, and Bony noted the increased engine beats and saw the line swinging to port, and the craft's stern came round. The line presently came to meet the sea off the beam, and the way on of the launch reduced the rate of line expenditure. The fish reduced its speed and he wound slack line on the reel drum. Water dripped to his knees. His back now was to the stern, his face almost directly confronting the dancing Joe, whose task was to keep the bow of the *Marlin* almost parallel with the line.

"He's coming up!" shouted Wilton, excitement unnecessarily raising his voice. "Fetch her round, Joe!"

Round came the stern. Round went the line and the rod tip until the line spun outward to the sea directly astern, giving Bony foot purchase on the stern rail and a clear fighting range. They could see the line lengthening above water as the fish, hundreds of yards away, was shooting to the surface at express speed. Up went Bony's rod tip against the weight at the far end. Down went the rod tip to produce slack line which was brought in to the reel drum. Again up and then down: up and then down. The angler's right hand ached with the rapid circular movement enforced by the winding handle. His left forearm ached with the incessant upward pull exerted on the rod every time he struck the fish. This time he was able to do all this without looking at his work, and thus he was able to watch the sea far astern, guessing where the fish would appear. His guess was right.

He and Wilton and Joe yelled together.

"There he goes! Look at him! Look at him!"

Up from the summit of a water mountain sprang the fish, six hundred yards away, a greyish torpedo enshrined in a rainbow. The water mountain passed from under it whilst yet it was above the sea, and consequently they did not see the mighty splash of its falling into a water valley.

"Go on, give it to 'im, Bony!" yelled Joe. "Sock it into 'im! You've got him! Don't let him have slack. Give it to 'im!"

"By heck, he's a record, Joe!" cried Wilton, exultation in his voice.

"No, he ain't, Jack, but he's a near record. How's the line on the reel?"

"Not enough if he runs far now. Begin to bring her round to follow the fish. Yes, there he goes."

Despite Bony's braking on the line the reel began again its scream, as the fish went deep and away at the speed of a fast car.

Bony's brain actually felt cold within his skull. It again became parted into two entities, one of which registered all sounds and movements made by his launchmen, the other coldly calculating, reasoning, seeking to forestall. This day he had the requisite knowledge of managing rod and reel and brake, but he still lacked the timing sense gained only by experience. He suffered no nervous complexes. He was unconscious of his body, but strangely conscious of his brain housed behind his eyes.

The thumb of the hand holding the rod he kept pressed to the taut line, estimating by its tautness the strain put upon it. When it became too great he eased the brake, and the reel's scream rose a note higher. The launch was under way, following the fish, but not overtaking it, reducing the expenditure of line the reserve of which was down to a hundred and fifty yards. Sweat poured from Bony's face, ran down his neck to saturate his shirt. The line often was so taut that Wilton despaired. He refrained from his urging, recognising that had he been in the chair he could have done no better than Bony was doing.

The screaming reel became silent, and instantly Joe swung the *Marlin*'s stern wide, bringing the line again back beyond the stern.

"What's 'e doin' now?" he demanded of Wilton.

"Dunno, unless he intends rolling a bit to take the trace round his tail and break it."

"Hell-'v-a-chance he's got of doing that with that nice strong trace," Joe shouted, and roared with laughter. "Stick to him, Bony! He's gonna try a few 'arty tugs."

And Joe was right. Up the line to the rod tip, and down through the line guides to Bony's hands came a succession of terrific tugs. Each tug tore line from the protesting reel despite the brakage placed on it.

"Careful!" pleaded Wilton. "Careful, or the line'll go, or the rod'll break. He's down deep, shaking his head or his tail, trying to snap the trace asunder. Let him to it. There's plenty of time. The more he fights now the less hard he'll be on line when he runs again. He's no chicken, bee-lieve me. You want to conserve your strength because you're going to be tired by the time you bring him to the gaff."

Joe reached forward and touched his partner with a foot. Wilton turned and Joe indicated the eastern horizon. There, low above the horizon, was a long, narrow black cloud.

Tight-lipped, Wilton passed into the cabin where he glanced at the barometer, and still tight-lipped he attended to the engine, checking oilers, checking the petrol in the tanks. When he emerged he stood close to Joe and said:

"Glass down to twenty-nine point four. The weather'll break with a howler."

Joe grinned, and all his whiskers seemed to stand out.

"Bit of bad luck, the weather," he said. "Hope the fish is tired time it strikes us, or you'll have to hold Bony into his chair. Just look at him now. Cold as ice inside and pourin' sweat outside. He's got the right temperament for sword-fishin'. Picking it up fast, ain't 'e?"

Wilton grinned. Once again he looked seaward: the thick-ness of the ribbon cloud on the horizon was increasing.

"The *Dolfin*'s coming in fast for home," he told Joe. "What do you reckon? Cut the line and make for Bermee?"

"Cut the line!" Joe blazed. "Cut the line with that fish on the other end of it! No fear. We'll run into Wapengo Inlet if the sea looks like we won't reach Bermee in time to get over the bar. The ruddy launch can sink before we lost that ruddy fish."

Wilton grinned, and patted his partner on the arm.

"Keep your eye on that weather," he urged, and went aft once again to stand behind his angler.

"How's he going?" he asked. "You've got a bit of line in, I see."

"Yes, but what I get in over a minute the fish takes out again in less than a second," panted Bony.

"Never mind. Make him fight all the time. Don't let up on him and give him a breather. Watch those rollers, too. Every time we heave over the back of one be easy on the brake because the strain becomes heavy. We don't want to lose that beauty now."

"How long's he been on?" Bony asked, between gasps.

"About thirty-five minutes. Getting tired?"

"More than a little. I'm not as young as I used to be. But what a fish, Jack! What a fish! Ah, come in a little nearer! No you don't. Ah . . . I'm holding you better now."

Bony gained a yard or two of line; held it whilst the rod became a bow; then he would lose a few feet despite all his own muscular effort, finely judging how to employ the brake without danger. And then into his radius of vision swept a cruiser-type launch painted silver-grey. It came in on the starboard side, and ran smartly parallel with the *Marlin* in order not to cross the angler's line. Bony saw a big man and a slim woman seated in the roomy cockpit. Another man stood in the shelter of the wheel-house. Yet another was dismantling a heavy game fishing-rod. The man and woman in the cockpit waved to him, and Bony managed to wave a hand in acknowledgment.

The sea was certainly 'getting up'; the rollers had now become huge mountains. When one was between them neither launch could be seen from the other. The big man seated with the woman in the anglers' chairs rose and pointed to the east, and Bony then saw the rising cloud belt sweeping towards the zenith. Joe shouted and waved his arms. After that the *Dolfin* quickly forged ahead and, passing across the *Marlin*'s bow, slid away shoreward.

The minutes were mounting against Bony. When the battle had lasted a full hour the gale struck them with wind and rain. The sun went out. The blue and white of the sea became green and white. The crests of the chop were whipped away in a general smother so that the green patches contracted and the white gashes spread to join in big areas.

"How's it going now?" asked the anxious Wilton.

"He's coming. But he's slow. It's like pulling at a whale," Bony sobbed.

"Keep going. You've got half your line in. He'll come faster and faster because he can't get any fresher."

The fish was still away to the north-east and the rising seas were attacking the *Marlin* broadside on. Joe edged her bow a little to take the crests on the port quarter. The launch bucked like a cork, and Wilton had hard work steadying Bony's chair to enable him to maintain a purchase with his feet on the stern rail. Foot by foot the dripping line was brought to the rod tip and down the guides to the reel drum.

"Storm blowing up?" asked Bony, the words rasping from his mouth.

"Bit of a squall," replied Wilton.

The rain hit the green areas of water, bounced, was whipped away into the suds; the upper slopes of the rollers were covered with angry crests. Wilton's uneasiness was caused by the prospect of the minor waves becoming added to the rollers and forming on them towering, curving, smashing walls of white water. Every minute the chance of making the bar at Wapengo Inlet was becoming poorer. He went back to Joe.

"What d'you think of it now?"

"Not too bad yet, Jack. How's the fish comin'?"

"Two hundred yards out. Another hour and we won't be able to get into Wapengo."

"Then we'll make down to Eden, Jack. This tub will ride anything. We've plenty of petrol. Take a look at the glass."

"Twenty-nine point three six," Wilton said on emerging from the cabin.

"She's gonna blow 'ard in a minute," predicted Joe, with amazing cheerfulness. "She can blow as 'ard as she likes s'long as we get that fish."

The fish was beaten, and had Bony been fresh a minute or two only would have sufficed to bring it to the launch, but he had by this time spent seventy minutes in a gruelling battle with a fish weighing several hundredweight. Now he realised that the wind had shifted from the west to the east, that it was rapidly gaining strength. He could see how it whipped off the weather-tops of the crests; how it drove short lines of suds scudding across the little patches of green water. The raindrops were big: each one that struck upon his arms and face and neck stung like the bites of green-head ants.

He knew that Wilton was again standing behind him, and he was forced to master his breathing in order to shout:

"I'm bringing him now. He's given in. It's like a ton weight at the bottom of a well."

"You're doing good-oh," Wilton hissed into his right ear. "Work him a bit faster. The sea's getting up, and we'll have to run for Wapengo Inlet. Wouldn't get to Burmee in time to navigate the bar."

Because the angler's arms felt filled with lead, and his back ached, he did not notice any trace of the anxiety growing in Wilton's mind. It was all very well for Joe to say they could run down to Eden if they couldn't chance the Wapengo bar. The *Marlin* wasn't a steamer, and the coast steamers sometimes ran for shelter. Brown eyes, screwed inward for protection from the rain and spray, calculated the amount of line still to be got in. He went back to Joe.

"Fish is pretty near," he said. "Get the gaff and ropes."

He took the wheel from Joe and Joe nimbly worked preparing for the ultimate conquest. Wilton, watching the on-coming seas and his angler's line, saw presently the bright metal swivel connecting the cord with the wire trace come up out of the water.

Now had arrived the most ticklish job of all, for there was no third man to take the wheel and keep the bow of the *Marlin* towards those vast white crests on each succeeding water mountain. He accelerated the engine to give the craft more speed and therefore more steering way. He watched Bony bringing his rod tip back towards him to take the trace. He saw Joe crouched immediately behind the angler with gaff pole and ropes expertly held.

With a bite of a rope he lashed the wheel, and sprang aft to take the trace. Luckily the fish was nearly dead, almost drowned. The launch bucked sickeningly, and her forehead dropped to bang on the wind'ard side of a roller. What a fish! The very biggest he had ever seen in the water: the biggest he had ever brought to the *Marlin*'s gaff. The great silver-green body slid through the surface suds when he hauled on the trace, bringing it alongside. In went the gaff: out came the pole: on to the gaff rope Joe threw all his weight.

Sheets of spray sprang upward from the side of the launch to be flicked away by the wind now becoming a dull roar. Bony lay back in his chair, panting, still gripping his rod, waiting for the announcement that his fish was secure.

Joe half-hitched his rope round a stern bit and sprang to the wheel to unslip the lashing. He was just in time to prevent the *Marlin* from swinging broadside to a vast cap of white water rearing above them. Wilton cut the line and took the trace end back to Joe, who now steered and held the line keeping the fish's head fast beside the launch. These men acted as though governed by one mind. Each move had been thought out before the fish had been brought in. Now Wilton entwined his feet round the arm-rest of Bony's chair, and, with a rope's noose in his hands, lay over the gunwale to slip the noose over the flailing tail. Time and again his head and shoulders were sent below the surface before his task was accomplished. Then he came struggling inboard, water pouring from him, pride and satisfaction like ecstasy shining in his water-clouded eyes. Above the roar of the wind and the sea came Joe's mighty voice.

"Got 'im! By hell, we've got 'im! Good for you, Bony."

Wilton slapped Bony's back till Bony began to cough.

"Five hundred and fifty pounds at least," he shouted. To Joe, and still shouting: "We'll never get him on board in this sea. We'll have to tow him."

"Sharks!" yelled Joe.

"Have to chance 'em taking a few pounds off him," Wilton yelled back. "He's fixed now. Make for Wapengo, and speed her up."

CHAPTER 11

"A Bit of a Sea!"

They stood, Bony and his launchmen, under the cabin roof
projecting aft to give shelter to the helmsman and the cabin
entrance. They were able to look through glass along the
fore-deck of the *Marlin* and see the whitish blur of land towards which engine and sea and wind combined to drive her
at abnormal speed. Wilton was at the wheel, and Joe stood
on Bony's other side munching a meat sandwich at least
three inches thick.

Now and then Joe chuckled as though at an unshared joke.
Not for several minutes did Bony grasp the reason. When he
did he was surprised: on Wilton's youthful face glowed intense happiness. He was seeing their reactions—not to the
storm of wind and the wave-crests fast becoming a menace
to so small a craft, but to the triumph of success.

He never had observed a prospector at the moment of un-
earthing a Welcome Nugget, but a prospector finding such a
nugget would look precisely as these two now did. On their
weather-touched faces was written plain a vast satisfaction
in achievement. The tautness of their nerves was betrayed
by the deliberateness of their actions.

Old hand that he was in the study of human reactions, he
was astonished at his own. His skin was clammy with sweat,
although his clothes were drenched by the rain that had
fallen sudden and swift before passing on to leave the sky
partially clear of cloud. No successful culmination of a man-
hunt ever had given him such exquisite satisfaction as he now

felt: his mind refused to be subdued; refused to cease its thrilling at vivid memory. It felt warm within his head. It was exhilarated to the point of intoxication: it gloried in its freedom at last to savour every moment of that epic fight with the fish now being towed astern.

The squall clouds were skidding across the tops of the hills, followed by individual clouds racing ahead of the *Marlin*. The sun was shining as though bravely defiant of a long belt of cloud lying above the eastern horizon, threatening, blue-black. The wind was roaring about every projection of the launch, and the sea was hissing and crashing like breaking glass. Coming from astern, the wind pressed their bodies into the shelter, forcing them to resist it with their hands against the ledge below the thick windows.

"Look at that ole wallerin' cow," urged Joe, jerking his head to the port window.

A steamer of some five thousand tons, painted white to her bridge with spray, was labouring northward to Sydney. Her stubby masts and squat funnel swayed west and then eastward as every gigantic roller passed under her. Her blunt bow was clotted with white water. Her black-painted sides were ribbed with it.

"Sooner be 'ere than on 'er," Joe said. "I'd be sick aboard 'er, I reckon."

Bony felt violent opposition to this idea until he realised that he agreed. That distant ship was indeed a 'wallower' while the *Marlin* was a wave-skimming bird. The land and the steamer were too distant to provide a basis for judging their own speed, but they could feel this speed alternately slackening and increasing. Each successive roller followed hard upon the *Marlin*; appeared to rear itself almost to the sky above her; remained like that for several seconds, as though gathering its maximum strength before springing forward to engulf a craft no larger in comparison than a mussel shell. The *Marlin* would appear to falter, to be paralysed, to be drawn back and under the towering wall of white-laced water; but always she managed to keep just ahead of the smashing weight. Then the foaming crest would boil under her and about her, embrace her with snowy arms, lift her high and with the assistance of the following wind carry her forward towards the land at the speed of a race-horse. Then slowly speed would diminish, the *Marlin* would be left behind by the eager wave rushing landward, left to sink in the steep water valley and to be threatened by yet another fearsome roller.

"How far d'you think we're off the Inlet, Joe?" Wilton asked, as one might ask the distance to a tram stop.

" 'Bout three miles. What d'you say?"

" 'Bout that. Think we'll get in over the bar?"

"The *Dolfin*'s made it. We'll soon know. If we're gonna go in, we want to make it afore this comin' squall strikes. Looks like we'll beat it. Hope so, any'ow. I'd sooner be eatin' old Rockaway's tucker in comfort than bitin' me finger-nails punching all the way day to Eden."

"That's Tathra down there, isn't it?" asked Bony. "What's wrong with going in there?"

"No shelter. No jetty for small craft. The place's no good in this kind of weather," answered Joe. "We'll make over the Wapengo bar—with a bit of luck."

"And if we have no luck?"

"I'm gonna take a look-see in a minute, and if our luck's out, well, it'll mean kicking down to Eden. I'd better see how the old bloke's coming on astern."

As light of foot as a young girl going to meet her lover, but with the inelegant movements of a wallower, Joe made his way aft between the two anglers' chairs to assure himself that the fish's towing-rope was secure. Wilton, observing Bony watching his partner, smiled broadly. The picture presented by the rear middle portion of Joe's anatomy was one never to be forgotten by Angler Bonaparte. It looked enormous within the confining limits of the after end of the launch, but against the momentary background of an appallingly rearing precipice of water it appeared correctly proportionate.

The oncoming wave raised the dead swordfish higher than the crouching Joe Peace. It was being towed tail first, and its tail fin came cutting through the white water as though it were the blade of a sword blackened by fire. When the *Marlin* was riding the roller's broad back Bony again looked at the wallowing steamer, and Wilton shouted to him:

"It makes a man feel seasick looking at her."

Turning to him Bony laughed. He was feeling peculiarly happy, almost light-headed.

"I ought to be seasick, but I'm not," he told Wilton. "The *Marlin* is like a bird, and I feel as though I were standing on a bird's back. I feel, Jack, like a man ought to feel always."

On Joe returning, Wilton gave up his stand at the wheel and passed down into the cabin to tend his engine. Joe winked and jerked his head back towards the towing fish.

"The old bloke's comin' along good-oh," he said, as a man might refer to someone on whom his pride is centred. " 'E might go six 'undred pounds, but I ain't sayin' he will. A nice fish, Bony. The people of Bermee will be glad to see 'im 'anging on the town triangle."

Absently he selected one of the two pipes thrust through his belt, and with remarkable dexterity applied the flame of a match to the dottle within its bowl. Never before had Bony smelled such tobacco, and hastily he rolled a cigarette and with much difficulty managed to light it. Pleasurably he inhaled, and moved as far from Joe as was possible. Wilton came to stand between them. And Joe said:

" 'Minds me of that time we 'ad Mr. and Mrs. Mack out

fishing in the *Marlin*. We was away out about six miles off Montague Island when the mercury, or whatever's in them barometers, leaked from under it, and an easterly comes roaring in without any kind of notice. Funniest easterly I ever seed. Any'ow, we advises 'ome and comfort at the toot sweet. Mr. Mack he says shoot 'er in. I yanks in the teasers, and then I goes aft to bring in the bait-fish and unship the rod. Mrs. Mack she says: 'Don't do that, Joe, we might happen to get a fish on the way in.' And sure enough we do. It takes Mr. Mack thirty-five minutes to bring him to the gaff, and by that time there's no hope of getting over the bar, and the sea wants to get up and kick us in the face.

"We punches away up to Montague Island, getting there near dark, and we ain't got no tucker and no bedding and the wind gets kind of coldish. Did the lady go crook? No. She says she's enjoying every minute of it. Can't I say I was. I kind of gets run down when I misses me tucker.

"Any'ow, we parks Mrs. Mack with the lighthouse women, and I tries to get tucker off the head keeper, but he gets nasty and wants to know what the hell we're doing on Montague, and don't we damn well know we ain't got no right to land? Couldn't blame him, 'cos their tucker supply is limited, and there ain't never no knowing when gales will stop a fresh supply being landed.

"The next day she blows harder than ever, and I managed to get a handful of tea and a loaf of bread and tin of dog. I seen Mrs. Mack and tells 'er it's no go attempting the Bermee bar that day, and I asks her how she's enjoying of herself. 'Oh,' she says, 'first rate, Joe. It's just too lovely for words and the people here are so kind.'

"So I goes back with me tin of dog and loaf of bread and handful of tea, and me and Mr. Mack and Jack, here, does a perish. The next day she's still blowing hard, and we runs out of terbacca. Orf I goes up to the lighthouse to borrow a shred or two. The head man 'e don't smoke, and the other two's a bit short. Still, one saves the sinking ship by comin' to light with a plug what he says he's been keeping as a stand-by in case of a drought.

"I takes this down to the *Marlin*, and Mr. Mack he cuts that plug into a fair three parts. 'Im and Jack, here, smokes fags and they chipped off the doings from their bits and I fills me pipe with the bit I got. An' stonker the crows if inside two minutes we wasn't all seasick, and the *Marlin* layin' in shelter as steady as anything.

"Terbacca! By cripes, it was terbacca. The next day she's as calm as tea in a cup, and off we goes to fetch Mrs. Mack down to the *Marlin* and away for home. There's me and Mr. Mack and Jack, here, doing a fast cure, and there's Mrs. Mack telling us what a lovely time she 'ad up at the lighthouse, and 'ow everything was lovely at sea, but she wisht she 'adn't run outer powder 'cos the air was makin' her nose red."

A series of chuckles emanated from Joe after this anecdote, and Bony was thankful that in the telling of it Joe had let his pipe go out. He thought that a remnant of that Montague Island tobacco must still linger in its bowl.

They could now see the rock-feet of the cliffs looming higher before the bow of the *Marlin*, see the foam leaping about them, shooting high up the agate-hard facets of iron escarpments. The short sand beaches were ribbed with swirling surf, and the lower slopes of the highlands behind them were stained with the white smoke of fine spindrift. Astern of them the deepening mass of blue-black cloud was racing to the zenith.

"I wish I had that swordie across the stern instead of dragging in tow," Wilton said, having flashed a glance round the compass quarters.

"Better not muck about with 'im now," was Joe's advice. "We'll have to get over that flamin' bar afore this weather strikes and raises a bit of a sea, or we're gonna be at sea all night and no tucker. I'll go for'ard and take a bird's eye view of the bar."

Wilton took the wheel and Joe clambered forward to stand holding to a mast stay and the mast. The wind tore at his well-washed dungaree trousers and blue pullover, and whipped outward from his round head the sparse greying hair. Bony would have liked much to join him, and said so; but Wilton said Joe would be back with his report in a second or two. They would attempt the bar if he advised it: otherwise they would have to fight the long night through making down to Eden. And that would be no pleasure trip with the seas coming abeam.

"Can you see the mouth of the Inlet?" Bony asked.

"Too right. Watch the bow: I'll point it straight at the bar. Wait! There . . . now!"

The position of the bar made Bony gasp. Between two low headlands the water leaped and seemingly burst upward in fountains of foam. The fury was worse there than along the short sand beaches. He saw the land extending westward between the headlands, but could see no welcoming reaches of placid water.

Joe came aft to drop down to them.

"In she goes," he said.

"All right. You take her in," Wilton replied.

Stepping back, Joe planted himself squarely in front of the wheel, and Wilton slipped down to the engine to give it a final inspection, for engine failure at one of the several critical moments ahead would spell certain disaster. The rollers now were becoming even more menacing, for the water was shallowing. Wilton reappeared and sat on the decking the better to control both the engine's speed and gear clutch. Bony saw, in the stern expression of his face, the mastery of mind over matter. The lips of the firm clean mouth were pressed tightly together. His gaze was centred on Joe's feet.

Joe was standing on his toes; his eyes almost closed. The pipe was still gripped by his teeth, but the bowl was raised to the level of his fringe of hair. At that angle it remained. He appeared to give as much attention to the sea astern as to the maelstrom ahead.

Joe stamped his left foot.

Wilton instantly put the *Marlin* hard astern. She began to wallow, sickeningly, lifelessly, as though she were foundering. The towed swordfish sank from sight. Out of the blue-black east reared a mighty roller. It seemed to Bony that it stopped in that terrifying attitude. He looked at Joe. Joe was watching it, waiting—and ahead waited the tossing chaos of water bordered by black rocks reaching to the sky.

All about the *Marlin* the water was white. The sun went out. There was no waning of its light. It just went out—flick. The summit of the following wave began to curve inward, its crest to topple forward over the *Marlin*. And Joe stamped his right foot and swung back to look ahead.

Instantly Wilton pulled back the propeller clutch and accelerated the engine to its greatest energy. The *Marlin* bucked her way forward, lifted her stern to the oncoming wave. On the wave's front floated high the dead swordfish, high above the launch. It appeared that the roller was about to toss the fish into the cockpit. When it failed to do this it came on and after the *Marlin* as though infuriated at being cheated.

The timbre of the wind rose to a high scream. Joe again stamped with his right foot, hard and often, but Wilton could get nothing more out of his engine. The crest of the wave began to fall forward—it crashed on to the towed fish, buried it deep, just missed the cockpit of the launch, boiled up under her and surrounded her with foam which the wind

ore away and sent in huge splathers directly into the shelter
where the three men were plastered with it.

Now the wave took charge of the launch, lifted her high,
propelled her forward with amazing speed. Bony now could
see through rents in a white curtain of spray the narrow
entrance of Wapengo Inlet, barely wider than a road. Before
the launch, bordering that roadway black rocks appeared to
be floating in bubbling quick-lime. To starboard a vast foun-
tain of foam shot skyward. The headland on either side
sprang to greet them, seemingly anxious to fall together and
devour them in a huge black maw.

The air above and about the *Marlin* was filled with streaks
of foam being carried past her by the wind. It was impossible
to face astern. The curtain ahead thinned magically, and
down in a valley, down far below the launch lay the comparatively calm water of the Inlet. They were being rushed
towards it on the heart of this roller that had caught them
away out beyond the bar.

The foam outboard lapped over the gunwale into the cockpit, but this they could not see, because they couldn't face
astern. The *Marlin* appeared to plane down to the still water
of the Inlet, until finally she shot on to its table flatness and
was moving into its widening lower reach.

Wilton eased the racing engine down to normal trolling
speed. The bowl of Joe's pipe came down to its normal position. Bony looking back, was amazed that they had passed
over and through such a roaring tumult. Even as he looked
a white sheet spring upward to hide it, sprang upward to
meet a deluge descending from the blue-black clouds.

"Hi! There's a shark after our fish!" Joe yelled.

"Too right, he is," agreed Wilton. "Come on! Get that
wordie aboard pronto. Never mind a drop of rain."

He pushed the gear stick into neutral and leaped after Joe,
who had jumped for the towing-rope. Joe's language would

not have disgraced a hell-ship's mate as he hauled on the towing-rope and dragged to the launch the great grey body of the swordfish, the fin of the shark coming after it. Bony engaged himself on the rope behind Joe, shouting with rage and energised by a spurious strength. Up came the tail of the swordfish, up and over the port edge of the stern. This edge dented deeply into the great rounded base of the tail which Wilton fought to manage so that either one of its diagonal fins would not jam against the stern rail.

The *Marlin* rocked in the flat water of the Inlet beneath the weight of the struggling men, and the fin of the shark zig-zagged and came closer and closer to the forepart of the swordfish still submerged. It was like dragging a bullock up a flight of stairs without the aid of a hoist. At last in board came the capture, and Joe yelled:

" 'Old 'im! "

Bony and Wilton ' 'eld 'im'. Joe came back to them with a Winchester repeating rifle, and he fired two shots at the base of the fin. The second shot evidently took effect, for the tail of the shark came right out of water to smash downward, sending outward sheets of spray before it disappeared.

"That'll lower 'is dignity a bit," Joe remarked, and came to accomplish the lashing of the swordfish to the stern bollards.

The wind had taken the *Marlin* near to a sand-bar. Wilton jumped to her wheel and thrust in the gear shaft.

Joe scratched his head.

"Five 'undred and seventy-five pounds," he estimated, shouting with his mouth close to Bony's left ear. The 'bit of a sea' and the crossing of that bar were not worthy of thought at this moment.

CHAPTER 12

The Rockaways

The *Marlin* was moving steadily ahead. Bony was aware of it in a detached way. He noticed the white wake streaming away astern. He was partially conscious of steeply rising land near to one side, and of a wide stretch of tortured water on the other. The movement of the launch, its lengthening wake that defied the onslaught of wind and rain, and the proximity of land, were of no import whatsoever. He was conscious of the rain penetrating his clothes and chilling his skin, and of the thin fall of water cascading from the down-turned rim of his old felt hat. Even this contained no importance.

There was only one thing that mattered, only the one thing, that black marlin swordfish lying athwart the stern of the launch. Mentally he groped to find an adjective suitably describing it, discarded many, and finally selected one which is overworked—tremendous. The fish dwarfed the width of the *Marlin*'s stern, for its great head and heavy sword projected beyond one side and its tail reached far beyond the other. Its glorious living iridescent blues and greens had long since vanished, being replaced by a general grey.

"What is the Australian weight record, Joe?" he asked, his voice subdued by the amazing fact that he had captured such a fish with such comparatively flimsy tackle.

"Six 'undred and seventy-two pounds," answered Joe. "Mr. J. Porter captured him back in thirty-seven. This bloke won't go as 'eavy, worse luck, but I'm a crab if 'e don't scale at more than five hundred and fifty. Ain't 'e a ruddy beaut?"

"And how long, d'you think did I take to bring him to the gaff?"

"Eighty-one minutes," promptly replied Joe. "That's a fact. I timed you. I always time an angler when a fish grabs 'is bait-fish."

"Eighty-one minutes! Was it that long?"

"Too right! You done extra well getting him to the gaff in that time in that sea running. Specially as 'ow 'e's only your second fish."

"You are being generous, Joe. I owe a great deal to you and Jack. I'd never——"

"Come for'ard, Joe, and make fast," shouted Wilton. Turning about, Bony saw that the *Marlin* was moving in behind the *Dolfin* to moor at a jetty.

He saw, too, through the descending wind-driven deluge a group of four people standing on the jetty waiting for them, and that the jetty joined a road which wound upward across the slope of a grassy hill to a large bungalow-type of house having tall chimneys and glass-protected verandas. The four people all wore oilskin coats and oilskin hats. One of them was a woman.

Joe, having clambered to the jetty with a mooring-line, shouted:

"Good day, Mr. Rockaway!"

No one of the group answered his greeting. Each member of it continued to stare downward at the fish lying athwart the *Marlin*'s stern. Joe had to pass behind them to take from Wilton the stern mooring-line.

"A nice fish, ain't 'e?" he persisted.

Bony betrayed small interest in the group. He observed that the girl nodded agreement with Joe's remark. but continued to regard the swordfish. Then the tallest of the three men jumped down to stand with Bony in the cockpit. For yet a few further seconds he gazed at the capture, before turning towards the detective. His eyes, light-blue in colouring, were wide open and very bright. He proffered a large but soft hand, and Bony took it.

"Heartiest congratulations, sir," he said, in tones soft like his hands. "My name is Rockaway."

"Thank you, Mr. Rockaway. My name is Bonaparte—Napoleon Bonaparte—and I can assure you that the Emperor himself could never have been more vain than I am this afternoon."

He saw the flash of interest that his remarkable name aroused in the mind of the big blue-eyed man; saw, too, that the interest was only of passing moment, quickly submerged by the greater interest in the huge fish. Rockaway looked upward at the woman, standing with the two men on the jetty, and asked, loudly:

"What d'you think of him, Mavis? A beauty, eh?"

"A dream out of the sea," she cried. "May I come down there?"

"Permit me!"

Bony jumped to the gunwale to offer her his hand. Looking upward he encountered large deep-blue eyes set in a face with Grecian contours. The face was devoid of expression, but the eyes were pools reflecting at the moment a keen pleasure. Gallantly, Bony assisted her down to the cockpit of the *Marlin*.

"Mavis, this is Mr. Bonaparte. Mr. Bonaparte, my daughter," Rockaway said without removing his gaze from the fish. "A tape, Dan! Fetch a tape."

"What will it weigh, do you think?" asked the girl.

"Can't make a good guess till we measure him," replied Rockaway. "More than five hundred pounds I'd say. What d'you think, Wilton?"

"Five 'undred and seventy pounds," Joe replied for his partner.

The tape appeared. Rockaway gave one end of it to his daughter, and, with as much enthusiasm as if the catch were theirs, between them they taped the black marlin. Bony stood back a little. He was faintly amused. Joe, with the two men on the jetty, squatted on his heels.

"Eleven feet eleven inches in length," Rockaway announced. Then: "Four feet ten inches in girth. Yes, according to the Catalina Formula, Joe's guess is near right. Again, Mr. Bonaparte, please accept my heartiest congratulations."

"And mine, too," added the girl, turning to face the delighted Bony, who bowed in his grand manner. Only Wilton, standing behind him, saw her eyes momentarily open wide. Bony said, grandly:

"You are exceedingly kind, and I much appreciate your warm sportsmanship. Your congratulations come as a fitting climax to an experience I never shall forget."

"How long did it take you to bring it to the gaff?" she asked.

He told her. Then: "Oh, if only I could capture a fish like that when the sea was like it was then! You know, you are extremely lucky, Mr. Bonaparte."

"And extremely wet," interjected Rockaway. "Come! We'll go aboard the *Dolfin* and drink a health to this prince of swordfish. You two men come along as well. And you, Dan and Dave. Come and drink to the biggest fish you are ever likely to see—bar the Australian record."

He passed first up to the jetty, where he assisted the girl from Bony, who again stood on the gunwale. He led the way along the jetty to the *Dolfin*, and down into the saloon. Outwardly the *Dolfin* was a gentleman's cruiser; inwardly it complied with the demands of a millionaire. The saloon was furnished in mahogany with red plush seating. With a slight flourish of his hands, Rockaway drew open the doors of a massive cabinet to disclose enough liquor to stock a club bar.

"Whisky, Mr. Bonaparte? A cocktail? Beer or stout?"

"Whisky, please. I am, as you observed, extremely wet."

"That can be remedied in a minute," Rockaway promised, himself attending to his daughter, their guests and their two launchmen. "You will be here all night for certain, although the glass is rising. To our deep regret we are unable to offer you the hospitality of our house as it is in chaos, being renovated throughout. However, you are very welcome to stay aboard the *Dolfin* whilst you're imprisoned in Wapengo Inlet. We will show you the pantry and Dan will demonstrate the working of the electric range to Wilton, here. Cigar?"

"No, thanks. A cigarette, perhaps. My papers have been ruined."

"Tell us something about your fight with that fish, Mr. Bonaparte, please," urged the girl, who now was seated on the edge of the dining-table, a cocktail in one hand, a cigarette in the other, her hat removed to uncover a crown of auburn glory. Twenty-four, no more, was Bony's swift estimate. It was peculiar how her face was never allied with her eyes in the expression of emotion. It was as though her face was enamelled, frozen by cosmetics, the application of which was not evident. Her gaze never left him whilst he related the battle, the four launchmen no less interested than she and her father.

Charming people, he judged them. They evinced no stain of snobbery, no hostility to his colour, no curiosity, as yet, about him. The man was large and jovial, and at this time Bony did not recall his flabby hand-grasp. The girl's beauty intrigued him, for never had he beheld beauty just like it. Once she closed her eyes the better to visualise what he was word-painting, and he thought then of feminine beauty painted on canvas. Her enthusiasm for swordfishing astounded him. He could understand it in her father.

When he had finished everyone spoke at the same time, and for a moment or two the small audience broke up into smaller groups to discuss this point and that. Presently, Rockaway said:

"Well, time flies. I'll hunt you up some dry clothes, Mr. Bonaparte. Dan, you fix Wilton and Peace with toggery and show them for'ard to the men's quarters. Afterwards, fix the shore cable to the launch so that the radiators can be turned on and the range used without regard for the batteries. Come along, Bonaparte. The mister stage is passed. I'm plain Rock to my friends."

"And I, Rock, am plain Bony to mine."

Bony was introduced to one of four cabins where he was shown bedding stacked in a locker above the bunk. Rockaway brought to him grey flannels and underwear and canvas shoes. He was the perfect host, providing even shaving gear and a dressing-gown.

"You'll find the shower for'ard of the engine-room," he said. "Consider everything aboard the *Dolfin* your own. I am really concerned that I am unable to offer you my house. Or that I am unable to remain here longer and see further to your comfort. My daughter and I are governed by a dictator who wears skirts and a look like a frying-pan. When the dinner gong is struck, we have to be on hand to answer it, or there's a scolding."

"You are, indeed, a friend in need, Rock."

"You and I have leaped to stand on common ground, Bony. So now, *au revoir*. I'll hope to see you first thing to-morrow. The sea will be down by the morning."

Quite a wonderful man, thought Bony whilst removing his sodden clothes. He heard Rockaway's voice up on the jetty. Later he heard the heavy steps of the man, Dan, pass along the gangway, and the thrump of his boots on the wooden jetty. When he sought the shower-room he could hear Wilton and Joe talking farther forward.

Twenty minutes later he was reclining on red plush and sipping a whisky-soda. His body felt delightfully warm and his muscles relaxed with exquisite pleasure. The Rockaways' kindness was, indeed, immense. They had treated him as an equal when unaware of his profession and reputation. He thought of them, brought them to the screen of his mind for further examination despite the fact that his mind wanted not the Rockaways but the swordfish displayed for its entertainment. That these Rockaways were English was proven by their accent. That the man was rich was evidenced by this magnificent launch and the big house situated on the hillside.

Wilton came in.

"Hullo! What have you there?"

Wilton's face was set. He placed on the shining mahogany table a Winchester repeating rifle. It was certainly not the one with which Joe had shot the shark. Joe came to stand just behind his partner, and Wilton said, leaning forward to the reclining Bony:

"Found this in a locker in the men's quarters. It's Bill Spinks's rifle. The one he had on the *Do-me*."

CHAPTER 13

A Lead at Last

Reclining on the red plush of the saloon settee, Bony's eyes were points of ice and the placidity of his slight body was unusual. From the rifle he gazed upward into Wilton's blazing brown eyes, to realise that in this young man were depths not previously suspected. The detective spoke softly with a metallic note in his voice. The placidity left him. He sat up. His nostrils quivered as the primitive man's nostrils quiver at the prospect of a hunt.

"Joe, go outside and see if anyone is in sight."

Joe's generous mouth was set in a leer. His eyes were small and agate hard. He left the saloon as silently as a cat. Bony said:

"How do you know, Jack, that this rifle belongs to Spinks?"

"Because the rear sight of this gun has been broken and repaired. Because I repaired the rear sight of Bill's Winchester repeater, .32. And because I recognise my own work on this repairing job," Wilton replied, to add with steady conviction: "This is Bill's rifle."

"Put it back exactly as you found it," instructed Bony.

"But it's——"

"Please," urged Bony.

Wilton took up the weapon and departed. Left alone, Bony smiled. The movement of his nostrils became more pronounced. The smile faded, vanished. Joe came in.

"There's nobody around," he reported. "Rain's liftin'.

136

Clouds gettin' higher and the wind easin' a bit. Fine day to-morrer. What d'you think about that gun?"

"It interests me, and I will continue to think of it," Bony conceded. "Meanwhile, Joe, get going on setting out a meal. We three will eat here. What's in the pantry?"

"Everythink in tins. Bread in the box. Fresh bread and fresh-looking butter."

"Then we'll feed royally. You fellows may drink beer if you wish, but I would like a pot of tea, strong tea. Tell Jack about the tea, will you?"

Fifteen minutes later they sat at the mahogany table, and to Bony's pleasure his launchmen preferred tea. Joe exhibited a slight nervousness in these surroundings, and remembered in time not to cool tea in the fragile blue saucer. He and Wilton were quiet, speaking rarely, obviously wait-ing upon their angler. Presently Bony said:

"I think, Jack, that we agreed the other afternoon that the *Dolfin* could have come in from the east to Swordfish Reef, and, unseen by any other craft, have met the *Do-me*."

"That's so. And the *Gladious* could have done it, too, re-member. Then there was that small steamer painted warship grey and reported east of Swordfish Reef by the *Orcades*."

"Yes, of course, that small steamer passed by the *Orcades*, so closely that the passengers were interested in it, as liner passengers are ever interested in anything. How long would it take, say, three men to paint the *Dolfin* all over with grey paint?"

Joe's valuable cup was nearly broken when it was set down violently on its saucer. The idea was not nearly as new to Wilton, who answered Bony's question.

"They could do it, I should think, in about three hours, just slapping on the paint."

"They could that," agreed Joe. "It was a dead calm day, too. There wouldn't have been no bother about painting the outside of the hull down to the water line. There were no waves to wash against a craft that could wash off paint just put on."

"The craft seen by the people on the *Orcades* was a steamer. It had a funnel," argued the detective.

"A coupler lengths of stove piping would do for a funnel," Joe decided.

"And the mast, being hinged to the deck, and in two pieces could have been shortened by a shorter top section," added Wilton. "Do'you think——"

Bony stopped him with a wave of a hand and a slight smile.

"We must be cautious. We mustn't manufacture facts to fit a theory. The man called Dan—what is he?"

"Dan Malone? He's the skipper of the *Dolfin*. He's a blue-nose fisherman. The other feller is Dave Marshall, come all the way from Cockney-land. Neither of 'em is any chop. They both worked for Rockaway when he first came to Bermee. Came here with Rockaway, in fact."

"Hum. They both look—er—tough. Do they mix at all with the Bermagui people?"

"Very little. I've seen 'em in the hotel at odd times," Joe replied.

"Indeed! Try to remember this: Did you happen to be in the hotel the night before that day the *Do-me* disappeared?"

"Yes, I was there 'aving a drink or two with Eddy Burns," Joe admitted.

"Were either or both these *Dolfin* men at the hotel that evening?"

Joe frowned, scowled, grunted. Then:

"No. But I remember seein' the Rockaway truck outside the garage. Parkins was doing somethink to it, I think. It was when I was goin' up the street to the pub—about nine o'clock."

"Without doubt we are progressing," drawled Bony, selecting a cigarette from one of Mr. Rockaway's expensive boxes. "How is it that you remember all this so clearly?"

" 'Cos I settled me slate bill at the hotel with a fiver Jack, here, give me the day afore the *Do-me* disappeared. Remember that fiver, Jack?"

"Yes. I got it from the bank when I went there to get house-keeping money for my mother."

"Then, Joe, do you remember if Mr. Ericson was about the hotel that evening?"

"He was all there. 'Im and some others were havin' a bit of a party in the back parlour."

"How do you know that?" pressed Bony. "Did you go into the back parlour and see Ericson?"

"No need to see him to know 'e was in there. I could 'ear 'is voice. The bar shutters were up, you understand."

"Oh! You are being very patient with me, Joe, and I thank you. Just one more question. Do you remember hearing Ericson, when in the back parlour, say anything about going the next day to Swordfish Reef after sharks?"

Again Joe scowled and grunted and hesitated.

"No-o . . . I can't say as 'ow I do."

Bony offered no assistance in clearing away the wreckage of the meal. With Rockaway's cigarettes on the table beside him he lay stretched along the settee, his eyes closed for periods, and those thin nostrils of his slowly expanding and relaxing. In the launch kitchenette, Joe observed to Wilton:

"That rifle's got 'im thinkin'. When you showed him that gun, I was forgettin' he was a d——. He's come to be like a bit of granite. Did you see 'is eyes when 'e was askin' all them questions?"

"Yes. And he looked like he does when he's fighting a swordie, Joe. It makes me feel kind of glad I've done nothing wrong."

"Me, too. I'll bet this Rockaway bloke 'ad somethink to do with the *Do-me*. Hope we're in at the final, Jack, old lad. Me and Dan's got a score to settle. He'll be in it as well. They're all crooks."

"We're only thinking so now," Wilton countered.

"I've thought it all along," Joe stoutly maintained. "I never took to that blue-nose Nova Scotia-man. Me—when the times comes, I'm gonna tear 'is guts right out. 'Peace,' 'e says to me one day on the jetty. 'Peace,' 'e says, 'I'll have you to know that I'm Captain Malone to you.' 'Im, a captain! Stiffen the crows! Why, Whiskers 'Arris on the *A.S.1* never wants 'is men to call 'im Captain 'Arris. Skipper's good enough for 'im."

Meanwhile Bony had gone up on deck to discover that the rain had stopped and that rifts in the spinning clouds supported the promise made by the barometer. Dusk was falling on a world weary of the wind but freshened by the rain.

Protected by the arms of the land, the jetty was situated on the north shore of the lower reach and within half a mile of the roaring bar. It was but half the distance to the big house built on the hill-side to which wound a road from the jetty's base. There were no other houses to be seen, and already in the windows of this one lights were gleaming. The landscape was losing its features, and the hill summits were hidden by the low cloud mist. Faintly Bony could hear dogs barking.

During his promenade round and round the *Dolfin*'s spacious decks, he peered often at the paintwork. Its colour was, of course, a silver-grey, and his keen eyes at once registered the fact that the paint was comparatively fresh and expertly applied. Once he halted to scratch the paintwork of the raised saloon roofing. He used his thumb-nail. He could discern no grey paint beneath the silver-grey. He was finding it most difficult to connect the Rockaways with the disappearance of the *Do-me* until he recalled Rockaway's handshake. Then he found it less difficult.

On going below he found clothes drying before two radiators, and the lights switched on in the saloon, the gangway between the cabins, and farther for'ard in the men's quarters from which drifted the voices of his launchmen. He called them to the saloon. Telling them to be seated, he began a long questioning regarding Wapengo Inlet, the depth of water in it, roads to it, streams running into it. From this emerged the fact that Joe Peace was far more familiar with Wapengo Inlet than was Jack Wilton. He had years before prospected the country for metals and timber suitable for railway sleepers. When the night blackened the opened port, he said to Joe:

"It's almost dark now, and I want Jack to assist me in making a thorough examination of this launch. Meanwhile I would like you to keep watch from the jetty, and to let us know instantly should you hear anyone approaching. We shall be some time, and you will not be able to smoke. Is there such a thing as a torch on the *Marlin*?"

"Two," Wilton replied. "But there's plenty aboard here, in the cabins, everywhere to hand."

Bony smiled, saying:

"If the batteries of one or more were found to be exhausted someone might wonder why they were used for so long."

Joe chuckled in his deep-chested way.

"Good for you, Bony," he said, with vast admiration. "Never give a shark a chance to bite you. I'll get them torches, and then I'll mount guard."

"How old is Joe, about?" Bony inquired of Wilton.

"Not as old as he looks, and tougher than he looks, too. He's about fifty, no older. He's a hell of a good man on a launch, and he can shift about quicker than anyone would think by looking at him."

"Have you known him long?"

"Most of my life. He used to work for my old man when I was a shrimp."

"Ah! I'm glad he's dependable, for one day I may want to depend on him very much. With regard to this search of ours, I want you to devote yourself to all lockers and receptacles. Remember to replace everything exactly as you find it. You may discover something you recognise as once belonging to the *Do-me*, or once in the possession of either Spinks or his mate. If you found a paint-brush, for instance, still stained with dark grey paint . . ."

"Might find such a brush in that shed on the shore back of the jetty. That's where all the paints and oils are kept."

"Oh! Do you happen to know the lay-out of the house? Ever been inside it?"

"Twice. But only as far as the kitchen."

"How many servants are employed?"

"There's the housekeeper, a thoroughly bad-tempered old bitch, a man cook, a butler, and Malone and Marshall. When the Rockaways have parties they get extra help from Bermee or Cobargo."

"And who, do you think, would be doing the renovations?"

"Lawson, I expect, from Bermagui. He generally does the renovating and repair work."

The examination of the *Dolfin* began from its bow where was a small hold to take the anchor and chain. Aft of this hold was a larger one in which were stowed a set of sails, stores, and drums of oil for the engine. The men's quarters were given minute attention, and this same thorough care was being applied to the examination of the sleeping cabins when Joe appeared, silently, to say that someone was approaching along the jetty.

"Go for'ard," Bony hastily instructed, easily falling into

the seaman's pronunciation of the word 'forward'. He himself passed aft to the saloon where he lay on the settee, lit a cigarette and took up a journal. He had barely settled when he heard footsteps on the jetty, and then the thrump of a man's boots on the deck above. The man descended the steps to the saloon entrance, and casually Bony half rose and looked round to see the man Dave Malone.

"Good night, Mr. Bonaparte," Malone said, unsmilingly.

"Good evening," responded Bony, mildly surveying the man.

"Mr. Rockaway sent me along to ask if you had everything needful."

"Everything. We lack for nothing. Please convey my thanks to Mr. Rockaway, and say I am most comfortably lodged and appreciative of his kindness."

"All right. Good night, Mr. Bonaparte."

"Good night."

Bony listened to the retreating footsteps until they were silenced by distance. Then he sprang for the steps and passed up on deck where he could again hear the departing footsteps. Joe came to stand with him.

"You stay here again, Joe, while we finish the examination down below."

An hour later the search was completed. It had produced no result.

"I'd like to look inside that paint and oil shed, Jack," Bony said when they were smoking and sipping coffee in the saloon. "Earlier in the evening I heard dogs near the house, so perhaps it would be unwise to examine the inside of the shed just now. I wonder now. Could you go along to it very early in the morning on the pretext of wanting to borrow a piece of waste or something?"

"Soon find an excuse," assented Wilton.

"Then go soon after daybreak and look for traces of dark-grey paint on brushes, in tins, and other receptacles. Now I'm off to bed."

Immediately Bony lay down in the luxurious bunk with its guard-rails of burnished copper, its pillows of down, its super-fine blankets, he slept. It seemed to him that he slept only a moment when he was awakened by Wilton to see sunlight streaming in through the open port. In Wilton's right hand was a paint-brush.

"Found it with a lot of others standing in water to prevent them going hard," he said, triumph in his voice and eyes. "Look!"

Bony's lips parted. His teeth gleamed. It was quite clear that when last used the brush had applied dark-grey paint.

"Grey kalsomine," Wilton explained. "A cold water paint."

"Were there any other brushes showing this colour?" he asked

"Two. Like this one, both six inches wide. Good for fast work. There's a heap of paint-tins and drums beyond the shed, but I didn't like being seen poking about it. There were no kalsomine packets or any kalsomine liquid, in the shed."

Bony sat up and reached for the box of cigarettes he had brought overnight from the saloon.

"You have done very well, Jack. How's the weather?"

"The sea's down. We can get over the bar as soon as you like. The sky's clear and the wind is coming from the south'ard."

"Then after breakfast, we will start back for Bermagui. I've a lot of work to get through in the shortest possible time. There will be no fishing to-day."

When, at seven o'clock, neither Rockaway nor his launch-men had appeared, Bony wrote a polite note of thanks and left it on the saloon table. At half-past seven the *Marlin* was at sea, heading northward for Bunga Head, a long swell coming abeam, a short chop and a following wind assisting her.

CHAPTER 14

"Who Did It?"

Shortly after ten-thirty the secretary of the Bermangui Big Game Anglers' Club announced the weight of Bony's second swordfish. The crowd on the jetty raised a cheer, and, when the *Marlin* was finally moored, strangers to Bony shook hands with him, and others asked for his autograph.

Joe's estimated weight was remarkably close, for the fish scaled at five hundred and eighty-one pounds. Suspended from the hoist at the head of the jetty it looked enormous, and subsequent pictures of it hanging on the town triangle, with Bony standing close beside it and holding one of Blade's spare rods, were even more impressive as the angler was dwarfed to almost a third its length. He did not get away for some time, having to submit to amateur photographers and more autograph-hunters.

The entire township was thrilled by his capture, and for three days people from inland towns and farms came to see and photograph it. The fame which came to Bony was to have repercussions he could not have foreseen.

Showered and shaved and dressed in usual day clothes, he spent an hour in Blade's office where he received reports from the secretary and Wilton concerning matters he thought it best for them to inquire into. After lunch he wrote at length to his wife and to the Chief Commissioner in Sydney, posting these letters himself. Later he visited Nott's Tea Rooms, where he was waited on by Marion Spinks. She exhibited just that degree of interest which caused Bony to suspect that had the fate of her brother been less uncertain his fine capture would have been given intense enthusiasm. He asked her if she still felt that William Spinks was not dead, and her answer was the same.

He was wondering what reliance could be placed on this example of affinity between twins as he walked up to the headland with his brief-case under an arm. He was no mocker of unexplained mental phenomena, being conversant with the astonishing power of telepathy possessed by his mother's people, and himself often having been guided aright by what he called intuition.

In him intuition was divorced from impressions of people and things. One of the first lessons he had learned in his profession of crime investigation was never to permit impressions of men and women to blossom into such importance that they swayed him to form judgments not based on cold facts. The final analysis which places a man on trial is not gained by impressions of his personality obtained by his accusers. They know well that the Lombroso school of criminology, defining criminals by their heads and countenances, is wholly in errror; that your smiling, easy-mannered, handsome man is often capable of slitting a human throat, and that your low-browed, ill-favoured man will just as often ask another to put an injured horse or a dog beyond its agony.

The point in any investigation arrived when a particular person came to the screen of Bony's mind for intimate examination. This was when a correlation of facts offered the possibility of this particular person having been in the position of being able to act in a particular manner. Such an examination was always due to facts and not to impressions.

This afternoon he found shelter from the wind (which

would have teased his papers) among the scrub facing the sea-ward edge of the grass-crowned headland, and some distance back from its blunt apex facing to the north. He was here able to look out over the sea to the long eastern horizon, as well as to the north where the summit of Montague Island and its lighthouse seemed to be fugitive from the massive Dromedary Mountain.

The sea was blue and green, and speckled with white horses running northward to ride down the long rollers still coming westward after the commotion of yesterday's storm. A hundred feet below where he lounged the grey and brown armour of the headland was being ceaselessly splashed by a white paint which gave no hope of permanency. Bony's remarkable eyes found the mast of two launches supported apparently not by a craft but by the hair-like line of the meeting of sea and sky. A third launch trolled miles out from the Brothers rocks, and Bony's mind was pricked with a pang of envy. Yet resolutely he exorcised the devil that was trying to tempt him from legitimate work.

He lay over on his chest and pressed his eyes to his crossed forearms the better to shut out memory of the sea and those launches trolling for swordfish, as well as to rest his aching eyes from the reflected glare. In this pseudo darkness he was able to throw upon the screen of his mind the picture of that key plan evolved by Blade and himself from the maps completed by the launchmen and from information received. On this plan the sea had been forced to retain the tracks of five motor-launches, a small steam launch, a trawler and an overseas liner. He continued to have faith that here was hidden a clue of vital importance once he obtained a lead indicating it.

Bony's belief that Time was his greatest ally was once more justified by the discovery of Spinks's rifle on board Rock-away's *Dolfin*. It did not occur to him that this was a lucky coincidence: that if the storm had not arisen, if the sword-fish had not taken his bait-fish when it did, they would not have been forced to shelter inside Wapengo Inlet, would not have met the Rockaways and been offered the hospitality of the *Dolfin*. If the rifle had not been presented to him by Time, Time eventually would have given him another lead. Time has been pictured as an old man, but Bony visualised Time as being a fair woman much like Dame Fortune who, if ignored, will bestow her many gifts.

On this occasion Time had been generous with her gifts to him. He had ignored her, wanting only the thrill of fighting fish, and she had insisted with her gifts on recalling him to the work which had brought him to Bermagui. Beside the rifle, she had presented him with several large-sized paint-brushes which pointed to the key plan on which was the track of a mysterious steam launch painted dark-grey, or war-ship grey. Had Blade and he not evolved that plan, the paint-brushes in Rockaway's shed would have had no significance whatsoever. The rifle could easily be explained. It could be said that a member of the *Dolfin*'s crew had found it on a beach, or beside a road, and was entirely ignorant of its connection with the *Do-me*.

The importance of the rifle, however, was greatly em-phasised by the discovery of the paint-brushes which formed the genesis of a trail that became more easy to follow the farther it went.

Bony had observed that the colour scheme of Rockaway's house was white and light-brown. His launch was painted a silver-grey, whilst his jetty was treated with a preparation containing tar. The house builder and decorator at Ber-magui, named Lawson, had informed Blade that the interior of Rockaway's house had been 'done' by him during August, and that nowhere had grey paint of any shade been used in the work.

For what purpose, therefore, had those several large paint-brushes in Rockaway's shed applied paint of a warship grey shade?

Blade's interview with the house decorator had produced further information of paramount interest. Rockaway had told Bony that he regretted being unable to entertain him at his house because it was in chaos due to the work of interior renovation. Lawson said he was not doing this, did not know who was doing it, and was not aware that it was being done. He had built the house, and since then had effected all repairs and renovations. He doubted that renovation was being carried out at this time.

Question: Was the renovating work being done with those several brushes still stained with dark-grey paint? If so, was not dark-grey paint an unusual colour to apply to the interior of a house?

Question: If Rockaway's statement regarding the condition of his house was false, what lay behind it? It was obvious that he was naturally generous, a true sportsman who would throw his house wide open to an angler experiencing adverse conditions, and not wishing to invite Bony to his house he had done the next most generous thing by presenting him with the use of his luxurious launch. The offer of hospitality had not been sought, nor had it been expected. Perhaps a few provisions to be gratefully returned at a future date, yes, when the engine cabin of the *Marlin* would have provided shelter for the night, if little comfort.

Again the key plan was screened. On 3rd October the *Dolfin* put to sea early to engage in swordfishing as there were two rods mounted in her stern. The trawler people last saw her at eight a.m. when she disappeared in the haze of the south-east. At approximately twenty minutes after noon of this day the officer of the watch and the quartermaster on duty on the liner *Orcades* sighted a small steam launch painted warship grey. They did not remember sighting the *Dolfin* at any time during their passage up the coast.

Was there not reason to assume that, after the *Dolfin* had been lost sight of by those on the trawler, those aboard her had hurriedly painted her a warship grey with those several large brushes found by Wilton in Rockaway's shed? They could have fashioned a funnel with a length of stove piping, and have put up the hinged mast having a shorter top-joint. The fact that the *Orcades* passed close to the grey-painted steam launch, reported to be longer than the average fishing launch, might have been engineered by those on the disguised *Dolfin* to attract attention and so divert possible suspicion from the *Dolfin* normally painted silver-grey.

Further to all this, Bony possessed authority to assume that Rockaway had pre-knowledge of the *Do-me*'s shark fishing trip to Swordfish Reef.

The evening prior to the disappearance of the *Do-me*, Rockaway's truck was repaired by Mr. Parkins, the garage owner. In the main bar parlour of the hotel, Ericson entertained several anglers and Blade that evening. Blade recalled that the prospective trip to Swordfish Reef was lengthily discussed. He remembered, too, seeing in the hotel both Malone and Marshall, Rockaway's launchmen.

There are three small parlours opening off the main bar, in another of which that evening lurked Joe and Eddy Burns, and according to Burns he distinctly remembered hearing Malone's harsh voice from the interior of the third parlour. So that Malone and Marshall could easily have heard the discussion in the main parlour about the trip to Swordfish Reef the following day. Through Malone, Rockaway could have learned that night of Ericson's intentions.

There was reason enough to assume all this; and to assume further that after those on the *Orcades* had lost sight of the dark-grey steam launch, that this launch ran westward to

Swordfish Reef to do what was done to the *Do-me* and those on board her. Then the disguised *Dolfin* cleared away out to sea to avoid being sighted by other launches. There she was equally able to escape the notice of steamers passing north or south, and only north or south. After dark she ran into Wapengo Inlet where work on removing the grey kalsomine or cold water paint was at once begun. During the night the warship-grey paint would be removed, and daylight would permit any remaining evidence of the kalsomine to be wiped away. Then, perhaps a coat of silver-grey paint would have been applied to make doubly sure that the temporary disguise was removed.

Again faced by the usual three questions: How was it done? Why was it done? Who did it? Bony was becoming confident of the answer to the third question. The answer to 'How was it done?' could for the present be left in abeyance, but the answer to the second question, 'Why was it done?' might well be gleaned from the fictitious diary he was compiling from data supplied by the Anglers' Club secretary, Ericson's cheque-book, a solicitor's statements, letters from Ericson to his friend the Chief Commissioner, and the weather records. The diary was fictitious only in that it was to be imagined that Ericson had kept it from day to day, from the time of his arrival at Bermagui to that day he had been murdered, or the day it was assumed that he was murdered.

Bony continued his work on this diary, and completed it about four o'clock. In a low voice he began to read it, finding that speaking decelerated the speed of his mind, thus making it digest each item in its turn. The diary thus read:

September 5. Arrived Bermagui by car and found quarters at the Bermagui Hotel. Weather squally and showery.

September 6. Arranged with Blade for oddments necessary to complete my gear for this tuna fishing. Also arranged with William Spinks about the hire of his launch, the *Do-me*. Met this evening five other anglers. (Note: Four of these anglers were known to Blade by previous visits. The fifth was a tourist from England, unknown to Blade, named Edwin Henderson. Henderson gave his Australian address the Australian Hotel, Melbourne.) Weather fine and wind moderating. Spent the evening in the parlour talking fish with Henderson and Blade.

September 7. Started fishing to-day. Weather fine and wind light, but was seasick off and on. Caught ten tuna ranging up to twelve pounds. Great sport with light tackle. Found *Do-me* to be a stout craft, and the two men keen on the job. Went to bed soon after dinner.

September 8. Weather good. Was not sick. Feeling very fit. Brought home fifteen tuna and numerous king-fish of no great weight. Put in the evening talking in the parlour with anglers.

September 9. Another good fishing day. Weather moderate.

September 10. Too rough to go out to-day. As time is of no value, I don't intend to suffer discomfort. Ordered a lunch hamper and tramped south along the road to Tathra from which base line stretches of coast were explored. Like this place very much. Went to bed early.

September 11. Two of the anglers departed. Fishing moderate. Weather stormy.

September 12. Fishing much better to-day. Paid hotel bill.

September 13. Henderson departed to-day for Melbourne. Says he will certainly come out again next year. Fishing fair but good in weight. Four ranged from sixteen to twenty-three pounds.

September 14. Fishing good. Paid Spinks week's hire of boat.

September 15. Too rough to fish. Walked to Tilba Tilba, there had lunch at the hotel, and returned late this afternoon. Found that two Sydney anglers and their wives had arrived.

September 16. Had a great day. Amazed by shoals of tuna south of Montague Island. Fought fish after fish till my arms ached. Gaffed a fine one which Blade weighed at thirty-one pounds. This is an astonishing coast for fish. Seen more to-day in the water than I have throughout my life. Talked with Blade in the parlour most of the evening.

September 17. Too rough to go out, although the others did whose time here is limited. Have the idea of settling here and so looked at property for sale. This place is a fisherman's paradise all right, and they tell me that the swordfishing is excellent from December to April. Went with a Mr. Pink and Blade to look at two properties on the outskirts of Bermagui. Saw a plot of land about five acres overlooking the township and the river and the bay. Could build there and be most happy. Blade a charming fellow and very helpful. Prices seem reasonable, but Australian State and Commonwealth Income Taxes on top of British taxes would be a burden unless I transferred my investments from England.

September 18. Good fishing but sea rough. Talked land and houses with Blade in parlour after dinner. Wrote to Henry and paid hotel account. (Henry—Commissioner of Police.)

September 19. Fishing good. Weather improved.

September 20. Rained all day, but sea fairly calm. Fishing good. Biggest tuna weighed twenty-nine pounds. Three more anglers arrived.

September 21. Another good day. Several anglers departed. Paid hire of launch.

September 22. Fishing excellent. Sea alive with tuna for miles and miles. Fished till tired out. No waiting between fish. This evening wrote Henry that I was seriously thinking of settling here, and of buying that five acres of land. Could build a nice place there, and have my own launch and run a garden. Told Blade about these dreams of mine, and he seemed delighted. Keen fellow, Blade, for his club and Bermagui.

September 23. Generally good day.

September 24. Weather fine and fishing fair.

September 25. Weather hazy and sea calm. Fishing again excellent. Paid hotel bill.

September 26. Too rough to fish. Had another tramp over those five acres. Talked about things with Spinks in the cabin of the *Marlin* during afternoon. Suggested I might buy a launch, and offered him a position of managing it for me. He seemed keen. Decided this evening to buy the five acres.

September 27. Too rough to go out first part of day, so hired a car and interviewed a solicitor at Cobargo to act for me *re* purchase of the five acres. Fishing good in the afternoon. Blade went out with me.

September 28. Weather still rough and fishing again good. Paid Spinks for hire of launch. Suggested that his mother and sister could live with him at my new house. Have extra rooms added if they would. Mother could cook and sister housemaid for me.

September 29. Weather moderating. Fishing superlative. Fished till I was tired. Then let Garroway and Spinks take a turn. Fished again till I could fish no more.

September 30. Too rough to go out. Prospected my five acres on which I have paid for option to purchase. Yarned with launchmen at the jetty all afternoon. Enjoyed their company much: heard many amusing and interesting stories of fishing and the coast. Was given details of a strange affair of many years ago which resulted in the naming of Mystery Bay, up the coast a little. Once a policeman always a policeman, I suppose, for I find I am attracted to a mystery just as much as in the old days.

October 1. Fishing wild and sea boisterous. Wrote Henry this evening telling him I had bought the land, and saying I would insist on him and Muriel coming down for the house warming.

October 2. Weather fine and warm. Fished till my arms ached. Biggest catch a twenty-four pounder. Saw a man named Rockaway on jetty when we got in. Rockaway had brought in a tuna which Blade announced to weigh sixty-seven pounds. Like Rockaway's launch, but it looks a little too expensive for my purse. Had a party to-night in the parlour, several anglers and Blade being my guests. Talked of trying Swordfish Reef to-morrow for sharks, Blade saying he could fit me up with heavy rod and line and trace and hooks.

October 3. Weather dead calm and sea flat. Hazy. Went straight out to Swordfish Reef. Last saw the launch *Snowy* at eight-five a.m. Last saw *Edith* making to the north-east at eighty-forty a.m. Last saw *Gladious*, south of us, at eleven-five a.m. Haze hid coast-line and low hills, but could see summit of Dromedary Mountain clear above the haze.

From this point Bony could proceed no further with Ericson's imagined diary. Its details were of necessity meagre, but in their sectioning under dates they formed the skeleton to which a host of details yet to be garnered could be added. Somewhere in that range of time recorded in the diary must lurk a fact which would point to the answers to the questions: How was it done? Why was it done? Who did it?

He was pensively rolling a cigarette when a shadow fell across his feet and a woman said, wonderingly:

"Hullo! What are you doing there?"

CHAPTER 15

Mrs. Spinks

"You haven't seen the *Do-me* by any chance, have you?" asked the gaunt, white-haired woman who was looking down at Bony. The brown eyes were burning with a strange heat, and the furrowed face was illumined by pathetic hope.

Knowing instantly who she was, Bony scrambled to his feet and bowed in his grand manner.

"How long have you been up here, mister?" she further asked.

"Several hours, Mrs. Spinks. But"—and he pointed to the litter of papers—"as you see, I have been studying."

Mrs. Spinks nodded, and then, whilst Bony was collecting his papers, she stood gazing away out over the blue and white carpet of the sea.

"The *Ivy*'s bringing home a swordie," she said.

"Oh! Where is she?" inquired Bony.

The woman pointed towards Montague Island, and Bony saw the distant launch carrying a flutter of blue at her masthead. The craft was so far away that he wondered at Mrs. Spinks naming her. He saw another launch, and he, too, pointed, saying:

"Out there is another launch. See?"

"That'll be the *Myoni*, mister. She's flying the red flag. Angler on her has brought a shark to the gaff. Yes, I know 'em all, all the Bermagui launches. I always watch for 'em coming home at eve, but I can't never see the *Do-me*. Oh— I can't never see the *Do-me*." Her hand firmly imprisoned

Bony's arm, held it strongly and without a tremor. The brown eyes blazed at his. "They all say the *Do-me* went down over Swordfish Reef, and that the sharks took my Bill and young Garroway and Mr. Ericson. They're liars, all of em."

"Let us hope so, Mrs. Spinks."

"Hope so! There's never no need to hope they're all liars. They are, I tell you. My Bill isn't dead."

"Isn't he?" queried Bony, his voice gentle.

"No, he's not. If he was dead I'd know of it, wouldn't I?"

"How would you know?"

"How would I know it, mister? I'd know it because I'm his mother, that's how I'd know it. Trust a mother to know if her only boy was drowned at sea. Trust me. Bill was a fine lad, and he's grown into a finer man. Steady as a rock, is my Bill. He's always loved me, always looked after me. Why, he never come home, not once, without giving me a good hug and kissing me. If the sea had took him he'd have let me know. He would have come in the spirit to stand close to me, to whisper to me that he was dead and that I wasn't to sorrow. And I wouldn't have, either. I'd have had to live on for a few more years and then he'd be waiting for me up on high, waiting to hug me again and kiss me. But don't you fret, mister. The sea didn't take him, and one day he'll come rolling home with young Garroway and Mr. Ericson."

"Yes, of course," Bony said. "I'd like to hear you tell me all about your son and the *Do-me*. Let's sit down on the grassy brow there, and watch the launches coming home while you tell me. Will you?"

He saw the generous mouth drop, and was made uneasy. He watched the defiance fade from her own eyes. When she spoke there was wistful eagerness in her voice.

"Would you really like me to tell you about Bill and the *Do-me*, mister? No one bar Marion ever wanted to hear about him and the launch he built all by himself. Cold, that's what everyone is. Even Marion gets a bit cold now and then. She's my girl, you know. She and Bill are twins. There weren't any others."

"I'd like to hear about them both and about the *Do-me* too. Come!" urged Bony. "Sit down here beside me and tell me everything. You said your son built the *Do-me*. Did it take him long?"

"A year. A full year, mister. He built her in his spare time. I helped to build her, too. He made me nail a deck plank into place just so it could be said I helped build her. I can't understand what's keeping them away for so long. Mr. Blade sends out my wireless messages when I ask him to, but Bill never answers them, and he doesn't come home. It's not like him, you know."

Bony puffed cigarette smoke.

"Perhaps," he suggested. "Perhaps your son and Mr. Ericson and young Garroway decided to go a long way away and fish. Perhaps they heard from one of the passing ships where there were many extra heavy tuna and sharks to be caught."

Mrs. Spinks moved her thin body the better to regard this very kind man who wanted to listen to her.

"D'you think that's how it is?" she insisted. "You might be right, mister. I didn't think of that."

Bony dared not look into the woman's wide eyes lit by the beacon of hope. He said:

"Did your son get on well with Mr. Ericson?"

The woman offered no reply. The work-toughened fingers of her right hand were being pressed to her lips. To the dancing, glittering, beautiful and cruel sea she said:

"Yes, that might be it. Bill and Mr. Ericson might have took it into their head to try New Zealand for the fishing. Mr. Ericson he liked Bill. He was thinkin' of buying himself a launch bigger and faster than the *Do-me*, and he was hinking of hiring Bill by the month to run her for him. Bill reckoned it would be good-oh. Regular wages would be better than the up and down fishing during the winter. Yes, they might have taken a run across to New Zealand on the spur of the moment. I never thought of that. And Bill could have got new underclothes in New Zealand, too. I needn't keep his out waiting for him. I can put 'em away."

"It appears that Mr. Ericson liked your son," Bony softly interjected, valiantly keeping from his voice the pity surging in his heart. And when she spoke again pride controlled her.

"Like my Bill! Everyone likes Bill. Why, a day or so before they went away Mr. Ericson was talking of buying that land of Watson's and building a house on it to live here for keeps. He said it would be a good idea if Bill ran his new launch, and for me and Marion to go and live with him, me to do the cooking and Marion the maiding. He liked my cooking, did Mr. Ericson, after I cooked a tunny he caught and sent out with young Garroway for their lunch. He said I was a splendid fish cook, and that only one cook in every hundred could cook fish properly. He was right, too. You want to have the fat hot but not too hot to burn, and when you steam fish you want it to steam slowly, not fast as though in a hurry to get it done with."

"Mr. Ericson had plenty of money, I understand," Bony suggested.

"Oh, I suppose so. He always paid Bill prompt every week 'cos he was staying for a long time. There's the *Edith* coming home."

"She's had no catch to-day."

"No. If the anglers caught swordies every time they went to sea there wouldn't be the sport there is in swordfishing."

"And isn't this the *Dolfin* coming along from the Three Brothers? It looks like her."

"That's her. Trim craft, ain't she, mister? She's coming

fast this way, too. Must be bringing in a swordie for weighing and recording. You'll see her mast go up presently, like as not, and the blue flag run to her truck. Mr. Rockaway doesn't bother to bring sharks to be weighed."

Bony watched the slim bow of the silver-grey launch cutting the water cleanly like a knife and thrusting outward sheets of spray. The *Dolfin*'s speed was much higher than that of the average launch: sixteen knots Joe said she could do.

"Her mast is hinged to the decking," the woman explained. "Mr. Rockaway likes the mast laid down. Says it makes the *Dolfin* more like a cruiser when her mast's laid flat. I like to see a mast up, myself. There, I thought so!"

They could observe a man working at what looked like a winch, and slowly the mast was seen to rise into position. Then to its summit was run the blue flag having the small white fish emblazoned on it.

The *Ivy* was about to pass over the bar with her capture of the day. The *Myoni* was drawing near the headland. She was flying the red shark flag, and, when a minute or two later she passed the headland, Bony and Mrs. Spinks could see the fish lashed across her stern. Her white paintwork reflected the light of the westering sun. Like birds homing to roost were these launches. Farther out the *Gladious* and the *Snowy* were coming in, their mastheads bare of bunting.

"Two swordies and a shark so far," Mrs. Spinks said. "Where's the *Vida* and the *Lily G. Excel*? Ah, there's the *Excel* coming in from Swordfish Reef. She's got no capture. The *Marlin*? But then Jack didn't go out to-day. Day off for Jack Wilton and that old fool of a Joe Peace. Jack's angler landed a good 'un, didn't he? Why, mister, you must be Jack's angler."

"Yes, that's so, Mrs. Spinks. I felt that I required a rest to-day."

"Of course. Any man would want a spell after fighting that five hundred and eighty-pounder. That will do Jack a lot of good, you know. It'll be in all the papers. Good lad is Jack Wilton. He's been long waitin' to marry Marion."

"Doesn't she like him enough?" inquired Bony, keenly watching the oncoming *Dolfin* riding down the chop and ignoring the rollers.

Mrs. Spinks audibly sighed.

"Marion's like me," she asserted. "She's waitin' for Bill and Mr. Ericson to come back home. You see, it's like this, Mr. Bonaparte—that's a funny name for a man to have: wasn't there an emperor or something of that name?—Jack Wilton's got his mother to keep and to think of. If he married Marion he'd have to look after me, too, until Bill came home. Still, that's not all. Marion always was a wilful girl, but in some ways she's very cautious. And it's no fault to be cautious in love, is it? Now if I went to cook for Mr. Ericson, and generally look after him, and Bill lived with Mr. Ericson, too, things would come straight for Marion and Jack. Jack's a good lad, but like all the fishermen here he finds money hard to earn during the winter."

"But there's plenty of fish to be caught for the market, isn't there?"

"They could all catch enough fish to sink their launches any week of the year. But there's no way of selling them. People in the cities don't like king-fish and tunny, it seems. They like sharks and flathead and other fish what feeds off offal."

Mrs. Spinks's eyes were flashing, and seeing that he was treading on soft ground, Bony switched back to Ericson and his plans.

"And you think that Mr. Ericson really intended building a home here and getting your son to run his own launch?"

"So he told Bill. Why, he was telling me, too, that evening

before they last went out. I was down on the jetty waiting to tell Bill about a telegram that had come from an angler who wanted the *Do-me* for a fortnight. When the *Do-me* come in, I give Bill the telegram, and Mr. Ericson and me was talking on the jetty when the *Dolfin* came in to get a fish weighed. Mr. Ericson asked me then if I would cook and housekeep for him, and he was talking about Marion doing the housemaiding when the *Dolfin* was being moored.

"All of us looked at the tunny what Mr. Rockaway had captured. Mr. Ericson was extra interested. He seemed to get suddenly very jealous of Mr. Rockaway, for off he goes along the jetty leaving me a bit surprised like and Mr. Rockaway with his mouth open like he was a fish out of water."

"That," Bony said slowly, "is most interesting. Was that the first time Mr. Ericson ever met Mr. Rockaway?"

"I don't know. Oh, I wish the *Do-me* would come in. I never liked Bill being out late and having to navigate the bar after dark. Especially when the tide's out as it will be to-night."

"Was Mr. Blade on the jetty waiting to weigh Mr. Rockaway's big tunny?" pressed Bony.

"Mr. Blade? Oh—Mr. Blade. No. He met Mr. Ericson on the shore. They spoke for a second or two. I remember that because that Dan Malone shouted to Mr. Blade to hurry along and weigh Mr. Rockaway's fish."

"Who else was standing on the jetty with you?" persisted Bony.

"I don't remember, mister. . . . Yes, I do. There was Alf Remmings, of the *Gladious*. He was there, because Bill give him the angler's telegram, and asked him if he would take the angler. Remmings said he would."

Bony was smiling faintly as he regarded the panoramic view of sea and land: he saw the highlands darkly gleaming beneath the sinking sun, saw the summit of Montague Island

and the lighthouse swimming on the horizon like a fabled
land waiting to be visited by Ulysses; he watched the nearing
Gladious and *Snowy,* and saw the sunlight reflected on the
silver-grey hull and the brasswork of the *Dolfin,* now about
to swing past the blunt tip of the headland. Mrs. Spinks
stood up to scan the steel-blue horizon.

"That's the *Canberra,*" she said, indicating a ship hull
down but whose decks and upper-works showed vividly
against the sky. "The *Orcades* will pass late to-morrow
afternoon. I always follow up the big ships in the papers.
Mr. Blade gets in wireless touch with them to ask if they've
seen the *Do-me,* and if so to tell my son to come home. He'll
be wantin' clean underclothes, and I've got 'em all ready laid
out for him."

"He'll come home when Mr. Ericson is ready," Bony said
softly. "You don't want to worry so much about those underclothes. And you don't want to worry about Bill. He'll be
all right. I must be getting along to the hotel for dinner. It's
getting late. Come along. We'll keep company."

"No."

The negative was spoken sharply. In the woman's brown
eyes again was rebellion.

"Very well, but I rather wanted you to tell me more about
Bill and Mr. Ericson and young Garroway."

"I'm not going. I want to stay here and watch for the
Do-me coming home."

Bony paused when some six or seven yards away from the
afflicted woman.

"You said, Mrs. Spinks, that everyone else was cold, that
they wouldn't listen to you speaking about Bill," he re-
minded her. "I'm not cold. I like to hear about Bill and
Mr. Ericson, and there you stand and say you are going to
let me go back to the hotel alone. Come along and talk about
Bill and Mr. Ericson and the *Do-me.*"

For the first time he saw Mrs. Spinks smile. She said, walking to him:

"It's nice to have someone to talk to, someone who will not say that Bill was taken by the sharks. He's a fine lad, my Bill."

She chatted about 'her boy' whilst accompanying Bony down past the Zane Grey shelter-shed to the road where they were met by Marion, who was hurrying to fetch her mother from her vigil.

"We have been gossiping about your brother and Mr. Ericson and the *Do-me*," Bony said cheerfully. "And we have decided that most likely Mr. Ericson persuaded your brother to go across to try the fishing in New Zealand waters. That is why they have been away so long. And, of course, over there they found the fishing so good that they forgot to send word."

"That's how it is, Marion," Mrs. Spinks cried, again smiling. Marion regarded her mother, a smile stillborn on her vivid face. She turned and walked with them to the hotel; and for the first time since the fourth of October, Mrs. Spinks went home without resisting.

While Bony was preparing himself for dinner, he thought it strange that those two women refused to believe that William Spinks was dead, were so emphatic in their belief that he still lived. And when he thought of that little scene on the jetty when Mr. Ericson walked away in a huff because Mr. Rockaway had captured a large tuna, he smiled at his mirror-reflected face and murmured:

"You are a very clever man, my dear Napoleon Bonaparte. Mrs. Spinks gave you this afternoon the authority for thinking along a certain line. Ah yes—this case is moving. But I can't think that those Spinks women are right in believing William Spinks to be still alive."

CHAPTER 16

Marine Surprises

The sixteenth of January produced pictures that were, with ease, to be brought to the screen of Bony's mind for many years.

It was a cool and brilliant day and, having caught a supply of bait-fish, Wilton directed Joe to take the *Marlin* away to the south-east and then follow Swordfish Reef to the north and Montague Island. And then, having attended to his engine, he came aft to sit in the spare angler's chair and roll a cigarette.

"I was talking to Mrs. Spinks yesterday afternoon," Bony said. "I was up on the headland working out a problem when she found me. It's more than a little strange that she and her daughter so firmly believe that Bill Spinks is still alive, don't you think?"

Wilton's brown face was newly shaved. His brown eyes directed their gaze over the sea, for long practice had given him the ability to occupy one part of his mind with talk and the other with the search for a fin.

"Not so strange as a man might think," he countered.

"Explain," lightly besought Bony.

"Well, you see, old man Spinks was no good, and before he slipped his anchor the family life was just plain hell. Fights, arguments, not much money, worry, and sheer damnation.

"When he died Mrs. Spinks was a bit of a wreck. Bill and Marion were then just over eighteen, and at once a big change came over Bill. It seemed to many of us that we'd been looking at him in a kind of fog, and that, after the old man drank himself to death, he stepped right out of the fog and became sort of real. Him and Marion and me had kept together at school. Always good pals. When we left school Bill went into the fog I was telling about. When he came out of it, he put it on me to be my mate, as I was fishing on me own, having got my old man's launch when he died a year before.

"Young Bill turned out a tiger for work, and I was able to lend him a hand, too. In less than a year Bill had paid off the debts and got the home on its feet, and Ma Spinks and Marion were living in peace and security. No more did Marion have to work out. Bill insisted on her staying home and helping to look after the mother. I never knew a feller who thought more of his mother than Bill did. He never left her in the morning without kissing her, and he never got home at night without kissing her. I suppose that after the hell they'd lived in for years they wanted the new life to be a kind of heaven."

Wilton left the chair and walked forward to take a long look at the sea. When he returned, Bony said, pleadingly:

"Well, go on with the real life story, Jack."

"Oh yes, Bill Spinks. Well, after he had been my mate for a couple of years he had money in the bank and the women were just happy and content. I've always loved Marion. Loved her when we was kids. And I wanted her to marry me. I knew she liked me; always had. I knew, too, there wasn't anybody else. But . . ."

"Just couldn't make up her mind about marrying, eh?"

"That's about how it was, right up to the time the *Do-me* vanished. Anyway, Bill saved money. Wouldn't drink or smoke or even go to the pictures. He began to talk about buying a launch that was likely to come on the market; then

he shifted off that idea and began to build the *Do-me* in his
spare time. Joe came back from deep-sea sailoring and I took
him on, and when we could we gave Bill a hand with his
building. Mrs. Spinks and Marion would come along sometimes and watch us working. And then Joe and me were out
of it. It was just them three, you see. They was a kind of
triangle nothing could bust—nothing but what must have
happened that day the *Do-me* never came back. I used to
get sore sometimes: jealous, I suppose. Yes . . . I reckon if
Bill was dead them two women would know about it."

"Tragedy that touches the dead blights the living, Jack,"
Bony murmured, and then became silent for a space.
Presently: "Still, if Bill Spinks is not dead, why doesn't he
come forward and tell us who shot Ericson and what became
of the *Do-me*?"

"Because he's not allowed to that's why."

"Not allowed to! Do you mean you think he is being held
prisoner somewhere?"

Wilton's gaze was seldom directed at Bony; even when he
answered this last question he continued the search for a fin.

"I don't know rightly what to think. He's not dead,
according to the women. If he is alive and was able he'd
have come forward. Not having come forward, and still
being alive, he must be kept somewhere against his will."

"Made prisoner by those who murdered Ericson?"

"Yes."

Bony sighed.

"I'm afraid, Jack, I can't agree with that theory," he said,
slowly. "It's now more than three months since the *Do-me*
disappeared, and those who would attack the *Do-me* at sea
and murder her angler are hardly likely to spare her crew.
To do otherwise would mean keeping Spinks and Garroway
prisoners for years—all their lives."

"It all sounds stupid, I know," Wilton admitted. Then,

as though after all there was possible basis for argument: "But the women still don't believe he's dead."

Bony persisted:

"During the Great War thousands of women wouldn't believe that their dear ones were dead; believed that one day they would come home from a prisoners' camp, or after a long period of mental aberration due to war."

"The same thing doesn't apply. Them three Spinks were extra close together. Besides, Bill and Marion are twins."

"And you believe Spinks to be alive because they believe it?"

"Yes. One day the mystery of the *Do-me* is going to be cleared up, and then Bill Spinks will come back to his home."

"That being so, Jack, Spinks might return to his home in the near future."

This made Wilton direct his gaze towards the half-caste who was faintly smiling.

"You know," Bony went on, "between the Spinks women and you I am beginning to think that Bill Spinks might be still alive. I shall have to take certain precautions when I wind up this investigation. I must think very seriously about it."

Wilton's brown eyes opened wide, and he said, as though breathless:

"D'you think you're getting near the end of the investigation?"

Bony nodded.

"Will you let Joe and me be in at the finish? Dan Malone is a tough customer, and that Dave Marshall's no mug in a scrap."

"Surely you are not accusing them and Mr. Rockaway . . ."

"What about that gun? What about them paint brushes? What about Rockaway saying his house was being done up when it wasn't? What about Rockaway and Mr. Ericson behaving as though they recognised each other that afternoon when the *Dolfin* brought in that big tunny? Remmings reckoned they recognised each other, anyhow?"

"Now, now, Jack," Bony said, reprovingly, "you must leave the speculating to me. When the time comes for the round-up, as they say in the moving pictures, I shall certainly ask you and Joe to be in it with me. But nothing to Joe yet, please."

"Right-oh. I'll go for'ard for a spell. There's lots of things I'd like to ask you. There's——"

"Don't, Jack. I hate telling lies," Bony cut in, laughingly.

"Hey, Jack! 'Way for'ard!" shouted Joe.

Wilton bounded to Joe's side, to stand with him for a second or two looking through the glass protecting helmsman and cabin. Then he was agilely scrambling forward to the mast, to stand there for a space. Bony raised himself above the cabin roof by standing on the gunwale, to see two miles directly ahead a rusty-hulled, black-funnelled ship wallowing along at slow speed. Wilton came aft.

"It looks to me like a shoal of tunny following that trawler," he shouted to permit Joe to hear.

"How do you make that out—about the shoal of tunny?" asked Bony.

"Compare the sea behind the trawler to the sea ahead of her."

"Ah! It looks darker behind the ship. The sea looks as though a fierce squall is tormenting it."

"'Tain't wind. It's surface fish. I can see the white water being splashed by 'em."

"So can I now. Why, there's miles of jumping fish. Tuna you think?"

"Maybe not. If they're tunny at this distance they're big 'uns for sure. Hey, Joe! Speed her up." To Bony, Wilton said: "If they should be tunny will you give 'em a go? I've a light rod and tackle down below."

Bony nodded, his blue eyes gleaming, his pulses racing.

"Keep your eye on your fish-bait," Wilton advised. "Likely enough outside that shoal will be swordies and sharks."

Bony dropped back to the cockpit to divide his attention between his bait-fish and the ship ahead. The quickened engine thrust the *Marlin* forward at increased speed, which added to the excitement coursing through his veins. Then Wilton beckoned him. He scrambled forward beside the mast, holding to it and to the port mast stay. Wilton was laughing, his eyes bright.

"Porpoises," he said. "There's thousands of 'em following the trawler. The trawl could only have been sunk again an hour back, and the crew have been cleaning up after the last catch, throwing overboard the small fish and remains of octopuses and sting-rays and that kind of gentry. Look! The sea's full of porpoises."

"Pity they weren't swordies," Joe yelled, now standing on the gunwale with his right foot to bring his head above the shelter structure, and steering with his left foot pressing hard on a spoke of the wheel. He continued to shout: "Who wants porpoises, any'ow? I don't. I want swordies and five 'undred-pounders at that."

Bony waved a hand in agreement with Joe, and then gave his attention to the extraordinary marine manifestation. Founts of white water spewed upward from the deep slate of the sea; a minute later countless 'humps' of fish appeared and disappeared every split second, the graceful backs of the mammals hurtling the chop upon the greater rollers. Quite unconcerned by the furious energy unloosed astern of her the trawler wallowed onward, her decks deserted of men, the lobster pot hoisted half up to her masthead signalling that her trawl was down and warning craft to keep wide of her stern.

Suddenly the *Marlin* was moving across a sea stiffened thick with fish. The porpoises swam in fours and fives and sixes, swam in all directions, amazingly escaping collision. They appeared beside the *Marlin*, dived under her, speeded alongside her to roll under her bow. Their humped backs could be seen southward and eastward, their total not to be estimated. They could be seen under the slopes of the rollers, superb masters of their environment.

"If I had to fall overboard I'd choose this place," Wilton said.

"Oh! Why?"

"Because it's a dead certainty there's no sharks here. These porpoises would smash a shark to pulp in less than a minute. Come up under him and slash at his belly as though each porpoise was a bullet out of a machine-gun. They ain't real fish, of course. They're mammals really, and that's why they've got to heave up out of the water now and then. You wouldn't think the sea could hold so many, would you?"

"I would not have thought that all the porpoises in all the oceans gathered together would number as many as these," Bony said. "Do they often gather together like this?"

Wilton shook his head.

"I've only seen 'em like this once before—years ago. We might as well get out from among 'em. There'll be no swordies hereabouts, either. Almost thick enough to walk on, ain't they?"

Back again in the cockpit Bony took position behind his rod, his mind awed by the mightiness of life all round the tiny craft. The strangely agitated sea appeared unable to reflect the sunlight and seemed heavy as though unseen oil flattened it. As Wilton had suggested, the mammals were so numerous as to give the idea that one could walk on them across the sea.

Wilton came aft and said to Joe:

"Bring her round. We'll range alongside that trawler and have a pitch."

Joe's face expanded in a grin of anticipation and he brought the *Marlin* round to an easterly course. Immediately she began to overhaul the trawler that had on her bow the cipher, *A.S.1.* Presently the *Marlin* was running with the bigger ship, a bare twenty yards separating them.

"They've finished cleaning up," Joe said, and chuckled at a joke he kept to himself. To Bony's quickened interest there was not a man to be seen on the trawler's deck, and Wilton explained that after the 'clean-up' the crew went off duty. They could see two officers on the glass-protected bridge; one of them came to the end to look downward at the little *Marlin*.

"*Marlin* ahoy!" he shouted between cupped hands. "How's the swordies?"

Wilton took over the wheel from the grinning Joe who came a little aft in order that his voice would not be deflected by the shelter structure. He also cupped his hands and distinctly, but with surprising volume, said:

"No respectable swordfish would be in the sea with that stinkpot afloat on it. You 'ad any bites to-day?"

"Only one. A bit of a nibble. We don't want no rod ticklers. Nothing less'n fifty-ton whales satisfies us when we does a bit of fishing with hand lines. How's your corns?"

"Itching to connect with yer stern, you lop-eared cast off," yelled Joe. " 'Ow's old Whiskers 'Arris to-day? Tell 'im a gentleman's down here wishing to 'ave a word or two with him."

The trawler officer continued to lean elegantly over the end of the bridge. He expectorated in a manner denoting careful practice. Then he said, conversationally:

"The captain is unable to oblige, you flat-footed, paunchy tadpole. The captain never speaks with ex-deck-hands who never wash their necks—you shark-eating old mother-basher."

Joe winked at Bony, cupped his hands and continued the chat.

"You tell ole Whiskers 'Arris that when I meets 'im again I'm gonna uncomb the tangle for 'im. I suppose he's down below, drunk again. I pity 'is poor missus and kids. And as for you, you la-de-da quean, I'm gonna spoil that nice uniform you wears ashore. You know, that one with all the yards of gold braid pinned to it. No wonder the price of fish in the cities is so high that people can't afford to eat fish. No wonder the Gov'ment provides soft jobs for their friends, sending them to sea in flash craft to look for fish. They gotta do somethink to make believe fish is scarce, 'cos you blokes is asleep 'arf the time. Why don't you wake up and catch fish, you scented barber's pole?"

Wilton had turned the bow of the *Marlin* away from the trawler and quickly they drew apart. The officer on the bridge and Joe continued their chat until both realised that the other could not possibly hear him. Then Joe turned to Bony, to say:

"I served a twelvemonth on 'er. That pup on the bridge thought a lot of 'isself even in them days. Not a bad sorta bloke, though."

"Zigzag her across the reef and make towards Montague," Wilton ordered.

Again Bony saw the sea above Swordfish Reef. To-day a steep chop marked its position, the waves close and ever-curling. They seemed to be barely moving like people who hurried, yet never arrived. The trawler already far astern sent a smoke plume from her funnel as though in derision of Joe Peace.

After two hours had passed in lethargic waiting, Montague Island appeared larger to Bony than ever before. Wilton, seated on the deck well forward stamped his foot. Instantly Joe became 'alive', raising himself above the shelter structure to hear his partner's observations.

"Swordie jumping! 'Way over there!'" shouted Wilton. "Speed her up."

Bony leaned far out the better to see forward past the *Marlin*'s side. He noted how quickly his pulses raced at the very mention of the king of fish. Then he saw the jumping swordfish. No doubt, the ancient originator of the story of Venus rising from the sea got his idea from a swordfish jumping. Bony saw the slim, beautiful figure glinting green within its rainbow sheath of spray.

"He's showin' orf," shouted Joe. "There's others about for 'im to do that. Keep an eye on yer bait-fish."

Again the great fish appeared to dance for a space on its tail, then slide down into the water at an angle.

Wilton waved a hand in a circular motion, and Joe steered the *Marlin* in giant circles about the place where the swordfish last leaped. Bony slipped on the body harness and attached it to the rod reel, then with gloved hands ready to control bait-fish and racing line, waited, his blood fired by expectation and the hope of seeing a fin. Presently Wilton came aft.

"There's plenty of birds south of the island," he announced. "Likely enough there's a big shoal or two of fish. If you'd like some quick sport I'll get the light rod and line ready."

Bony nodded. He still hoped to see a fin. The *Marlin* continued a straight course to the north, and in less than half an hour those on her saw ahead the water lashed to fury and darkened as though by a fierce wind squall.

The porpoises had been tightly packed in the water astern of the trawler, and their number within sight at any one instant had been astonishing but the *Marlin* trolled on to an area of hundreds of acres almost solid with fish. With the light line and tackle Bony brought to the launch fish after fish that all weighed in the vicinity of ten pounds. They were blue-fin tuna, firm and rounded, strong and desperate fighters. In twenty minutes Bony gave it up. It was too much like hard work, this incessant reeling of fish to the light gaff wielded by Wilton. There was no chance of missing a strike. If one fish got off the feathered hook another would take it. When one fish was drawn towards the launch it would be followed closely by hundreds of others.

"More fish in that shoal than would be wanted to feed Australia for a year," Wilton said, seriously. "If all the fish in that shoal was put aboard a twenty thousand ton ship they'd sink her. And, Bony, Australia imports every year more than a million pounds' worth of tinned fish."

"So I've heard," Bony said. "And I recently heard Joe refer to the various governments sending out ships to look for fish along our coasts. I wonder if they have ever heard of Bermagui and Montague Island. I don't suppose so. There's enough fish in this sea to provide us all with fish at a penny a pound. Yes, Jack, it's a mad world, and it's getting madder every year."

An hour later they trolled in water clear of shoal fish only to pass into another area crowded with countless billions of king-fish averaging four pounds each in weight.

"And men on the basic wage working in the cities and wondering how to feed the kids," Wilton said, bitterly. "And fishermen along this coast struggling to make a living in a limited market."

Again they got free into clear water, and Bony watched the receding area of tortured sea whilst he wondered at the selfishness of man which denied a stupendous harvest of the sea to the hungry. As he had said, it is a mad world.

Wilton was standing up for'ard and Joe was talking to Bony when the giant reel abruptly began its screaming. Three pairs of eyes at once were focused on the water astern of the launch. There was no commotion. The reel continued its high note, and the line was racing fast down into the clear green depths. Bony jumped for his place at the rod, slipped on his gloves and released the brake and controlled the line running off the drum of the reel. He did not see the glance of approval pass between his launchmen.

"What took the bait-fish?" Joe demanded.

"Don't know. Never saw it go. Did you, Bony?"

"I was not watching," Bony admitted.

"Sounds like it was a swordie galloping away with the bait-fish," Wilton surmised.

"A bit too steady for a swordie," Joe doubted. "More like a shark."

"Perhaps," Wilton conceded. "Hope it's not a hammerhead. We'll be hanging around a long time if it is."

" 'Tain't a 'ammerhead," Joe argued. "He's going too far and too fast for a hammerhead. Might be a mako. Hope so. I like to lower their dignity."

"More than half my line is out," Bony cried, that longed-for thrill of exultation coursing through his veins like fire. "Shall I strike him?"

"Might be as well," assented Wilton, standing at his angler's back.

Bony applied brakage and struck. There was no give in the weight at the end of those hundreds of yards of line buried in the sea. There was no pause in the scream of the reel.

"Shark all right," confidently predicted Joe. "He's going south. A swordie would get away to the north-east. Hullo! Look! He's coming up. He's a mako for sure."

Bony was gaining line and striking as rapidly as he could. He was experiencing pride in the fact that Wilton was not telling him what to do. Then he shouted when his launch-men shouted, for they all saw leap half-way out of the water a greyish shape having an eel-like head. The head shook, epitomising rage and hate. They could see its fearsome mouth snapping at the wire trace they could not see. They could see the whitish circle on the broad triangular dorsal fin marking probably the most ferocious species of shark.

"He's a good 'un," yelled Joe, his back to the wheel. "Sock it into 'im. 'E can't throw a bait like a swordie can. What goes into 'is mouth stays there. Go on, Bony, sock it into 'im."

Thirty minutes passed before the sweat-drenched Bony saw the bright swivel connecting line with trace come up out of the sea. He thought then that victory was near, but the brute decided to prolong the fight and went away with two hundred yards of Bony's line. That two hundred yards of line took Bony another twenty minutes to regain, and then, when Wilton was about to grasp the trace with gloved hands preparatory to bringing the fish closer for Joe to gaff, the shark attacked the *Marlin*. The craft shuddered from the blow delivered by a battering ram weighing four hundred pounds. The battering ram ran away with a hundred yards of line, and 'played' for a space with the exhausted angler. It again attacked the *Marlin* ten minutes later, heaving itself nearly clear of the sea in effort to get into the cockpit at the angler himself.

That made Bony feel cold beneath the heat of battle, and Joe yelled and danced and waved a bar of iron. After that, and five more minutes of struggle, the shark gave in. It was drawn to the side of the launch and expertly gaffed. Joe made fast the gaff rope to a bollard. Sheets of spray leaped upward further to cool the angler and to be ignored by the launchmen. Wilton hung on to the thin trace, taking the vicious tugs of the brute's head, and then Joe leaned over the gunwale and proceeded to lower the brute's dignity with the iron bar. That done, he stood up and turned to face the triumphant angler.

"That's fixed 'im," he said, grinning. "I like taking it outer them sort. They ain't no fit companions for young gals."

CHAPTER 17

Intuition

The Sydney newspapers arriving at Bermagui on 17th January contained matter highly gratifying to Bony but annoying to Inspector Napoleon Bonaparte.

He had had an unfortunate day at sea, having lost a striped marlin swordfish through haste in bringing it to the gaff in short time. Then a seal had followed the *Marlin* for two hours, apparently to gain relief from boredom. Its presence keeping away probable swordfish from Bony's bait-fish, Wilton and Joe between them did everything possible trying to 'lose' it. They put the launch at top speed to tire the seal, but it evidently liked speed. Every time it went below the surface the *Marlin* was put hard to port or starboard with the hope of escaping, but on coming again to the surface the seal would raise itself high out of water, look about like a crop-eared dog, spot the launch and come tearing along after it. Short of shooting it there was no getting rid of its unwelcome presence until it chose to leave, and neither Bony nor his launchmen thought to do that.

Then, when returning to his hotel after this unfortunate day, Blade called him into his office.

"These newspaper reports will interest you," Blade told him. "The papers arrived this afternoon."

He displayed several sheets on which he had enclosed matter with neat blue crosses. Bony's attention was at once attracted by the headline over one of the reports. It read:

"Brisbane Detective-Inspector Captures Giant Swordfish."

Two inches were given to facts of the capture of Bony's second fish and its weight and measurements. Four inches were given to him:

"There is, of course, in Australia only one Mr. Napoleon Bonaparte. He is an inspector attached to the Criminal Investigation Branch in Brisbane, a man whose career is as romantic as it is remarkable. It is said that he has never failed successfully to finalise a case assigned to him, and that his bush craft and gifts have raised him high in the estimation of his superiors. His presence at Bermagui probably indicates that he is enjoying a busman's holiday; for the disappearance of a launch off Bermagui, and the subsequent recovery in a ship's trawl of the mutilated head of the angler who disappeared with the launch, a relic which unmistakably proved that the unfortunate man was shot, presents one of the most baffling mysteries of modern times."

Yet another Sydney daily mentioned Bony's profession and hinted that he was taking a busman's holiday. It added:

"His record of successes has created strong confidence in him by his superiors, and on several occasions he has been loaned to the Police Departments of other States to clear up a particularly difficult case. Should D-I Bonaparte really be working on the *Do-me* case, it may be taken for granted that startling developments will ultimately take place."

Setting the papers down on Blade's desk, Bony walked to the door where he stood and pondered on this particular 'startling development'. Blade came to stand behind him his face troubled.

"I feel that I am partially responsible," he said. "Not, however, for the information concerning your profession and presence at Bermagui. Those secrets have been well kept by all you took into your confidence. We're not gossipers."

When Bony turned to the club secretary he was smiling although his eyes were serious.

"It is obvious, Blade, that the facts concerning me were given by editorial direction."

"I am glad you accept that," Blade hurriedly cut in. "It has been my practice to post the newspapers with any unusual happening down here, and, of course, your five hundred and eighty-pounder swordie was an unusual happening. It's good for the town and the club, you understand. I hope that the unfortunate revelation won't have any serious effect on your investigation."

"I think not, Blade, and it is not worth worrying about really. It will cause comment, and people here will want to know why I am enjoying myself fishing for swordfish if I am investigating the disappearance of the *Do-me*; and they will want to know why I am not investigating the disappearance if I am really here on holidays." Bony chuckled. "And I was thinking of capturing half a dozen more swordies before I finalised this investigation. Now, I will have to work."

"Are you making any headway at all?"

"Yes, a little, a little. I am almost in the position of being able to say how it was done and who did it. I am waiting to know why it was done. That is strictly between ourselves. Ah—here's Constable Telfer."

"Afternoon, Mr. Bonaparte," the man with the big hands, the tough and big body, and the red and tough face said in cheerful greeting. He glanced at Blade, hesitating to speak further. Bony said:

"Did the inquiry about dark-grey kalsomine paint bear fruit?"

"Yes. The party bought ten packets of dark-grey kalsomine on 11th September at Milton's hardware store in Cobargo."

"Oh! That, Telfer, is most satisfactory. By the way, I will probably be out fishing to-morrow, and should Sergeant Allen, or another officer arrive when I am away, I want you to be careful not to disclose an item of interest concerning our work on this *Do-me* case. We are not going to permit any loss of credit to ourselves."

The constable's face and eyes indicated happiness.

"In fact, Telfer, it would be well for you, and you too, Blade, to be extremely dense and mentally vague. Allen might ask if you know a man having blue eyes and soft hands, a commanding presence and an English accent, and in age about sixty. I am expecting Allen or another officer to bring me important information concerning the man I have just described, and he may think himself sufficiently clever to put one over on poor old Bony. Keep him occupied, therefore, with subjects such as the weather."

"I'll do my best to keep him interested," Blade assented.

"And I'll be a gawk from Woop-Woop," Telfer added, delighted by the prospect.

"I am sure that we, with the possible assistance of the Cobargo uniformed police, can deal with our own affairs," Bony said. "My impression of Allen is that he wouldn't hesitate to steal a march, and it is he who is likely to convey the information, being so familiar with the ground. Now I must prepare for dinner. I am displeased with myself for having lost a swordie through sheer brainless stupidity. *Au revoir!*"

"Must we let the Cobargo crowd in on this job?" Telfer asked, doubtfully.

Bony nodded.

"There are more bolt-holes than you and I could cover, and more than one rabbit."

When he had gone Telfer regarded the club secretary. Blade smiled and said:

"He said that you and he wouldn't be able to manage all the bolt-holes. He didn't include me, but I am going to look after one of those bolt-holes, and you're not going to stop me."

"I don't aim to." Telfer sighed and added: "I wish I could get results like he does, and go fishing while I'm doing it. When I think of all the nights I've stopped up out of bed teasing my nit-wit brain to work out a theory or two about the *Do-me*, and him away fishing and doing his real job at the same time, I reckon I ought to get away from The Force and take on wood chopping."

At dinner Bony had to assure his table companion, Mr. Emery, that although he was a detective-inspector he was really and truly on holiday and not at all interested in the fate of the *Do-me*. He did this with no betrayal of 'hate' of telling lies. He could 'sense' the additional interest in him exhibited by everyone about him. In itself this interest fed his abnormal vanity, but beneath the pleasure it gave him lurked a feeling of annoyance. Time had forestalled him, had played a trick on him by revealing him to this Bermagui world before he was ready for the revelation.

When it was dark he strolled along the main street pausing to gaze at the captures suspended on the town triangle. His own gigantic swordfish, due to be removed the following day, was also displayed, and he felt secret satisfaction that those brought in this day were in comparison mere tiddlers. Afterwards, he strolled on along the road to Cobargo, turned to the skirting higher land. He saw a light shining from an unguarded window; eventually he knocked on the door of the small hut in which this window was built.

"Come in!" called Joe Peace.

Bony entered. Joe was seated at a roughly made table.

The stove gleamed with fat which had escaped from the frying-pan now on the wooden floor and occupying the interest of four large black and white cats. There was a bunk on which was a toss of blankets, indicating that Joe 'made' his bed after he got into it. Above the table was suspended an oil lamp, polished and wick-trimmed, the only article showing evidence of constant care. Joe stood up.

"Why, Mr. Bonaparte! Come in. Shut the flamin' door, please. The draught makes the lamp smoke. Here, take a pew."

He offered his visitor a petrol case.

"Had dinner, I suppose? If not, I can soon lash up a feed of some sort," he said.

"Thanks, Joe. I've had dinner," Bony told him. "I've just dropped in for a few moments. Didn't think you would mind."

"Course not. Glad to see you. I've just finished me grub. I'll clear the decks and feed me animals, and then we can settle down for a chin-wag. Me joint ain't none too flash, but I'm a great one for peace and quiet. Can't understand any bloke wantin' to git married. Can you?"

Verbally Bony agreed, but he thought that marriage would have improved Joe's surroundings. The place was spotlessly clean, but its contents were in fearful confusion. Joe went out, and the four cats went with him. He closed the door and was away for two minutes. On returning, the cats came in with him. He gave them milk in a pie-dish, and meat on a plate, and the plate and dish he subsequently washed with his own utensils. Then, seated opposite Bony and smoking a cigar his guest had presented, with the four cats purring and cleaning themselves on the table between them, he ceased his careless talking and waited to learn the purpose of the visit.

"I understand, Joe, that once you did some prospecting about Wapengo Inlet," Bony began.

"Too right I did. Went into that country years ago looking for colours and sleeper timber. Found plenty of timber but no metal. Gold must be there, though, washed down outer them 'ills."

"Was that before Rockaway settled there?"

"Years before."

"By the way, Joe, how does Rockaway get his mail and papers?"

"Tatter comes for 'em on 'is moter-bike. 'Tain't far on a moter-bike. Two miles from the 'ouse to the Tathra road, and seventeen to Bermee. 'E's a bit of a scorcher is Tatter, and the Rockaways don't 'ave dinner till eight."

"Oh! What is this Tatter?"

" 'E's the butler. When the truck isn't in, Tatter makes the trip for the mail and papers."

"What kind of man is he to look at?"

"Tatter? A biggish sorta bloke. Done a bit with the gloves at some time. 'E's never run foul of me—yet."

"There is a man cook, isn't there?"

"Yes. 'Is name's Jules. Don't see much of 'im. Bit of weed is Monsoo Jules."

"A Frenchman?"

Joe nodded and blew cigar smoke at the cats. They objected, and one jumped lightly to Bony's shoulder, where it settled and purred.

"How long has this Jules and Tatter been with Rockaway?" was Bony's next question.

"Like the others they come 'ere with Rockaway. Even Mrs. Light, the 'ouse-keeper, came with Rockaway and the gal. Some says that Mrs. Light uster be lady's maid to Mrs. Rockaway afore she kicked orf. She's a sour old cow. . . . You like cats?"

"Much, and dogs, too," replied Bony, who was stroking the animal on his shoulder.

"Can't says as 'ow I'm partial to dogs," admitted Joe, and Bony guessed that he was the cats' defender against the attacks of local dogs. He gazed steadily at Joe, saying:

"When you were prospecting at Wapengo Inlet, did you discover any caves or natural holes in the ground?"

Joe regarded Bony from beyond a pall of smoke.

"It's funny you asking me that," he said slowly. "Me and Jack was talkin' of caves and things last night. There's a longish cave less'n 'arf a mile from Rockaway's 'ouse. It goes away back under to top of the 'ill. Just the place for ole Rockaway to plant anybody he wanted to keep quiet—blokes like Bill Spinks and young Garroway, f'instance."

"Indeed!" Steadily Bony regarded Joe through the smoke. "Do you, too, think they are still alive?"

"Can't say as I do. But Jack does, and he thinks it because the Spinks women won't admit they're dead."

"Where is the entrance to this cavern—from the house?"

"It's straight up the 'ill from the 'ouse. You see, the 'ill top is sorta 'ollow. Sandstone and granite, and the sandstone 'a washed out leavin' the granite cap still there. It's a good place all right. Small entrance what could be easily blocked from outside."

"Although we are unable to believe that Spinks and Garroway are alive, that cave would be a good place to keep them in for months?"

"For years. As I told you, the entrance is small and can be easily blocked from outside. There's only one 'ole in the roof and a rock could be rolled over that. Any'ow, it's too high from the floor to reach and escape that way. Still, what would be the sense of killin' Ericson and not them what saw the killin' done?"

Bony slowly nodded in agreement, and for a space they were silent. Then he said:

"I would much like to examine that cave you speak of, Joe. Although we do not believe those two men to be alive, I must not disregard the possibility. The time has almost arrived to take a certain path of action, and before that action is undertaken I must be sure that the lives of possible prisoners are not endangered. I wonder, now. Would you accompany me, say to-morrow night, down to Wapengo Inlet and there take a look around?"

"Would I! Too right I would," replied Joe, his mouth a-leer, his small eyes agate hard. "Thinking of Bill and young Garroway makes me kind of take a step or two to believin' they're alive."

"Well," and Bony lifted the cat from his shoulder, "I'll let you know to-morrow about the expedition to Wapengo Inlet. Meanwhile I rely on your silence. When we do act we must act swiftly."

"You can rely on me, Mr. Bonaparte. I ain't married, for a woman to get anythink outer me."

On reaching the hotel, Bony passed at once to his room which was on the ground floor. There he opened his brief-case to refresh his mind on the statement made to Sergeant Allen by Eddy Burns.

He was standing at the table set before the window that opened on to the yard and garages, the case on the table, its contents not yet withdrawn. Slowly his slight body stiffened until it became utterly immobile. That 'sixth' sense named by him intuition, was unaccountably aroused, its physical effect being a tingling sensation at the back of his head.

For quite a minute he remained standing thus, and then his nostrils expanded and relaxed. In this time his maternal blood conquered his white blood, and he became primitive, super alert, controlled by the nervous reflexes of primitive man and animals. Swiftly immobility fled, to be replaced by feverish activity.

He made a thorough search of the room and his possessions, but everything was in order. He examined the brief-case and the papers within, but found no clue to possible interference. He remembered exactly how last he had placed the papers in the case, and they tallied now.

"Strange!" he murmured.

The tingling feeling had passed, and again he was normal. The cause he attributed to a condition of health, for there was nothing within the room, or in the air, to have warned him of danger. It was then a quarter to eleven, and he took the brief-case to the licensee with the request that it be locked in the office safe.

He joined Emery in the main bar parlour, and for half an hour talked fishing over a drink or two. When he went to bed it was to sleep without delay. He was awakened by a small voice full of menace.

"Get up and dress. Don't so much as whisper, or I'll spatter the walls with your brains."

CHAPTER 18

Taken for a Ride

A detective is menaced by physical violence much less often than Hollywood would have us believe; and during Napoleon Bonaparte's career threat to his life had been a rare phenomenon. He had himself never effected an arrest, his custom being to fade away after having placed the keystone of an investigation into position.

Mentally alert the moment the sound of the small voice penetrated to his subconscious, he recognised instantly the thing that pressed coldly and roundly against the back of his head. He was lying on his right side, facing the wall, and from behind him the small voice continued:

"Light, Dave."

The electric light went on. Bony blinked. He continued to lie still.

"Get up," ordered the small voice.

Obeying, he swung his legs over the edge of the bed, to stare at the round orifice of the pistol barrel, the hatchet face of Dan Malone above the weapon, and Dave Marshall who stood by the door with his hand still raised to the light switch. Then his gaze encountered the pale-blue eyes of the North American, to see in them no anger, no emotion, only a dead cold purpose.

"You gotta chance of living," Malone said, and Bony noted his power of speaking distinctly and yet so softly that one had to strain hearing. "If you don't do as you're told, when

you're told, I'll snuff you right out. It's up to you. Dres
and make no sound."

To comply with the instruction was to exhibit commo
sense. The unusual situation produced the same mental stat
as that created in Bony's mind by a fighting swordfish. I
divided his mind, one part of it now seeking to cope with thi
second 'startling development', whilst the other part wa
astonished by the facility with which the pistol barrel re
mained in exact alignment with the centre of his forehea
no matter his movements. The situation was ordinary be
cause of the entire absence of melodrama in Malone's voic
and facial expression. His threats were horrifying onl
through their implication. They were spoken in the calm
cold manner of the doctor stating that the patient woul
die of starvation if he would not eat. There was in Malone
threats just that degree of certainty, and it angered Bon
because of its affront to his dignity.

He was at last dressed in the clothes he had worn at dinne
and when on his visit to Joe Peace. It was Dave Marshal
who handed to him his wristlet watch, who packed his toile
things into the smaller of his suit-cases, who glanced insid
the wardrobe to see there Bony's old fishing togs and shoe
It was Malone who continued to menace him with the pisto
who did the ordering, who now said:

"Sit down at the table and write a letter I'll dictate
There's your writing tablet and pens and ink. Head th
letter 'Thursday night'." Bony prepared himself to write
and Malone continued:

" 'Dear Mrs. Steele. I have found it necessary to leave lat
this evening on very important business which I expect wil
keep me away for several days. Don't worry about th
account. A man in my position can't bilk' "—Bony shud
dered—" 'any one. Please tell Jack Wilton of my absence
and ask him to hold himself in readiness for my return

ours faithfully.' Sign it properly. Good! Now put the
etter into an envelope and address it to Mrs. Steele,
ermagui Hotel."

Bony complied with the order, and was then told to stand
nd face about. Malone now came to stand beside him, to
ip his left hand round Bony's right arm, to cross his right
rm over his chest and press the barrel of the pistol against
ony's right side.

"We're going for a walk like this," Malone said, without
motion. "We're going to tread very lightly so's not to wake
nybody up. If you don't tread softly enough to please me,
r if you shout or play the fool, you'll be dead afore you
now it. Ready, Dave?"

Marshall was standing by the door and light switch, the
arge and heavy suit-case on the floor beside the small and
ghter one at his feet. He nodded. The light went out
nd the door was opened, although Bony could not hear its
movement.

Malone waited for three seconds, when Marshall flashed on
hand torch having its beam semi-masked by a handkerchief.
n this subdued light Malone escorted Bony out of the room,
long the corridor, down a short flight of steps, and so out
to the yard. By keeping to the wall of the building they
scaped treading on the yard gravel. They passed along the
drive-in', Marshall following with the suit-cases and his
orch switched off, and where the drive-in debouched on to
he sidewalk of the street they were met by a third man who
hispered to Malone that there was no one about, and that
o sleepless guest was lounging on the hotel balcony.

Bony was conducted directly across the road to the open
rassland separating the township from the inner beach, and
here they walked parallel with the road, moving without
ound on the grass, until they were out of the township. They
ere obliged to walk on the road when crossing the bridge

of a narrow creek, and again when well beyond the jett
where they were obliged to cross the bridge over th
Bermaguee River. After that they kept to the grass verge c
the road for nearly a mile when they arrived at the junctio
of the Tilba Tilba and Cobargo roads well beyond the la:
house of the scattered settlement. There, in the deep shado
of the forest trees waited a car.

It was a new machine of an expensive make. Marsha
placed the suit-cases in the luggage compartment and steppe
into the rear seat. Malone and the third man squeezed Bon
into the car to sit beside Marshall, and after him steppe
Malone, the third man taking the wheel. Not until th
machine was well away from the road junction did the drive
switch on the head-lamps.

With a calm he certainly did not feel, Bony said:

"Perhaps one of you have a cigarette?"

The request appeared to reduce the tension in the me
either side of him, for Malone chuckled, saying:

"Give Mr. Bonaparte a fag, Dave. He deserves one fc
being a good little nigger boy."

"Your kindness charms me," Bony said, cuttingly—afte
Marshall had held a match to the cigarette. "It would be to
much, of course, to ask where we are going. As your accer
betrays your origin, and your actions confirm your accen
I have authority to assume that you are, to use your ow
picturesque idiom, taking me for a ride."

Again Malone chuckled, coldly and without humour.

"That's the name for it, Mr. Bonaparte, although in you
case we don't aim to stop the bus and take you for a littl
walk before bumping you off."

"Ah! You have, then, another idea?"

"That's telling," Malone guardedly fenced. "We're goi
to take great and particular care of you, any'ow. Can't hav
niggers like you snoopin' around, drawin' plans of the shij

ping and what not, and pinching paint-brushes when no-buddy's around. People who stick their dirty noses into other people's business git burnt sooner or later. Ain't that so, Mr. Tatter?"

"That is so, Captain Malone," replied the driver in precise English.

The driver, then, was Rockaway's butler, the fellow who often came to town on a motor-cycle for the mail and papers. Malone, however, appeared to be the leader of this party which might have no connection with the Rockaways, father and daughter. Bony hoped this was so, for he continued to feel a degree of warmth towards the man who had so hospitably welcomed him at Wapengo Inlet, who was so enthusiastically an angler, and so charmingly oblivious to the colour of his guest.

In less than half an hour of swift driving they passed through the end of a town, turning right to cross a bridge. The stars informed the alert detective that the general direction of travel was changed from west to south, and when they skirted a second town he observed that the general direction of travel was eastward. The farther they progressed the rougher became the roads until they left the made roads and followed a winding track through close-packed scrub trees.

The car had traversed this track for nearly two miles when into the radius of the head-lamps slid a large bungalow type house. The track could be seen to pass along the front of this house, and arriving at it the speed was reduced when passing it, reduced to a crawl to swing right and enter a large shed the doors of which were wide open.

The head-lamps illuminated the interior of the place, a large garage, for there was a truck, a light sports car, a motor-cycle, drums of petrol and of oil, a lathe and trade benches. The car engine was stopped, and Bony could hear the garage doors being closed. The interior electric lights came on and the car's lamps were switched off.

"Come on, we git out here," Malone ordered, himself first to leave the car. Bony dutifully followed—to see Rockaway leaning against the mudguard of the sports model and a lean man crossing from the double doors he had closed. Rockaway said, conversationally:

"Well, Mr. Bonaparte, we meet again in adverse circumstances. It is to be regretted, for my admiration is sincere for one who has captured a five-hundred-pound swordie."

Bony bowed in his grand manner. Now that the situation seemed likely to develop melodramatically, he was feeling a little more at his ease. There was more warmth in Rockaway than in Malone, although Rockaway might prove to be equally deadly. Tatter went to the doors. The thin man stood beside Rockaway, and Malone took station a little to the front of Bonaparte. Marshall was lifting the suit-cases from the car.

"The circumstances controlling our first meeting, as well as this one, were not of my choosing, Mr. Rockaway," Bony said, to add grandiloquently: "You will, perhaps, gratify my curiosity concerning the reason for this remarkable conduct."

"Certainly, Mr. Bonaparte," the big man readily assented. "A certain cause is having a series of effects. The cause being your inquisitiveness and the effects so far being certain newspaper reports hinting that you are taking a busman's holiday, examination of your papers proving that you have become deeply interested in the fate of the *Do-me*, and your abduction from your bed and escort to this place."

"Ah! So someone did examine the papers in my brief-case," Bony exclaimed. "It is strange, for although I could obtain absolutely no proof that the case has been tampered with, I yet was warned by a sixth sense I name intuition."

"Yes. You see, Mr. Bonaparte, during your absence from the hotel this evening, or rather last evening, Tatter, my butler, examined your personal effects, and in your brief-case saw those maps and plans and reports and statements you have compiled concerning the missing *Do-me*. Before your absence from the hotel presented him with the opportunity of looking over those papers he had no chance of receiving instructions from me, and so he replaced the brief-case exactly as he had found it. Having at one time been a most successful burglar, for you to have discovered any article misplaced would have cast reflection on his reputation."

"I can assure you that his reputation remains untarnished," Bony said, slightly smiling.

"I am glad to know that. Of course, he did quite right to leave the brief-case in your suit-case, and as Marshall has brought both your suit-cases here we will go into your papers more fully. Get me the brief-case, Dave."

Marshall opened the larger of Bony's suit-cases and began to tumble out on the floor its contents. Bony, watching him, saw first bewilderment and then chagrin on his rat face.

"It's—it's not here," he stuttered.

"Oh!" Mr. Rockaway said slowly. "In which case did you place Mr. Bonaparte's brief-case, Tatter?"

"In the large one," replied Tatter, from the doors.

"Well, it ain't here," Marshall said.

"That's where I put it," averred Tatter. "That's where I found it in the first place. I remember the incident perfectly."

"Well, well!" Rockaway said, in his voice for the first time a discordant note. "Surely, Malone, you realised the importance of Mr. Bonaparte's brief-case and checked up on Tatter's statement? It would have taken only a second."

"Tatter said he knew it was in the big suit-case," Malone answered.

"Tatter said this and Tatter said that, you fool," Rockaway exclaimed. "Unless I am with you to guide your every step you are lost. Now, Mr. Bonaparte, please assist us. What became of your brief-case?"

"It was like this, Mr. Rockaway," Bony replied easily. "On my return to the hotel last evening I had occasion to refresh my mind on a point of my investigation into your strange activities, and my sixth sense informed me that that brief-case had been tampered with. In order to secure it against another invasion, I took it along to Constable Telfer for safe keeping."

"That's a lie," Marshall burst out. "You never left the pub after you got back there. We was watching the place from eleven o'clock."

"Well, Mr. Bonaparte, what became of the brief-case?" persisted the fresh-complexioned, suave-voiced big man. "Come, we are unable to waste time."

"It is in Constable Telfer's safe."

Mr. Rockaway sighed. Then he said:

"Knock him down, Malone."

There was no delay. Malone's iron-hard fist crashed against the point of Bony's jaw, producing a grating sound in his ears, lights before his eyes, and a vast pain in his brain. A second blow was given by the floor of the garage, producing nausea in his stomach. He experienced an intense longing to be supported by Mother Earth, but he was dragged to his feet. The lighting within the garage appeared dim, as though a shadow fell between its illuminated objects and Bony's eyes. Beyond this shadow stood Rockaway and the others. Malone stood nearer than they. He had let go his hold on Bony. Rockaway's voice seemed to issue from a great distance.

"Now, Mr. Bonaparte, what *did* you do with the brief-case?"

Bony blinked his eyes to banish the unreal shadow. He

fought to regain mental poise. A warmth of peculiar origin was passing up his neck to heat his brain, to burn his eyes, and even then his mind was divided so that he wondered at this until he understood that it was actually mounting anger. He was astonished by the fact of being in this instance unable to control this growing heat despite his effort to discipline himself. Almost all his life he had regarded anger as the blunted weapon of the weak man to be scorned by a cultured man such as he.

"The brief-case, Mr. Bonaparte," Rockaway said again.

"I took it . . ." Bony began when the self-discipline imposed over many years vanished. The heat in his brain had become too fierce for longer control, and abruptly his mother's blood took charge of him, made him one with her and her people. That sneering brute close to him had knocked him down, had called him a nigger boy, had treated him as though he, Napoleon Bonaparte, was a nomad of the bush.

Bony actually screamed when he leaped at Malone, standing only three feet from him, wolfishly waiting the order to again knock him down. Bony's transformed face astonished the Bluenose to the extent of delaying his defensive action for a split second, for Bony's face had become jet-black in colour, his eyes glaring blue orbs set in seas of white, while his teeth reflected the light like the fangs of a young dog. Before Malone could act, Bony's fingers were crunching into his throat with a strength extraordinary in a man so light of body. And like the grip of a bull-dog those hands were not to be prized away until it was too late to revive Captain Malone.

Never before in his life had his aboriginal instincts so controlled Napoleon Bonaparte to the exclusion of that other complex part of him inherited from his father and on which was based so magnificent a pride. Reason had fled before the primitive lust to destroy. He had Malone sagging, was sup-

porting the heavy body with his two hands, when he heard
Rockaway say, still casual and cool:

"Knock him out, someone. Don't kill the fool. We must
have that brief-case."

Bony began to scream with laughter at the sight of
Malone's awful face: blue-black, tongue protruding, glassy
eyes rolling horribly in their sockets. Then abruptly his
laughter was cut off. A flare of flame swept across his eyes,
to be followed by a night in which thought and being had
no entity.

CHAPTER 19

Telfer Doesn't Like It

Throughout the swordfishing season, Edward Blade invariably opened his office at seven o'clock each morning to attend to the requirements of launchmen preparing for the day's angling, and usually he went home again at eight for breakfast to return at nine o'clock. By nine, when all the anglers had gone out, there was correspondence to be dealt with among other demands.

On returning to his office after breakfast on the morning of 18th January, Blade was surprised by Jack Wilton, who was waiting for him when he and his launch and his angler should have been at sea.

"Hullo! What's your trouble, Jack?" he asked, unlocking the office door and leading the other inside.

"I've been waiting for Mr. Bonaparte since seven o'clock this morning," Jack explained. "As he didn't turn up at the jetty by half-past eight I went to the hotel to see what was wrong. It seems that he's gone away. He left this letter in his room for Mrs. Steele and me."

Blade accepted and read Malone's dictated letter with a heavy frown between his widely spaced eyes. He re-read it several times, before looking up to stare at the puzzled launchman. Without commenting he passed to his table and there turned over filed papers until he displayed the hiring contract of fishing tackle signed by 'Napoleon Bonaparte' The letter addressed to Mrs. Steele, the licensee, was signed 'Nap Bonaparte'. From the examination of the two signatures, Blade glanced up at the waiting Wilton, to say:

"It seems plain enough, Jack. Something had happened which has taken Mr. Bonaparte away for a few days. Still . . ."

"Joe says that Mr. Bonaparte visited him at his shack last night, when Mr. Bonaparte said nothing to him about going away. In fact, he promised Joe to decide about something when out fishing to-day."

"Oh! What time was that, when Mr. Bonaparte left Joe's place?"

"About half-past ten."

"Yes, that would be about right. I heard him talking to Mr. Emery in the main bar parlour at eleven. They were comparing their plans for the fishing to-day. And now I come to recall it, I heard Mr. Bonaparte say to Mr. Emery that they had better be off to bed as there was another day's angling in front of them." Again the club secretary read the letter, and again he stared pensively at Jack Wilton. "I can't make it out. He must have decided to go away after he left Emery to go to bed. Do you know if he took any luggage with him?"

"Yes. Mrs. Steele went to his room after I had been there and taken the letter to her. Mr. Bonaparte's two suit-cases are not there now, and the bed was just like he had slept in it."

"That makes it stranger still," Blade murmured. "I've seen those cases. One was pretty heavy and a good size. He must have left in a car. Couldn't leave Bermagui with those cases any other way. You wait here. I'll go along and have a word with Telfer."

The constable was found engaged with his office work. He read the letter addressed to Mrs. Steele, and then he listened to Blade's vague misgivings. After that he pushed aside his papers and stood up, saying:

"I don't like it."

Again he read the letter, and again he said:

"I don't like it."

On their way to the hotel Blade mentioned Bony's visit to Joe, and his subsequent chat with Emery in the parlour. He also insisted that Bony would have taken a car in which to leave Bermagui because of his heavy suit-case which, with the lighter one, had gone with him. They sought Mrs. Steele, who conducted them to Bony's room. She said:

"The maid has just finished tidying."

Telfer glanced inquiringly about the room. He walked to the table and stared down at the pens and ink and the writing block.

"You came here a while back with Jack Wilton, Mrs. Steele. How was the room then?" he questioned.

"Just as usual after a gentleman has left it. The bed was unmade and the ash-tray was almost filled with cigarette ash and stubs. Mr. Bonaparte's fishing clothes are in the wardrobe. He's taken everything else with him."

"Oh! The place didn't look as if he had left in a great hurry?"

"No."

"Nothing was upset?"

"No."

"When did you last see Mr. Bonaparte?"

"About ten to eleven. He came to ask me to put his brief-case in my safe in the office. Then he went into the main parlour and talked with Mr. Emery."

Telfer's brows shot upward, and Blade said softly:

"Oh! Ah!"

"I hope there's nothing wrong, Mr. Telfer?" Mrs. Steele said, suddenly anxious.

"Don't know yet," Telfer admitted. "Anyway, keep quiet about our interest in Mr. Bonaparte. Did he say anything, or hint to anyone that he might be leaving?"

"Not a word. Not even a hint, Mr. Telfer. In fact, he was telling Mr. Emery that he was going to persuade Jack Wilton to troll to-day around Montague as he hasn't been up there yet."

Telfer stared at her in his disconcerting manner.

"We'll go along to your office," he said, decisively. "I'd like a look at that brief-case."

In procession they passed along the corridor, down the short flight of steps, into the original building, and so to the small office built beneath the staircase. Telfer motioned Mrs. Steele and Blade to go in. He himself casually toured the parlours and the bar before joining the licensee and the club secretary. Mrs. Steele had opened her safe, and she produced Bony's brief-case. Telfer unlatched it and swiftly glanced over the papers whilst being watched by the others. When he replaced them and fastened the case, he said:

"I'll take charge of this, Mrs. Steele."

"But," objected Mrs. Steele, "Mr. Bonaparte told me to take great care of it and to give it to no one but himself."

"It'll be all right," Telfer told her. "He didn't say how long he would want you to keep it?"

"No."

"Did he seem worried?"

"Oh no. He was just as nice and smiling as always."

"Did he use the telephone last night, do you know?"

"I don't think so. I can find out for sure from the barman."

"I'd like to know—for sure."

Mrs. Steele was away for a few minutes, to inform them on her return that no one had used the telephone after five o'clock the previous afternoon.

"I do hope nothing is wrong, Mr. Telfer," she said, earnestly. "What with the *Do-me* and poor Mr. Ericson——"

"You just say nothing about anything to anyone," Telfer told her. "You'll oblige me by doing just that."

"Oh, I'll not gossip."

"Good woman! Come on, Blade."

Silently they walked to Blade's office which was nearer than the Police Station, and there Telfer said slowly, ponderously:

"I still don't like it. Why the devil would Inspector Bonaparte say nothing about going away? He goes to bed as usual, and then he gets up and dresses and packs his two suit-cases and clears out when he's expectin' a C.I.B. man here to-day with important information. Why? Tell me that."

"I can't, Telfer. The point is, how did he leave Bermagui? He must have hired a car to go away in, having those suit-cases. He couldn't go away by any other means. Whose car did he hire?"

"Yes, whose? We must find that out. I wonder why he visited Joe last night. We'll find that out, too. Meanwhile I'll take the brief-case along to my office, and hunt up the night telephone operator. You could, if you like, see Smale and Parkins about the hired car. There's no others he could have taken."

They met again in the street an hour later, when Blade said that neither Smale nor Parkins had taken the detective away from Bermagui, and Telfer said that Bony had not asked for a telephone connection the previous day. Guarded inquiries had established the fact that no one within the hotel and no one living along the only street of the township had heard a car arriving at or leaving the hotel after ten o'clock the previous evening.

"I was mooching about till midnight," Telfer stated, "and I didn't see or hear a car anywhere. I'm liking it now less than ever. I wonder if he went away in a launch."

"He might have done that, but if so wouldn't he have chosen the *Marlin*?"

"Well, there's Wilton down outside your place. Let's go along and see if he noticed any launch missing early this morning." They had almost reached Blade's office when the policeman halted, and said: "I can hear an aeroplane."

Blade listened.

"Yes. I can hear it, too. Coming from the north, from Sydney. It might be bringing the C.I.B. man Bonaparte's expecting."

"If it should be like that, remember that we promised Bonaparte to be dumb," urged Telfer, who was becoming increasingly anxious that through Bony's unaccountable absence all credit would be withdrawn from him. "It wouldn't do to blab out everything we know, which isn't much, just because the inspector went away for a day or two."

"Still . . ." and Blade hesitated. "It's all too mysterious for my liking. And we know he strongly suspected the Rockaway people."

"We'll wait, anyway, before we disobey Inspector Bonaparte's orders," Telfer countered stiffly. "Let's go on and question Wilton about the launches."

Jack Wilton was invited to follow them into Blade's office, and there he was asked if any launch was out when he first went down to the jetty that morning.

"No, they were all at the jetty," Wilton replied. "The only launches that have gone out took anglers with 'em. If Mr. Bonaparte went away in a launch instead of a car, then that launch got back before I went down at six this morning."

"Humph! Where's Joe?"

"I think he's in the garage soldering some hooks to traces."

"Well, slip in there and bring him here."

Joe appeared in less than a minute—as the aeroplane was roaring overhead on its way to the landing-ground. Telfer became brisk.

"Now, Joe, I understand that Mr. Bonaparte paid you a visit last evening. What for?"

Joe's face expanded in a mirthless grin.

"'E come to see me cats."

"What else?"

"To ask kindly after me 'ealth."

"Didn't he make you a promise to decide about something when you were at sea to-day?"

Joe considered his reply before giving it. Then:

"Well, he was thinkin' of me and 'im doing a bit of prospectin' down around Wapengo Inlet."

"Oh! He was, was he! Why?"

"Struth! Why does a bloke go prospectin' if it ain't for metal?"

"Rot, Joe. Now look here. We think that something serious has happened to Mr. Bonaparte," Telfer said, confidingly. "It's up to us to get together and find out just what has happened to him. What do you think, Jack?"

"I think like you do, but Joe won't talk." Wilton answered.

"I promised 'im I wouldn't," Joe cut in. "It was a little private matter between me and 'im, and it ain't got nothin' to do with 'im goin' away."

"How do you know it hasn't?"

A car hummed by the office building, and Blade knew it was driven by Smale, who was under contract to meet all planes.

"'Cos it 'asn't, that's all."

"You'll excuse me saying so, Joe Peace, but you're an obstinate old fool," Telfer told him with slow deliberation. "After Mr. Bonaparte left you last night he returned to the hotel, had a drink with Mr. Emery, and then went to bed.

This morning he has gone, with his suit-cases, leaving a note to say he'll be back some time. Supposing—I say supposing—the people who murdered Ericson got wind they were being cornered and to save themselves took Mr. Bonaparte away, intending to put him out safely? Come on, we've got to find him. Tell us everything he talked about last night."

"Well, 'e talked about cats and dogs and gold and caves and the Rockaway push."

Further to this Joe would not add, and the purple-faced constable could question no further because Smale was returning from the landing-ground. He emitted a long-drawn sigh of exasperation.

"You two fellers quit for the time being," he said, addressing Wilton. "And keep your mouths shut tight."

He followed the launchmen as far as the door from which position he gazed along the road to Wapengo at the oncoming car. Blade joined him, saying:

"I think that what Joe said about the conversation with Mr. Bonaparte is substantially correct. Joe wants to make a mystery of the entire visit."

"Maybe you're right," Telfer conceded. "Ah—thought so! Here's D.-S. Allen."

The man who stepped from the car halted opposite the office was big and lean and efficient in action and appearance. He strode smartly towards Telfer, who had stepped down from the club office to meet him. And he said, as though words were time wasted:

"Day, Telfer!'

"Good day, Sergeant. You on the job again?"

"Yes. Mr. Bonaparte out to-day?"

"Yes."

"All right! I'll go on to the hotel and fix a room. See you later."

The two men watched him being driven to the hotel, and the constable said, gravely:

"I'm liking it less and less. He'll be expecting Bonaparte back on the *Marlin* this evening, and when he learns that Bonaparte didn't go fishing to-day, and that he left some time during the night, I'm going to get it well and truly in the neck. Darned if I know what best to do. Anyway, I'm going home for dinner."

An hour later, when he returned, he found Blade studying a large scale map of the district.

"I been thinking," he told Blade. "Perhaps one of the fellers at Cobargo saw or heard a car pass through there from here. Mind me using your phone?"

"Go ahead. Then we'll test an idea of my own," Blade said, using a pair of compasses with which to measure distances on the map.

Telfer was engaged four minutes, and, looking up, Blade saw him staring at the ceiling.

"Mounted Constable Earle lives near the Cobargo bridge," he said slowly. "Earle says he heard a car enter Cobargo from the Bermagui road, pass over the bridge, and take the road to Bega. Bonaparte might have been in that car. Time— two-twenty a.m."

"That's quite likely, Telfer. Now listen to my idea. Bonaparte visited Joe last night and they talked about Wapengo Inlet. Supposing that after he went to bed he decided to prospect the Rockaways' place, and so packed up and got himself driven, say, to Lacy's or Milton's at the back of the Inlet, and from there do his prospecting?"

"Then why go all the way round through Cobargo and Bega, and then across Dr. George Mountain? Why didn't he take the direct coast road?"

"Because the night being dead quiet, he knew someone here would hear the car departing."

"Where did he get the car, and when did he order it?" Telfer demanded, triumphantly. "And why didn't he take the brief-case?"

"Oh, search me!" Blade answered despairingly.

"No, that won't work out, old man. What I think is this. Assuming that Bonaparte was right on the track of them that killed Ericson—and he was suspecting the Rockaway crowd, wasn't he—and assuming they are the guilty parties, they'd have knowledge who and what Bonaparte was late yesterday afternoon when Tatter came with the mail. He reads a newspaper, and he telephones old Rockaway about it. He was in town till late last night. I saw him in the pub. Then the car comes in and parks outside the town, and Tatter and the rest pounce on Bonaparte when he's in bed and take him for a ride, as they say on the pictures. I'll check up on that car Earle heard early this morning."

Again he applied himself to the telephone, and when he had done he was smiling a grim and broad smile.

"Gellibrand, down at Tanja, says he heard a car coming along the Dr. George Mountain road at half-past three this morning. It was so unusual that he got up and looked out of his window. He saw the car pass his house, and he recognised it as Rockaway's Southern Star. Says he'll swear to it."

After this neither spoke for a full minute; when the silence was broken it was done by Telfer, with positive reluctance in his voice.

"I'll have to make a full report to D.-S. Allen. If I don't I'll be put on tramp. Blast! What did he want to come butting in for? The Cobargo crowd and us could have cleaned up this business."

"That's your best course," Blade urged. "I've been looking at this letter addressed to Mrs. Steele, and it makes me almost sure that it's been dictated."

"How?"

"Well, look at the word 'bilk'. Compare it with the other words. It's written raggedly, as though the writer hesitated to write it. I can't fancy myself hearing Bonaparte speaking such a word. But, Telfer, old man, I've heard Malone use the word more often than once. Then look at the signature here on this contract for fishing tackle. It's in full—Napoleon Bonaparte. On the letter it's just Nap Bonaparte. He was a proud man, Telfer, and secretly proud of his name. I don't think he'd sign Nap at any time. In this case he might have done so to lead us to believe he wrote at dictation. Yes, Allen will have to know all about it. But you can present to him a good case, can't you?"

Telfer grinned. He was standing by the seated secretary, and he patted Blade on the back, saying:

"Thanks to you. I'll hop along to Allen right away."

Blade saw nothing more of Telfer until the constable saluted him from Smale's car. Beside him sat D.-S. Allen. The car took the road to Cobargo. It was then four o'clock.

After that Blade found work impossible, for a 'why' insistently knocked on the door of his mind. Why were those two going to Cobargo? He watched the car round the bend back of the jetty, saw it disappear behind the bank of the higher land, saw it reappear speeding in front of a dust cloud, saw it crossing the bridge over the Bermaguee River, watched it until it again disappeared just before reaching the road junction where Rockaway's car had waited for Bony and his abductors.

The sun shone full upon the seated secretary, who absently greeted, or returned the greetings of, passers-by. With the same degree of absent-mindedness he saw the homing launches, and for the first time was thankful that not one of them flew a capture flag. He should have gone home for dinner at six, but he continued to sit on his doorstep.

It was a launch that brought him to his feet as though jerked to them by a rope.

The *Marlin* was passing across the inner bay towards the headland and the open sea. It was almost seven o'clock, and quite loudly Edward Blade said to the world in general:

"Where the hell are those two fellows going at this time of day?" Then he hurried into the office, strode to his table, glared at the map almost covering his table. "Damn it all!" he cried aloud. "Why didn't I concentrate on that brief-case? Either Bonaparte made up his mind to leave the pub before he went to bed, and decided to plant his brief-case in the hotel safe, or he expected a move from the Rockaway crowd and had it locked up for safety. And then they got him. That's it, then they got him. I'm left here like a dolt while Allen and Telfer and the rest scoop the pool. And I'll bet Wilton and old Joe Peace are headed for Wapengo Inlet, too."

Mr. Parkins looked in through the doorway.

"You going dippy—talking to yourself like that?" he inquired.

"*Going* dippy! I *am* dippy," Blade shouted.

CHAPTER 20

Men in Chains

Napoleon Bonaparte returned to consciousness of life by a series of steps. Between each step must have been a long period of unconsciousness, because he remembered a world that appeared to whirl at dizzy speed by a mechanism that ticked, then a surrounding void which pulsated, and then dark sea on which he softly floated whilst a fire of pain slowly consumed him.

Finally he awoke to reality to discover himself lying in a large cavern dimly illuminated by shafts of sunlight joining the sandy floor with the shadowy roof. The ticking noise was made by dripping water, the pulsating sound was produced by a man snoring, and the soft sea was but a narrow mattress on which he was lying. Pain within his head was so severe that the snoring of the man and the dripping of the water combined to aggravate an agony that could not be borne silently.

Anguish wrenched from him a loud groan. The sound of it evidently disturbed the sleeper, for his snoring ceased. Then a voice called:

"Hi, Bill, the bloke's coming round. Hi, Bill, wake up."

"Wha's that?" another man sleepily asked.

"The new bloke's coming round, Bill," the first voice replied. "By the sound of 'im he's crook."

Bony, lying upon his chest and the left side of his face, heard movements and then saw a shadowy figure moving towards him from a dark corner of the cavern. It approached on its hands and knees, and when it entered one of the shafts of sunlight gleaming like pillars supporting the roof, pain was temporarily beaten back by wonder the apparition engendered. Its face was dead white. The large eyes were blue-black, the hair which fell to the naked shoulders was black, and the black and ragged beard fell down in front of the chest. As it moved the links of a chain clinked.

Farther back from this man was another, also on his hands and knees, a younger man whose hair and beard were red, and when he, too, passed through a light-bar, his eyes were revealed as pale blue and his face the colour of chalk.

They arrived, these two wild creatures, at Bony's side, to gaze silently down at him, pity in their eyes, forgetful of their own conditions.

"I want a drink," besought Bony.

"Fetch the dipper, Bob," ordered Blackbeard, and Red-beard turned and crawled away. Again Bony's pain was weakened by the sight of the chain round Redbeard's waist from which other chains were passed back to secure his ankles, forcing his feet up off the ground, permitting him to proceed on his hands and knees, but preventing him from standing.

"Think you could turn over?" asked Blackbeard. "Try!"

Bony wanted only to lie still, but Blackbeard insisted and gently turned him over. Then, slipping an arm under the mattress, he raised Bony upward the better to drink from the dipper of water brought by Redbeard.

"You got a devil of a wallop on the head," Blackbeard said, softly and sympathetically. "They let you down here last night, and as we have no light at night we didn't know if you was alive or dead, and we couldn't do nothing but roll you on to this mattress. Come aside a bit so's not to wet the mattress, and I'll bathe the wound on your scalp."

"You are———"

"Better not talk now. There's plenty of time to talk. We been here a long time, and you may be here a long time, too."

Bony closed his eyes, gratefully relaxing. The cold water was a salve, and, whilst Blackbeard was sponging his head with a rag, Redbeard kept up a monologue.

"Funny sorta bloke, ain't he? Indian he looks like. Never seen 'im before. Musta run foul of that Bluenose, Malone. Cripes! I'd like to get me teeth inter 'is throat like old Parkins's bull-terrier. What a 'ell of a bash 'e got on 'is head. Someone must 'ave swiped 'im with a anvil or something. Any'ow, we've someone to talk to. I'm tired of playing five-stones and making irrigation channels on the floor to run water on to the spuds and things. That's last year's. More water? All right!"

Gradually the pain within Bony's head was subdued, and the lesser smart of the scalp wound proved an anodyne to the greater. Gently Blackbeard laid him down, and Bony said to him:

"Thanks. The pain's easier. Who are you?"

Blackbeard's eyes widened and he answered:

"I'm Bill Spinks, and this is my mate, Bob Garroway. Who are you? How did you come to get thrown in here?"

Bony essayed a smile and it hurt.

"I'm only a fool fly caught in a web I should have seen ten miles away," he replied. "I'm supposed to be a detective."

"A d., eh!" exclaimed Garroway.

"Yes. And so you two are Spinks and Garroway! After all your sister and mother, Spinks, were right in refusing to believe you were dead."

"Are they all right? When did you see them last?" Spinks eagerly demanded to know.

"I saw and talked with them only yesterday, or maybe the day before. After the *Do-me* vanished Jack Wilton and Joe began a subscription, and a Mr. Emery came in very hand-

somely, so that your sister was able to take over Nott's Tea
Rooms. Mr. Blade is helping, too, with the books and advice.
See if I've any tobacco and papers and matches in my pockets,
will you?"

Mention of tobacco produced an animal-like cry from
Garroway, who came rapidly forward like a huge spider and
would have mauled Bony's person had not Spinks struck
him away.

"Keep your distance, Bob," roared Spinks, and young
Garroway crouched and began to whimper. To Bony, Spinks
explained apologetically: "We been here a long time, Bob
and me. It 'asn't been too interesting with nothing to do
and nothing to occupy ourselves bar thinking and thinking
what was going to happen to us and what was happening to
them at 'ome. The place has got on Bob's nerves, and sometimes he isn't himself. . . . Here's a tin nearly full of fine-
cut, and matches and papers, too."

"Then roll me a cigarette, and you two help yourselves.
Tell me about the *Do-me*. You can call me Bony. All my
friends call me Bony. Afterwards, perhaps, I'll feel a little
better and try to get out. They haven't chained me, have
they?"

"No. They put chains on us because——"

"Let that wait. Tell me about the *Do-me* from the beginning."

"All right!" agreed Spinks, busy with cigarette making.
"Keep back, Bob. You'll get your smoke, don't worry. The
dirty swine could have given us a bit of tobacco and a paper
to read now and then, 'stead of keeping us here as if we was
a couple of lions. About the poor old *Do-me*! Well, the
yarn begins this way.

"We went out to Swordfish Reef to try for sharks—me
and Bob, here, and Mr. Ericson. He was a very decent kind
of chap was Mr. Ericson, down here for the tunny fishing.

When he asked if sharks could be captured with rod and line, we told him they could, and we got Mr. Blade to fix up a line and reel and rod like for swordfishing.

"The sea was as flat as a board that day, and there was a haze lying low over it. We lost sight of the *Edith* and *Snowy* early in the piece, and after a time we lost sight of the *Gladious*, too. When we got out to the reef we seen it was just on the boil. You could follow its position running up to Montague by the water just boiling on top of it, making a kind of sea track.

"We couldn't see the coast, only the top of Dromedary Mountain, and we began to follow the reef towards Montague Island. Perhaps you know the coast and the Island?"

"Yes," replied Bony. "And I've been out to Swordfish Reef and seen the water boiling above it just as you describe."

"Oh! That'll make it easier for me to tell you. I suppose Marion and Jack Wilton got spliced?"

"No. Jack told me that he thought your sister couldn't make up her mind to marry him. It's a pity. Jack is a fine fellow and he has loved your sister for years."

"Yes, that's so. And if ever we get out of here she's going to make up her mind and quick, too. You can leave that part of it to me."

"Too right, 'e can, Bill," supported young Garroway.

"Shut up, Bob, while I tell Bony about the *Do-me*. As I was saying, we were trolling for sharks northward along Swordfish Reef when there came out of the haze to the east a steam launch painted a dark grey. She was a bit ahead of us, and me and Bob couldn't make her out. She was a stranger to us. Any'ow, she still kept on her course to east'ard, and I seen that if we kept on our course to nor'ard there'd likely enough be a collision.

"When the two craft got to about fifty yards from each

other, Bob, here sings out that the grey launch's funnel looks kind of funny. There's a feller standing against it, and presently he jumps around and down comes the funnel to be chucked overboard. Then Bob sings out that the feller what threw the funnel overboard is Dave Marshall, one of Rockaway's men, and I knew he was right when I made out Dan Malone at the wheel. Then I recognised the *Dolfin* under the grey paint. It gets me beat. I can't make it out why the *Dolfin's* been painted grey and why she was showing a dummy funnel.

"She still comes along on her east'ard course, and I seen that if I didn't push the *Do-me* hard a port there'd be a collision for sure. And just then Mr. Ericson shouts out 'fish-oh'. I looks astern and there's one mako shark coming on fast after the bait-fish, and two more farther astern and a bit wide. That's all I can see of them, because I had to go hard to port to miss the *Dolfin* who didn't change her course by so much as a hair.

"I shouts at Malone, asking him what the devil he thinks he's doing, but he doesn't answer. Our speed was the usual trolling speed of three miles to the hour, and the *Dolfin's* speed is about eight until she draws level with us when Malone cuts her down to our speed. So we gets to running side by side, about a yard separating us, and Marshall goes down and takes the wheel and Malone comes to stand on the low cabin roof staring down at us.

"I can hear Mr. Ericson reeling in the bait-fish before the mako could strike and probably take the line under the *Dolfin* and foul it in her propeller. He's swearing a bit, and I don't blame him. I says to Malone:

" 'What's your ruddy game?'

" 'Stop your engine,' he shouts at me, and with that he pulls out an automatic pistol and aims it at me. The sea was so calm and the craft were keeping such even pace that I could understand that Malone could shoot me without much chance of missing.

"So I threw the propeller shaft out of gear and cut off the engine ignition. Over me shoulder I saw Mr. Ericson stand up in the cockpit behind his chair, and then step up on the gunwale.

" 'Put that gun away, Canadian Jack,' he said, and at the same time he tells him that he whips an automatic out of a pocket.

"But Malone had the advantage. What happened was too quick for me to follow, but Malone fired one shot and Mr. Ericson went at the knees and he dropped straight down over the side, the pistol still held in his right hand. Although the launch propellers ain't biting the water, the craft are still moving forward fairly fast, and astern of us I seen the bubbles rising from Mr. Ericson and the water stained with his blood. I can't look at nothing else but them bubbles getting farther and farther astern, and then over 'em and among 'em was that mako shark, and the fins of the other two less'n two fathoms away. The water blackened a bit, and I knew them three brutes were fighting over Mr. Ericson.

"Me and Bob, here, began to curse Malone for the dirty murdering swine he is; but he keeps cool and says if we don't go aboard the *Dolfin*, quick and easy, he'll put us down with the sharks, too. We can't do nothing but obey his orders, and Marshall comes with ropes and binds our hands behind our backs so hard that it hurt. Then they takes us below and locks us into a cabin apiece.

"After that I heard the *Dolfin*'s propeller bite water and the engine accelerate, and I looked out of the port. I couldn't see nothing, and I couldn't think of much else beside this act of piracy on the high sea and the murder of poor Mr. Ericson. Then the *Dolfin* got a bump. She was being made fast to the *Do-me*, I guessed. A minute later the *Dolfin* went.

ahead, and I knew by the way she was labouring that she wa
towing my launch. I could hear hammering going on, and
it didn't seem to be on the *Dolfin*.

"Presently we crossed the water road above Swordfish Reef
and I seen then that we were heading east and out to sea.
stayed by the port wondering what was going to happen
next. Judging by the speed of the *Dolfin*, and guessing th
time we'd been towing the *Do-me*, I seen that we'd crossed
Continental Reef and was well out in the extra deep water
beyond the Continental Shelf, where the bottom's mile
below. Then the *Dolfin* slowed down and stopped.

"There was another bump when the *Do-me* coming on
behind hit her stern. I could hear Malone talking to
Marshall, and then Marshall shouts 'right-ho', and the *Dolfin*
gets away again as fast as she could. After a while she slewed
to starboard, and that brings me looking at the *Do-me*
lying still a quarter of a mile off. Then the *Dolfin* stop
again.

"I was wondering what it all meant when the *Do-me* gave
a kind of shudder and the water sort of boiled up around
her. Soon after that she began to settle, and I knew they'd
blown out her bottom. She went down by the bow. They'd
taken Mr. Ericson's rod away from the chair, and I sort of
knew they had put it into the cabin, with all other movabl
things, and then had hammered shut the cabin door. Ther
wasn't to be no wreckage floating."

Spinks ceased speaking, and Bony watched the bright drop
of water trickle down his ashen face into his black beard
He said nothing, and Spinks went on with heartbreak in hi
voice:

"She went down bow first. I saw her go down. She wa
my launch, was the *Do-me*. I built her. Mother christene
her with a bottle of wine. We'd got all right, mother and m
and Marion, just got sort of settled down. Owed nothing

ou see. And then they come along and kill my angler and
ink my launch."

Bob Garroway began to shout oaths and curses against
Rockaway and his men, and Spinks sprawled forward towards him and shouted at him to "shut up". Confinement
or more than three months had made almost beasts of them,
nd Garroway, still shouting his vile oaths, ran away on
is hands and knees like a loathsome spider. Bony could
ear him whimpering in a dark corner of the cavern, and he
ould see Spinks's face working whilst he fought to regain
ontrol of himself.

"He's getting on my nerves, is Bob. He's given me a bit
f trouble, like. Always growling as though it's my fault
ve're chained in here like a couple of mad dogs."

"Roll me a cigarette," Bony asked, soothingly. "What
appened after the *Do-me* sank?"

"After she sank! Oh, we went on out to sea. The *Dolfin*
ust pottered about for hours. Once Malone put on speed
or half an hour—she can do about sixteen knots, you know
—and I thought it was likely that she was getting out of the
vay of a steamer. She could that, you see, with the haze
ying low on the water and her painted dark grey, without
he steamer people spotting her. After dark she ran east for
oast, and it must have been after eleven that night when
ve got over the Wapengo bar. Soon as we moored to the
etty I heard Rockaway say to Malone:

" 'Did you manage it, Dan?'

" 'Yes,' said Malone. 'But Ericson drew a gun and I was
orced to drop him.'

" 'You would be,' says Rockaway, sneering like. 'And,
suppose, you were obliged to shoot the launchmen,
oo?'

" 'No, we got 'em down below,' says Malone. 'Anyhow,
ou needn't worry. There's no evidence afloat. We sunk the

Do-me and watched for flotsam. We left nothing. A schoo of mako sharks took charge of Ericson's body.'

" 'Ah, well, I suppose you always will be a fool, Dan, says Rockaway. 'Having committed one murder you migh just as well have committed two more and have done th job properly.'

" 'Oh!' says Malone. 'If that's all that's necessary to pleas you, we can soon take the two below out to sea and drown 'em.'

" 'And get back here about dawn and have daylight show ing us getting the kalsomine off the *Dolfin*,' sneers Rockaway 'Every time I'm not with you to lead you as if you were a sheep you go and half do a job. You were always like that You and Marshall take the men along to the cave and chain them as was arranged, and then come back here quick and get the kalsomine off. It'll be light in four hours.'

"And so," continued Spinks, "they brought us here. The entrance is 'way back there. They levered a great boulder against the entrance, and since then they've lowered tucker down to us through that hole in the roof. If we could have broken these chains one could have got atop the shoulder of the other and climbed free through that hole, but th chains won't let us stand up, and they took good care to bar off all loose rock we could have broken the chains with They had everything nicely worked out, and Mr. Ericson might have been with us to-day if he hadn't draw'd his pisto on Malone."

"We got cramp in our legs at first," cried Garroway from the corner to which he had run.

"Yes, we got cramp in our legs," Spinks said. "It was bac at times. Used to make us howl, it did, but afterwards w didn't get the cramp. But our knees got sore crawling abou on 'em. Passing time was about the worst. I asked Malon one day for something to read, and he said we needn't bothe

ose Rockaway was getting to believe we'd be better off
rowned.

"We lost count of the days, too. I don't know the month
is now. Then we played five-stones and after that we
layed at irrigation with the stream flowing across the place,
inking the sand patches either side was paddocks. Then
ob got so that he thought I was to blame for us being here.
e lost his block once or twice and took to me. I had to keep
holt on myself, or perhaps Rockaway would have had to
rown only one of us. It's been crook all right. Like being
the condemned cell, I should say, not knowing when they
ould be coming to take us to sea and drown us in deep
ater."

Bony could not see Garroway, but he could hear him
uttering. Spinks, squatting beside Bony, became silent.
e stared upward at the jagged hole in the roof as, likely
ough, he had stared for hours. Then Garroway began to
y, miserably, and Spinks shouted:

"Stop that, Bob, or I'll dong you one."

Bony shivered. His head still pained badly; but it was
ot the pain that made him shiver.

CHAPTER 21

Joe is Unleashed

It was quite dark when, a few minutes after ten o'clock, Jac
Wilton took the *Marlin* over the bar and into Wapeng
Inlet under the command of his mate who stood beside th
mast and issued his steering orders by stamping his feet i
accordance with an arranged code. The stars were cool an
faintly masked by a high-level haze, and the wind was blow
ing steadily from the south. The roar of the ocean obliterate
the cries of water birds and the plopping of surface fish.

Inside the bar, the *Marlin*'s engine was stopped, and whil
still moving she was steered into the lee of a land bluff an
there anchored. This operation produced no noise, becau
Joe had replaced the chain with a two-inch rope. Now pr
tected by the bluff from the wind and the ocean surges l
the bar, the launch rode easily and safely.

The two men launched a small dinghy, and lowered the
selves into it. Wilton took the oars and Joe the tiller. Fifte
minutes later they were at Rockaway's private jetty.

Standing up in the cockleshell of a boat, and balancir
themselves and it by holding to the jetty, they were able
bring their eyes just above the decking and see the upp
portion of the *Dolfin* and the several lights within the dista
house on the hill-side They saw, too, the reflection on th
water of a light shining through one of the *Dolfin*'s port
and from its position knew that it came from the engin
room.

"Someone aboard," whispered Joe.

"Must be," agreed Wilton. "They wouldn't leave the light n needlessly."

"What about prospectin'?" inquired Joe, and Wilton saw ιe movement of his hand down to the business end of a ιonkey wrench keeping company with his pipes thrust :tween his paunch and his belt.

"No rough stuff, you old idiot. We've got nothing on these 2ople, remember. We're just a couple of nosey parkers espassing on other people's property. To date I'm a fool ting on the beliefs of another one."

"Then what do we do—stay 'ere all night?"

"We've got to find out who's aboard the *Dolfin*, and then ok into that cave you've been talking about. Sit down, ıd I'll work the dinghy along closer to the launch."

By hauling on the jetty decking, Wilton with his feet oved the dinghy under him along the jetty's side farthest om the *Dolfin* until he drew opposite her cockpit. Here, hen Joe stood up, his shoulders as well as his head were ιove the level of the decking. Somewhere below, probably the engine-room as the light there was the only one itched on, a man was whistling the 'Dead March in ul'. Joe shifted his head nearer to his partner and ιispered:

"Cheerful, ain't 'e?"

Wilton hissed for silence. He wanted to listen to a peculiar ιise ashore.

"Someone's coming down with the hand-cart," he said ftly.

They could hear the crunching of the iron-shod wheels on e small gravel of the road leading from the house to the tty. Inside the *Dolfin* a spanner was dropped, but the man ere continued his doleful whistling. Then along the jetty nbers travelled the vibrations set up by the cart's wheels .ssing over the cross planking.

" 'E's bringin' the flamin' cart out here," whispered Jo

"Yes, and we're a bit too close. Move the dinghy seawa a fathom or two." With their feet they pushed the boat alo the jetty until they gained position opposite the *Dolfi* smart bow which was the farthest part of her from the sho "That's better," Wilton said. "We can see and not chan being seen. They must be bringing stores or petrol aboa for the fishing to-morrow."

"This time o' night!" scoffed Joe.

The rumble of the wheels on the planking of the jet steadily became louder, and presently they could make o the cart and the man who was pushing it. The cart push halted the vehicle opposite the *Dolfin*'s cockpit, raised t handles to slide something off it on to the jetty, and th drew the cart back for a yard or so. He called out loudly:

"Are you there, David?"

It was Rockaway's butler, Tatter, the precise of spee A spanner was tossed among others in a box down in t engine-room. The whistling of the Dead March cease followed by rubber-soled shoes applied lightly to wood, a then there appeared the man, Marshall.

"How is the work going?" asked Tatter.

"Oh, I found the perishing fault. A cog in the timi gear had broken and I've just about fixed another in place. You got Malone out there?"

"Yes. Mr. Rockaway says we are to treat Captain Malo with all respect. Captain Malone had many good poir despite his mental cloudiness and inability to live rig unless instructed. We are to put the Captain in Cabin On

"Captain me aunt's bootlace," snorted Marshall.

"He liked to be called Captain," Tatter said gent "Come now, let us take him to Cabin One."

Joe thrust an elbow into Wilton's ribs, and Marshall sa

"That's a good job, any'ow. Is the Boss sticking to

plans?"

"He has effected slight alterations," replied Tatter. "He thought it best to suggest to Miss Rockaway that she take a holiday in Melbourne, and so she left about five o'clock in the sports car. Her absence clears the decks as it were, and Mr. Rockaway has become more himself. When we have attended to Captain Malone, I am to go to Bermagui for Mr. Bonaparte's brief-case which you and Captain Malone so stupidly overlooked. I anticipate no difficulty with the hotel safe."

"How do we know it's in the hotel safe and not in Telfer's safe as Bonaparte said?" Marshall asked, surlily.

"Because, David, we know that after Mr. Bonaparte returned to the hotel last night he did not again leave it. He persisted in saying that he had persuaded Telfer to lock it up in his safe so that we would be baffled. However, should I not find the case in the hotel safe I will have to look for it in Constable Telfer's safe. Mr. Rockaway must have the brief-case.

"I shall be back not later than three o'clock, when you and I are to bring the prisoners down on the cart. It may be necessary to quieten them with something. We need anticipate no trouble from Mr. Bonaparte as he is extremely low: he had not recovered consciousness when I took the prisoners their day's rations at one, or at seven when again I visited the jail. You struck him much too hard, David, and Mr. Rockaway is greatly displeased.

"And so," went on the somewhat remarkable Tatter, "having the evidence in our possession, that is the brief-case in Mr. Rockaway's hands and the prisoners down below on the *Dolfin*, all the evidence is to be destroyed. You are to take the *Dolfin* to sea as soon as it is light, and I am to go with you. We are to go beyond the Continental Shelf where the water is especially deep."

"I don't like it, Tatter," Marshall said, slowly.

"I don't like it either, David. But then I don't like shaving and I don't like reading morbid books. If Captain Malone had been a man of reasoning he would have done the work more thoroughly when he and you sank the *Do-me*, and we would have been spared this distasteful task of drowning three men in very deep water. Still, we ought not to think badly of Captain Malone now that he is dead."

From their lower elevation, Wilton and Joe saw the men lift the corpse from the jetty flooring and carry it aboard the *Dolfin*. They could hear Marshall and Tatter talking like men moving a piano, and a light went on in Cabin One.

"By hell, they're unholy swine," Wilton whispered gratingly.

"Casual, ain't they?" Joe said, cheerfully. "What did I tell you? They got Bill and young Garroway planted in that cave, and per'aps Mr. Bonaparte's with 'em. Now's our chance to mop up them two down below. Then there'll be only Jules and old Rockaway."

At this moment of crisis Wilton was amazed by the clarity and the speed of his own mind. He clearly understood several significant facts and was able to appreciate the degree of their significance. On equal terms, he and Joe would be a good match for Tatter and Marshall. The element of surprise would be to their own advantage. But victory over these two was not assured, and if he and Joe met defeat the fate of Spinks and Garroway, and Bonaparte if he still lived, would certainly be sure. He had in the dinghy beneath his feet a single-shot rifle, and Joe's weapon was only a monkey wrench. And then Tatter was to leave immediately on a burgling expedition and would be away for several hours. He was the most dangerous of the bunch, and must be allowed to go. Then Marshall could be dealt with.

"You keep quiet and do nothing," he fiercely whispered to Joe.

"We gotta begin somewhere and sometime," argued Joe. Again he was commanded to keep quiet.

Shortly after that Tatter and Marshall reappeared on the jetty. Tatter said:

"It is eleven-thirty, David. I must be going. Report to Mr. Rockaway when you have tested the engine and tidied up."

"All right! I'll have everything for the trip outside ready in less'n half an hour. And you go careful up in Bermagui. So long."

Marshall turned back to the *Dolfin* and Tatter raised the handles of the cart and pushed it away along the jetty. Wilton waited anxiously, listening to the sound of the cart's wheels until it left the jetty and began the short road journey to the house. Joe fidgeted, irritating his partner. Marshall began again the doleful whistling of the Dead March, and now and then dropped his tools loudly in the box containing others. And then the watchers saw a light glare from beside the house, and heard the throbbing of Tatter's motor engine. Wilton waited until the noise of the engine was swallowed by the low roar of the surf outside the bar. At last he unleashed Joe.

"Now you can get aboard and take position on the cabin roof. Wait there for Marshall to come up. Make no mistake about him. If he starts yelling he'll complicate matters."

"Leave it to me," pleaded Joe, and without sound he clambered up to the jetty, leaving Wilton to push with his feet the dinghy until it was directly opposite the *Dolfin*'s cockpit.

He was glad, was this earnest young fisherman, that he had not acted when Joe urged action, that he had been cautious and allowed Tatter to go. With Malone dead and

Tatter out of the way for a few hours, Joe and he coul‹ clean up this bunch of murderous crooks one by one. H marvelled at Marion's faith in her 'feeling' that her brothe was not dead, and the road into the future, with her besid him, glowed bright with promise. It was worth daring foı and he would dare a great deal more now that hesitan suspicion was vitalised by fact.

He was thinking sadly of Napoleon Bonaparte, hopin‹ that he would be found alive, recalling the man's likeabl personality and those wonderful minutes when he fought giant swordfish in a rising gale. The light in the engine-roon was switched off, and he heard Marshall's feet padding tc wards the companion-way. He saw Joe's bulk move slightly was gratified to see Joe's arm rise high, and in his hand th two-foot-long monkey wrench.

Joe made no mistake, for he had served apprenticeshiı to this trade of violence early in life on the waterfronts of dozen notorious cities. Marshall made no out-cry. He san‹ beneath the wrench to fall down the companion-way, an‹ with astonishing agility Joe was after him.

" 'E's ours," he said to Wilton who had sprung to the jett and then to the launch's cockpit. "Get a torch."

Wilton went below, lifted a torch from a hook at th entrance to the saloon and masked its light with a handkeı chief. Between them they so trussed Marshall that sel: release was impossible, for they displayed their mastery ‹ rope and of rope knots. At speed they worked, and then the rolled the unconscious man under the saloon table and ra: up on deck.

Now continuing the plan worked out when on the way t Wapengo Inlet, they lowered the *Dolfin*'s dinghy into th water and cast off the launch's mooring ropes. Joe jumpe to the jetty with a boat-hook, and from there pushed th launch seaward. The wind obtained its hold and assiste him until he was forced to let her go. Without a word to Wilton he turned and ambled shoreward along the jetty, leaving his partner aboard the *Dolfin* busy with the anchor and its long heavy chain.

Twenty minutes later the *Dolfin* was nearing the southern shore of the Inlet and nearer the bar whose roaring voice effectually engulfed the noise made by the anchor chain when Wilton let go. He waited a minute to be sure the anchor held fast, and then he stepped down into the dinghy and rowed for the jetty against wind and current, with the lights in Rockaway's house harbour lights to guide him.

He was half-way across the Inlet when from the big house came a low thunderous crash. His harbour lights went out.

Joe, meanwhile, had gained the entrance to the cavern he knew so well by having camped in it for several lengthy periods while really prospecting. There he discovered a huge boulder pressing hard into the entrance which debouched on to a narrow, flat and grassy ledge. He remembered this boulder which had stood for centuries just beside the entrance, and he knew well that its change of position was not due to accident. Up the hill slope he scrambled to reach the hole in the roof of the cavern down through which Bony had been lowered and by means of which food had been given daily to the imprisoned Spinks and his mate. On his chest, Joe peered down the dark orifice the size of a manhole and two feet thick.

"You there, Bill?" he called.

Garroway answered him and then frantically cried:

"Bill! Wake up, Bill! Ole Joe Peace is at the 'ole in the roof. Wake up, Bill. Are you dead?"

"What's that? Help! I musta been dozing. What d'you say?"

"It's me, Joe. I'm up at the 'ole in the roof, Bill."

"Joe Peace! You old devil, Joe!" cried Spinks. "Cripes!

I'm glad to hear your voice. Where's Bony?"

"I dunno. Ain't 'e down with you?"

"No. We watched for the house people through a chink between the entrance wall and the boulder they levered acrost it, and when Tatter came twice Bony pretended to be still out to it. He's only been gone less'n half-hour. Me and Bob, here, got close together, and when Bony stepped up on us we gripped him by the feet and lifted him up so's he could catch a holt on the roof hole. We got chains on us so that we can't stand. Get us out, Joe, quick. I want to get me hands on Rockaway."

"I'll get you out, Bill, and get them chains off you, too. Wait a tick."

Joe slid down the slope with care not to dislodge loose surface stones. At the entrance he tested his strength against the boulder, and from within the cave, Spinks advised him to look about for a pole and a smaller stone that had been used for leverage.

Joe found the pole and the stone, and setting the stone in position he laid the end of the pole under the boulder and across the stone. But, try as he might, exerting all his strength, he could only move the boulder a foot. It fell back into its position when he eased the levering pole.

Undaunted he moved stone and pole to the other side of the boulder and tried again, and again could move the great weight but not sufficiently to clear it of the entrance. Still undaunted he took a purchase with the pole at another angle and this time found he could master the boulder with the slight slope away from the entrance to assist him. Grunting with effort, sweat streaming from his face and neck and arms, he put every ounce of power into a grand final pull on the levering pole. Over went the boulder, to stay poised for a split second on the edge of the narrow ledge, then to topple over and down the hill-side.

Joe laughed as he gasped for air. Then he slapped his thighs, and urged Spinks and Garroway, who were at the entrance, to just wait and listen. Immediately below was Rockaway's fine house.

CHAPTER 22

Mr. Rockaway is Upset

Mr. Rockaway was not happy.

Unhappiness produced a remarkable change in Mr. Rockaway, as though it were that strange drug used by Dr. Jekyll. Normally, Mr. Rockaway's long white hair was carefully brushed back from a magnificent forehead, his blue eyes were indicative of the joy of living, and his fresh-complexioned, large but not over-fleshed face bore an expression of good-will towards all men.

This evening whilst sitting at his desk in his sumptuously appointed study his hair was ruffled, his eyes were small and hard and his mouth was drawn into a fixed scowl. He was unhappy because Fate had thrown a bar into the machine of contentment and peace he had created beside this sylvan inlet, wrecking the creation. The bar was ex-Superintendent Ericson, late of New Scotland Yard; and then, when he had begun to re-build the machine, Fate had wrecked it again in the person of this Bonaparte fellow. And to crown every thing poor old Dan Malone must go and get strangled.

Poor old Dan! His brain was weak but his loyalty was as strong as steel, and to go and end like that was a crying shame.

That Dan Malone has messed up the *Do-me* business was less that unfortunate man's fault than his own. He ought to have gone out with Dave and Dan on the *Dolfin* that day, when there would not have been all this bother of sending Tatter to burgle a safe after ten years' retirement from his profession, and then having to send him and Marshall to sea the next morning and drown three men, two of whom should have been disposed of when Ericson was shot. Yes, he was a fool to have expected so much from poor old Dan.

Of course, he was a fool. Living here and quietly enjoying life had sapped his mentality. He had lost his punch. Here he was thinking of poor old Dan as weak-minded when he himself was a thundering sight worse. When the *Dolfin* brought back Spinks and Garroway he should have ordered poor old Dan to go out to sea straight away and drown them. But he hadn't, and there was the kick. Throughout his long and somewhat exciting career he always had avoided murder because an early study of this crime convinced him that murder is an excessive spur to police activity, and that one murder very often demands another. And then there always had been the unpleasant thought of a rope about his neck.

Of course, Mavis was a disturbing influence clouding his matured judgment. Like her mother she was soft-hearted, and once she knew about the prisoners in the cavern she opposed their disposal in deep water. That created a problem the solution of which was extremely difficult if the disposal of the prisoners in deep water was not to be accepted. Retirement from business and settlement in a place like this free from the probability of enforced imprisonment, and with unlimited angling nearly all the year round, had not been accomplished easily, and a move to another place to achieve the same objective would be much more difficult. He had hated to think of leaving this machine he had created, and he wasn't going to leave it.

Ah well! He had got rid of Mavis for a week or two, and she would spend a devil of a lot of money. But now he could clean up the mess made by poor old Dan and prolonged by Mavis who was so like her wonderful mother. He could still hear the dwindling hum of Tatter's motor-bike, and with satisfaction he counted on having Bonaparte's brief-case in his hands within three hours. With the evidence in that case destroyed, and with the prisoners, including Bonaparte if he still lived, drowned in deep water, the rocks lying in the stream of his life would have been removed and the stream once again would run quietly and smoothly. And then, hey ho! for the swordfishing in earnest.

Mr. Rockaway was sitting facing the tall french windows with his back to the door. So intense was his grief at the passing of Captain Malone, he failed to hear the infinitesimal sound of oil being squirted into the lock of the door and about the handles and catch. The uneconomic application of oil prevented Mr. Rockaway from hearing the handle turned and the catch drawn inward to permit the door being opened. Rich though he was he would have denied the necessity of the oiling, but the person outside obviously thought otherwise, because having opened the door a fraction, he squirted more oil into the hinges.

Even when in possession of a large amount of oil it was no mean feat to enter the room without Mr. Rockaway being aware of it. It was a still greater feat for the intruder to close and lock the door without disturbing Mr. Rockaway's train of thought.

However, Mr. Napoleon Bonaparte was wholly successful.

If unhappiness was a drug converting Dr. Jekyll Rockaway into Mr. Hyde Rockaway, the effect of pain and mental anguish produced by the sufferings of others was similar in Bonaparte, Inspector, C.I.B. His general appearance was the antithesis of that of the being known to his colleagues. The veneer of civilisation, so thin in the most gently nurtured of us, was entirely absent. He was wearing nothing. A film of oil caused his body to gleam like new bronze. His hair was matted with blood. His eyes were big, and the whites were now blood-shot. His lips were widely parted, revealing his teeth like the fangs of a young dog.

The oil-can he had obtained from the garage he had left

outside the door, but he had with him an old shot-gun he had discovered in the garage and had loaded with number BB shot which, as everyone knows, is substantial in size. Mr. Rockaway was oblivious to Bony's advance from the door to a position behind his back, of the gun being pointed at him and the pink-nailed finger touching the gun's front trigger.

Soundlessly, Bony blew between pursed lips, and the white hair on the crown of Mr. Rockaway's head trembled in the miniature breeze. With slight irritability, Mr. Rockaway turned round in his chair. The degree of shock he received can be understood. He was like a man petrified by the sight of a car rushing straight at him.

Bony had observed in the face of the man above the menacing pistol resolution to be obeyed. Mr. Rockaway now saw above the muzzle of the double-barrelled gun a human face implacably determined to kill. He knew that, should he move a fraction of an inch, he would die instantly, and he did not want to die instantly. When he was dead he would not be able to enjoy life, to live well, to feel the stupendous thrill of fighting a swordfish. He knew, too, that had he wished to move he could not. Even his hearing was affected. He could see Bony's lips moving, but the sound of the words spoken by Bony appeared to come from another direction.

"Malone was just an ordinary brute," Bony said, sibilantly. "He killed Ericson swiftly because he thought himself in danger. You, you are much worse than Malone, much worse than a brute. You are something inexpressibly foul to have condemned two men to a semi-solitary confinement for more than three months, chaining them so that the use of their legs was cruelly restricted, with probable crippling for life, denying them mental recreation in reading and the ordinary common necessaries of life.

"I am going to give you a chance to live, Rockaway, not because you deserve it but because it pleases me to give it.

It pleases me to give it because I dislike using this gun with which to kill you, a gun being an impersonal method of destroying vermin. I want to feel you dying. I want to feel you struggling futilely in my hands while you are dying—as Malone did. In a moment I am going to drop this gun and employ my hands in your destruction."

The paralysing inertia of the nightmare still imprisoned Mr. Rockaway. He now tried to move and he tried to speak, but he was unable to do one or the other. He thought that his mind was cracking when the electric light blinked once. He thought how strange it was that he continued to gaze at a limited circle in the centre of which were two blazing orbs of blue surrounded by scarlet. Although he was unable to look away from those orbs he did see the rusty gun fall to the carpeted floor and wondered why it did not discharge. He saw, too, Bony's dark hands rise and slowly approach him, their fingers distended and curved. He wanted to gain relief from the paralysing inertia by screaming, but he could not even scream.

At this instant Joe's boulder arrived, its last bounce on the hill-side having blinked the electric light.

The rear of the house faced a low cliff cut into the hill-side where a level building area had been formed, and the chimney carrying smoke from the kitchen range was built into this rear wall. The boulder struck the chimney a few feet above the range, passed cleanly through the brickwork, sped through the large kitchen to crash into the passage between it and the dining-room, and there to fall through the floor and sever the electric light and power lines.

There followed an instant of complete silence. Then began a roar of extraordinary intensity when the tall brick chimney fell and cut through the roof and the kitchen ceiling. It collected all of Mr. Rockaway's table china from the racks and glass-fronted cupboards, and reached the linoed door in a succession of thuds.

The sound effects of Joe's boulder produced opposite results in the two men facing each other in the study. They momentarily froze Napoleon Bonaparte, and they released Mr. Rockaway from the bonds of inertia. He leaped to his feet, sending the chair over against Bony's legs, and rushed towards the door. But the light was out and he became lost, so that he crashed into an antique Venetian cabinet containing still more antique Chinese porcelain. On his rebound from this he felt Bony's hands clutching at his coat, and he then provided proof of his abhorrence of being throttled by screaming, or rather squealing much like a rabbit when caught in a gin trap.

When he stopped to take in air he heard Bony laughing like a devil, and he again screamed, this time keeping it up. He saw the faint grey oblongs of the french windows and dashed to them, but he did not see his own desk and fell sprawling over it. Now he felt Bony's hands on the back of his legs, felt them slip up his back towards his neck. It was not a soothing feeling, and he continued to scream.

Bony's hands were at his shoulders when the door was smashed in and the windows crashed inward to admit half a dozen burly men. One of them flashed a torch, and the remainder fell on Mr. Rockaway and Bony and tore them asunder at the instant Bony's hands closed on Mr. Rockaway's throat and stopped his screaming.

More men entered the untidy study. More torches were flashed on. Mr. Rockaway recognised the intruders as policemen and he craved their protection. Bony recognised among the visitors Detective-Sergeant Allen and Constable Telfer. It was only then that he was recalled to his educational attainments, his professional rank, and his pride in his father's race. He was overwhelmed by a flood of shame that had nothing to do with his nakedness.

CHAPTER 23

Bony Again Rises

When Mr. Rockaway's many clocks struck the hour of two in the morning he was seated in his own luxurious car in mixed company. Besides several policemen, under Sergeant Lester, were his cook and his housekeeper, and Dave Marshall who was still thoroughly indisposed. The rough road over Dr. George Mountain was no sedative to Marshall's violent headache, but this route to Bega was dictated by the police desire to leave Bermagui and Tatter severely alone.

The damage occasioned to the electric light and power lines by Joe's boulder had been repaired, and behind carefully drawn curtains much activity followed the departure of the prisoners. Detective-Sergeant Allen decided to wait at the house for Tatter's return in preference to going to Bermagui after him, or attempting to arrest him on the road coming from the township, this decision being largely based on knowledge of Tatter's past and his known character.

A constable was stationed outside the house to give warning of Tatter's approach along the private road. Another was stationed at the front door in conformity with routine, and a third, who was a first-aid expert, was detained to attend Bony, Spinks and his mate. Wilton assisted him, and Joe maintained the supply of hot water.

When Mr. Rockaway's numerous clocks chimed the hour of three in the morning Bony, Allen and Telfer sat in the study sipping coffee and eating ham sandwiches, while in the lounge Spinks and Garroway, bathed and barbered and haved and massaged, were being dined on the best that the absent Mr. Rockaway could supply.

Bony, also having bathed and resumed his clothing, was in a state of mind most despondent, and he listened to Detective-Sergeant Allen with no great attention. Allen was disclosing the basis of his decision to take Tatter here on his return from Bermagui, but Bony revealed an irritating lack of interest in Tatter.

His careful descriptions of Rockaway and his daughter, Malone and Marshall, sent to the New South Wales Commissioner of Police, with the suggestion that Scotland Yard be asked immediately if these men were known prior to Superintendent Ericson's retirement, had resulted in money being spent like water on beam wireless and cable services both in Sydney and London, and the dispatch to Bermagui of D.-S. Allen to act under and with D.-I. Napoleon Bonaparte.

Rockaway was thought to be an Australian who emerged as a financier and company promoter in London in the year 1910. Shortly after the war he failed, but made a comeback in 1924, rising to rocket heights in three years. Unlike so many of his kind he chose his own time to get out—with a sum estimated at a round million. His confidential valet, David Marsden, disappeared with him and his daughter in 1927.

Superintendent Ericson, then inspector, was assigned to the Rockaway case, and his prolonged examination of Rockaway's activities revealed close association with a firm of blackmailers having branches in all European capitals. The managing director of this firm was a Mr. Lumley-Saunders whose hobby was safe-breaking, and his partner was a well-known character known by the cognomen of Canadian Jack.

From data supplied by Inspector Bonaparte, Scotland Yard was confident that Rockaway was the financier and

company promoter named Elson, Marshall was his vale
named Marsden, while Malone was Canadian Jack. The
London people inquired about Lumley-Saunders, asking i
he was under suspicion and carefully describing his appear
ance and habits. His appearance tallied closely with Tatter
and Tatter's expedition to break open the Bermagui hote
safe indicated him to be Lumley-Saunders.

Messages from London revealed that Scotland Yard wa
gravely anxious about Tatter, issuing warnings to the New
South Wales Commissioners that Lumley-Saunders wa
wanted for homicide in several countries. He was known
to be a shoot-at-sight, a cold and deliberate snake of a man
whose apprehension would require care and efficiency
Hence Allen's growing anxiety lest Tatter had somehow
received warning of the raid, his chagrin that, not having
followed the private road from their cars hidden in the
scrub off the Coast Road, they had missed him. Further
when informed of Tatter's expedition it was too late to ge
after him, too dangerous to bail him up at the hotel
The wise course, it was thought, was to await Tatter'
return.

Reduced to a cringing wretch by Bony's unorthodox be
haviour in his study, Elson, alias Rockaway, had confirmed
the information supplied from London and admitted that
Tatter was Lumley-Saunders. He was vehement in his asser
tion that the original plan to prevent Ericson betraying them
after he recognised him on the *Dolfin* was to confine him
and his launchmen until such time as arrangements could
be made for the gang to transfer to another country. He
swore that Tatter and Malone would have overruled his
objections to the killing of the two launchmen had it not
been for his daughter who threatened them all with dis
closure if murder was done. She on her part agreed not to
visit the prisoners in the cavern or arrange for their escape.

She had not known of the abduction of Bony, and she had been persuaded to leave on an extended holiday.

When the clocks announced the time as four o'clock, Allen was intensely worried. By now, of course, Sergeant Lester would have warned the police in all towns to watch for Tatter on his motor-cycle and to stop all cars passing through towns in the hunt for him. Constable Telfer being here at Wapengo Inlet, Bermagui was without police protection, whilst only one man was on duty at Cobargo.

"We'd better get along to Bermagui and find out what's happened there," Allen said. To this Bony objected.

"Wait for daylight," he advised. "Should we meet Tatter returning to Wapengo Inlet we will have light to stop him and capture him. In the dark he would have a greater chance of escaping us. We will leave here on the truck in the garage, transfer to your police car and in that proceed to Bermagui. Even had Joe and Wilton remembered to tell us about Tatter's destination before they went out to bring the *Dolfin* back to the jetty I would have counselled waiting here for him. When we did learn from Rockaway the object of Tatter's expedition, after assuring the safe removal from the cave of Spinks and Garroway, it was too late."

"Well, he must have received warning somehow or he'd have been back by now. You've done all right, but I'm likely to get it in the neck if Tatter kills anyone or get clear away."

"I shall smooth that over, my dear Allen, but you cannot smooth over a matter concerning me. I can but express regret for what has happened. Although probably you and Lester will be sufficiently generous not to mention in your reports the condition of mental degeneracy you found me suffering from when you burst into Rockaway's study, I myself will never overlook it or cease to regret it. Of course, I was unaware that Joe had listened to a conversation between Telfer

THE MYSTERY OF SWORDFISH REEF

and Blade in the latter's office, and that in consequence of that and my conversation with Joe the preceding evening he and Wilton had arrived at the Inlet via the sea. Nor did I know you and Lester were nearing the house via the land or that Wilton and Joe had accounted for Marshall, and myself for Malone—for I was not sure I had killed him. Even in spite of the fact that I thought I was faced with the task of overcoming the entire gang, there is no excuse for my primitive attack on Rockaway. No, not even when my very natural indignation at the treatment received by Spinks and his mate is taken into account.

"I am entitled to credit, and I am going to see that Telfer is given credit to the furtherance of his career. Before ever Mrs. Spinks told me that Ericson and Rockaway had met at the Bermagui jetty and recognised each other as enemies, I was sure that the genesis of the *Do-me* affair was to be discovered in Ericson's professional career before his retirement.

"It has not been an easy case, Allen, and one wrongly begun by you who did not give sufficient attention to the locality of the crime"—Allen shuddered at memory of his sea-sickness—"I hope, at a later date, that from my papers you will clearly see how important it is to reconstruct the crime and its background. Even on unstatic water objects can be traced and their movements established. For me, however, the satisfaction gained from success has been spoiled by my own extraordinary exhibition of loss of personal control, proving that, despite everything I am a savage."

Bony's gaze fell to the task of making another cigarette, and Allen brazenly winked at Telfer who had been a silent listener.

"A savage with guts is a better man than a civilised man like Rockaway who becomes a yellow craven when his number goes up," Allen said quietly. "I would have acted as you did, knowing that I was alone against a gang and that the sound of a gun-shot would have brought the others on me. Darn it! I can't see that you've anything to reproach yourself with."

Bony sighed.

"You cannot understand me, Allen," he said softly.

After Bony had made certain arrangements with Wilton, he left with Allen and Telfer and two constables, for Bermagui. Nothing was seen of Lumley-Saunders, alias Tatter, and the arrival at Bermagui found Allen greatly depressed.

It was five o'clock when they reached the end of the single street, to observe Mr. Blade standing nonchalantly in the doorway of his office. This abnormality in the life of Bermagui was emphasised by the appearance of Mr. Parkins outside his garage, and several men and women outside the hotel farther along the street.

"Here's evidence of Tatter," moaned Allen. "Pull up, driver. We'll interview the club secretary."

Blade declined to leave his doorway when the police car halted opposite it, and Bony and Allen with Telfer alighted and walked to him. He was freshly shaved and as neatly dressed as always. He smiled at them, and then with concern said:

"You have been hurt, Mr. Bonaparte! Badly?"

"I could have suffered worse," answered Bony. "Have you by any chance seen or heard anything of Rockaway's butler, Tatter?"

"Yes, Mr. Bonaparte. I have both seen and heard of him. I first heard of him about one o'clock when he stopped his motor-bike about a mile down the coast road. I knew it was his machine by the sound of its engine, and I wondered why he was coming to Bermagui at such an hour, and why he stopped his machine a mile out of town. Being annoyed because Sergeant Allen and Constable Telfer left me behind after I was promised a front seat at a certain show, I dressed and prospected the town, as Joe would say. I saw Tatter enter the town by the back, and I followed him to see him break into the hotel. . . ."

Blade purposely discontinued his narrative on the pretext of lighting a cigarette. The cigarette seemed difficult to light.

"Well, what did you do then?" asked the anxious Allen.

Blade casually lit a cigarette, and then, as casually, he said:

"Oh, I followed him into the hotel."

"Go on, man, go on," implored Allen.

"As I said, I followed Tatter into the hotel. I was still feeling much annoyed at being left behind by you and Constable Telfer. I came on Tatter kneeling before the hotel safe. His hand-torch was switched on, and beside him was laid out an array of implements. So, you see, I collared him."

"Did you? Good man!" shouted Allen. "Where is he? Don't say he got away."

"He didn't get away. It's only secretive, sly policemen who get away from me. Tatter, on seeing me, drew a gun and fired but missed. He had a gun in a holster under each arm-pit—automatics. I took them from him and held him until the barman came and assisted me to secure him."

Telfer was actually gaping. Sergeant Allen merely stared with eyes like a child's glass marbles.

"You caught him—Tatter?" he said, doubtfully. "What did you do with him?"

Mr. Parkins, who had come to stand close, chuckled.

"What he done with him isn't so important as what he did to him," he interjected.

Mr. Blade smiled.

"You see, before I suffered a long illness I was a wrestler," he explained. "I caught Tatter with a flying tackle. Then

I picked him up and gave him an aeroplane spin, and finally I applied an Indian deathlock. As he had fired at me, and as you had left me behind to twiddle my thumbs, I didn't give him a sporting chance. I had him brought here, and you can now take charge of him."

He stepped aside to disclose Tatter lying on the office floor, efficiently bound and gagged.

"I gagged him because of his language," Blade said apologetically.

At seven o'clock a small boy came racing from the headland to give Bony certain information. Four minutes later Bony knocked on the door of Nott's Tea Rooms. The street was deserted.

"May I come in?" he asked Mrs. Spinks, who opened the door.

"Why yes, of course," replied Mrs. Spinks. "You're Jack's angler, aren't you? What's happened to your poor head?"

"Nothing of much importance. It got in the way of something," Bony said. "Is Miss Spinks at home?"

Mrs. Spinks called loudly for Marion, and again Bony had to make light of his head injury.

"It's a little early, I know," he said quietly, "but I rather want you both to accompany me to the headland where I want to show you something of great interest."

"The headland! Yes! I was up there last evening looking for the *Do-me*," said Mrs. Spinks. "Oh, why doesn't the *Do-me* come back?"

"Your son and young Garroway will come home one of these days," Bony predicted, to add brightly: "But to-day I've something fine to show you. I'm not going to tell you now what it is. I want it to be a surprise. Come along! Leave everything, and come along with me."

The street was still deserted when he escorted them past

the hotel, where no one stood, past the Zane Grey shelter-shed, and so up the little path leading to the grass-crowned headland that had witnessed the agony of a distraught woman. He led them to the seaward edge of the great rock barrier protecting the town, hoping they would not notice the unusual activity of care down in the street they had left.

"Why, it must be late," explained Mrs. Spinks. "All the launches are coming out."

"Yes, so they are, Mother," agreed Marion.

"And look! Here's the *Marlin* coming up from the south, Marion."

"That's so, Mother. There's old Joe Peace standing against the mast. Is Jack bringing home a big swordie, Mr. Bonaparte?"

"Something of the kind," Bony evasively replied. "Just wait a minute and you'll both see my surprise."

The *Marlin* was coming close to the foot of the headland, her bow gently pushing aside white water. The sea was carpeted with cavorting white horses running over bars of blue and green.

"I can't see a swordie on the *Marlin*'s stern," Mrs. Spinks said disappointedly. "I can see that worthless Joe Peace against the mast, and I can see Jack Wilton standing on the gun'le and steering with a foot."

"And I can see——" Marion turned round to face Bony who was standing a little to the rear. Her mother was too interested by the oncoming *Marlin* to notice how she stepped close to Bony and impulsively clasped his arms above the elbows. The girl's face had become milk-white, her lustrous eyes great black opals. Her lips were parted slightly, and there was a catch in her breathing. She fought to speak, gained control of her voice and was about to say something when Bony gently pressed the tips of his fingers against her mouth.

The *Marlin* was within three hundred yards of them. Bony stepped to the side of the elder woman and softly offered her a pair of binoculars. With the eagerness of a child she accepted them from him, raised them to her eyes, and then out over the dancing water rang her loud cry:

"It's Bill! It's my boy, Bill! Bill! Bill! Bill!"

Back to them came the response.

"Mother! Marion! We're coming home!"

Mother and daughter were clinging to each other as the *Marlin* rounded the headland to be met by every launch at Bermagui and escorted across the inner bay to the river bar.

"Come!" urged Bony. "We must be at the jetty to welcome them."

Mrs. Spinks began to run, crying loudly: "It's Bill! It's my boy coming home!"

Bony accompanied them to the little path leading down to the road. Mr. Parkins waited there for them with his car. Bony stopped and watched. He saw Mr. Parkins urge them to get into his car. He saw them drive off along the single street. He saw Mr. Emery's tub move away after it, and other cars and trucks appear to form a long procession which rushed at unlawful speed down the street and along the curving road to the jetty. Bony watched the *Marlin* go in behind the promontory protecting the river's mouth. He watched until the last of the sea procession disappeared behind the promontory. The road beyond the jetty was blackened by cars, the jetty was blackened by people. He could hear the people cheering.

He was happy because he felt he had atoned for that fall from the height to which his pride and natural gifts had lifted him. But, when he turned to face the glittering sea in time to watch, far away, a beautiful fish dancing on its tail, memory of his temporary fall was expunged from his mind.

Further adventures of Detective-Inspector
Napoleon Bonaparte by

ARTHUR UPFIELD

"In modern detective fiction Bony has a place
of his own—at the top."

Oxford Mail